THE ANTHILL

by the same author

THE LUCKY ONES

JULIANNE PACHICO

The Anthill

FABER & FABER

First published in the UK in 2020
by Faber & Faber Ltd
Bloomsbury House
74–77 Great Russell Street
London WC1B 3DA

Typeset by Typo•glyphix, Burton-on-Trent DE14 3HE
Printed and bound by CPI Group (UK) Ltd, Croydon CR0 4YY

Quotations from: *The Para-State* (p. 68, 2016) by Aldo Civico by
permission of University of California Press, Oakland, California;
'Unspeakable Things Unspoken', Toni Morrison: originally delivered as a
Tanner Lecture on Human Values at the University of Michigan, 1988

The right of Julianne Pachico to be identified as author of this work
has been asserted in accordance with Section 77 of the Copyright,
Designs and Patents Act 1988

*This book is a work of fiction. Any references to historical events, real people, or
real places are used fictitiously. Other names, characters, places, and events are
products of the author's imagination, and any resemblance to actual events or
places or persons, living or dead, is entirely coincidental.*

A CIP record for this book
is available from the British Library

ISBN 978–0–571–33146–8

2 4 6 8 10 9 7 5 3 1

I wondered too, as Georges Bataille suggested, that if in the pleasure of inflicting death and torture, there is also a quality of childhood, of a life 'unbounded by civilized properties'.

—Aldo Civico, *The Para-State: An Ethnography of Colombia's Death Squads*

Invisible things are not necessarily 'not-there'; . . . a void may be empty but not be a vacuum.

—Toni Morrison, 'Unspeakable Things Unspoken'

CONTENTS

PART I

YOU

LALO

The bus route down from the Medellín airport doesn't make you nauseous like it used to, not like when you were last driven on it twenty years ago, an eight-year-old girl on her way to Heathrow. Now you're twenty-eight and the road is still one sharp curved turn after another, past restaurants with names like Sancho Paisa and trashy nightclubs like Oh My Sweet Jesus. Grinning statues of machete-wielding farmers, Texaco gas station stars. PANADERÍA signs on every corner, scraggly half-dead grass on the side of the highway. And down there in the valley below is the city – your city – its far-off lights lurking like tiny star clusters from a distant galaxy, awaiting your arrival.

When you get off the bus at the Sandiego mall, a girl in a collared shirt heaves your suitcase into the front seat of a cab, paying no mind to your apologetic warning of *Careful, it's very heavy.* You overtip her out of nervousness and she bows her head: —Thank you, miss. The taxi driver gets lost and keeps refusing to go down the street you insist is correct, based on the directions saved on your phone. —I really think it's this way, you say, as he turns the steering wheel in the opposite direction of where you're pointing.

By the time the driver has managed to lurch your suitcase on to the pavement, a man has come out of the building. He stands at an awkward distance, arms crossed, like he doesn't want to get too close. You pay the taxi driver in exact change and he says, —Thank you, beautiful.

When the taxi finally drives off it feels like the man has been standing there an uncomfortably long time. His head is shaved close to the scalp and he's wearing a long-sleeved white shirt that hangs past his wrists and white exercise sweatpants with a black line running down the sides. Even his tennis shoes are white: a clean white, like they've just been purchased. He could be an assistant football coach, or a sports-shoe salesman.

—. . . Matty? you say.

But the man shakes his head. —He's not here, he says. He should be back soon. But he told us you were coming. Don't worry, he left very specific instructions.

—Instructions, you say.

—That's correct.

A shudder jolts through your torso but you're able to restrain yourself: hopefully it looks more like a twitch, rather than a violent spasm. An unexpectedly chill breeze makes you grateful for your tights, impulsively purchased at the last minute from Terminal 3's Boots pharmacy. One of the few memories you have left of Medellín (cradled close to your body, carefully, like you're carrying a basket of eggs) is the temperate weather. *Welcome to the City of Eternal Spring* – that's what the pilot said on the loudspeaker. But you don't recall Medellín being this cool in the evening.

The man reaches for your suitcase. —This is embarrassing, he says, but I didn't grab my keys. We'll have to knock hard and hope somebody's listening.

His shirtsleeve has risen up his arm. On the back of his

hand, you see what looks like scar tissue: puckered wrinkled holes, lumpy like the bark of a tree.

—No problem, you say. Totally fine. (Apparently you've turned into a US cheerleader, all optimistic pep talk.)

—Or I'll tell you what, he says. Are you hungry? Do you want to go get a drink? Let's take the suitcase and come right back.

—Um, you say. You look down the road. An old woman has come out of a building and is placing a fat garbage bag by a tree. It all seems domestic enough. Sure, you say. Why not.

Your suitcase makes a terrible rasping sound every time it goes over a crack in the pavement. He walks quickly despite dragging your suitcase along and doesn't seem bothered when it sways dangerously after going over a ledge. Following him down the street, like a duckling trailing after its mother, you tell him about airport security. When you'd sent your suitcase through the conveyor belt, the lady looking at the X-ray screen had furrowed her brow. She'd leaned to the left, Tower of Pisa style, and tried to catch your eye.

Did you pack boxes in here? she'd asked. *Dozens of them?* Making a rectangular shape with her hands.

—Books, you tell the man now as he pauses by the traffic lights. I brought too many books with me. I'm sorry it's so heavy.

—I'd never expect a woman's suitcase to not be, he says. Watch out, here come the motos.

An army of helmeted figures on motorcycles buzz by, an angry swarm. You take a step back, swallowing hard. You hope you're not standing inappropriately close to him. He has a strong smell of BO, a musky scent you never encounter in

5

London, not even in the sweatiest, swampiest hours on the Tube. Why is being back in Colombia a reminder that you have a physical body, that it's an actual thing existing in space?

—Those motos sound like insects, you say. From a monster movie.

He makes a face as though what you've said is very strange and he needs to struggle to understand it.

—If you ever get lost, he says, tell the taxi driver to take you to the Anthill headquarters. Tell him Circular, and then these numbers . . .

—I know, you say. I have the address. (You don't add *How else would I have got here?*)

—Or, he says, just tell them, 'The Anthill headquarters, please.' If you're anywhere near this neighbourhood they'll know exactly what you mean.

You nod, refraining from thanking him, the most tepid of feminist victories.

—I don't mean to be condescending, he says, suitcase wobbling wildly as he steps off the pavement. I just want you to be safe. Mattías would kill me if I didn't protect you. Like, literally kill me.

He makes a gesture across his stomach, velociraptor-claw style. On your face: the slowest of smiles.

—Would he, now, you say, and the feeling of gratitude spreading through your stomach is like something warm getting spilled.

The restaurant is comida pacífica, food from the coast. He orders you a portion of fried fish, which seems a bit heavy for this time of night, but since no one has brought you a menu it feels fussy to request one. For himself, he orders a plate

6

with all the sides (plantain, cabbage, coconut rice) but nothing else.

—I don't eat animals, he says, moving his knife and fork out of the way as the waitress sets down a basket full of popcorn. But I ordered you ocean fish. Not river. Whenever you can, get ocean.

—Aren't we a bit far from the ocean?

—Not at all. He shoves a handful of popcorn into his mouth. The owners of this place, their family lives in Chocó. They ship it here direct in special ice containers. Trust me, whenever you can, avoid fish from the river. No tilapia or carp ever; it's bad for the environment. Have you ever been to the Pacific coast?

—No. I never had the chance to travel when I lived here.

—You didn't? the man says, tilting his head in the universal manner that signifies *Tell me more.*

You tell him the basics, speed-dating style. Your Colombian mother, killed in a traffic accident when you were eight. Your British father, a lawyer who sent you to English boarding school. He followed you to England soon after, moving back into his family home in the south-west. He's still living there – at least, you haven't heard otherwise.

—Does it look the way you remember it? the man says, taking the beers directly from the waitress before she has a chance to set them down. Medellín, I mean.

—I have a really bad memory, you say, raising the bottle to your lips. I was only eight when I left.

The man nods, as if this is acceptable. He starts talking about himself. In the time it takes you to need a second round of beers, you learn his name is Lalo, he's a freelance writer, he just came back from a three-week camping trip on the Pacific coast of Chocó, and he's been volunteering at the Anthill since the day it opened, over three years ago.

—Working at the Anthill saved my life, he says, as you use your tongue to poke at a popcorn kernel stuck in your molar. It did! I would have been lost without it! But remind me again – how is it you know Mattías?

You pinch at the flap of skin beside your thumb, then your index finger, descending down your hand like a musical scale. If you pinch hard enough, you can almost feel the redness. — We grew up together, you say. We lived in the same house when we were kids. (You almost don't say it, but then go ahead anyway, brutally, like it's nothing.) We were best friends. Why . . . What did Mattías say about me?

—Exactly that, Lalo says, rotating his beer so that the logo faces him. He said exactly that. How lovely the two of you were able to get back in touch. Did he contact you first? Or—

—No, you say quickly. I, ah, got his email. From a mutual friend.

Lalo picks at the label on his bottle. —Mattías always talks about your father – how he's been a great friend of the Anthill and all that. Financially, I mean.

This is news to you. —He has?

—Of course! He's even said that if it weren't for your father's contributions, the Anthill wouldn't exist. Mattías went to so many people! He must have raised around twenty thousand dollars in the beginning! He's very grateful to your father, obviously.

—Grateful, you echo. Of course.

When the waitress asks if you'd like another drink, you don't even let her finish the sentence before blurting out, —Yes.

8

As you push the slice of lime down the bottle's neck, Lalo gives you the basic lowdown about the Anthill. —The Anthill children come every day, he says, the lime fizzing in your beer. Five days a week. Fridays are different; that's when we serve Community Meal. We offer all kinds of classes: art, sports, English, computers for the teens. We only have three computers, unfortunately. How long are you in Medellín for? Will you be staying here your whole trip? You could teach English. Or anything you want, really.

—I don't exactly have a plan, you say, not mentioning your one-way ticket, purchased with your associate tutor stipend. I just thought it'd be good to come back for a bit. It's been so long.

—Will you be working on anything while you're here?

—What do you mean?

He drums his fingers on the table. —Like on a book, or something.

—Oh, I'm not a writer.

—Oh!

He sits there, looking at you. So you say, —I study literature. And teach it, I guess.

A young man carrying a stack of CDs approaches the table. He says he's from Venezuela, that this is a rap single he wrote and recorded himself, that he'd appreciate any help you're able to provide, God willing. Lalo gives him a crumpled-up bill, you give him a coin, but neither of you accepts a CD. After he leaves, Lalo says, —A lot of people are coming to Medellín these days to be writers. A lot of volunteers. I'm working on a book about Medellín myself, actually. You wouldn't be alone!

You shake your head. You almost don't say it, then go ahead anyway, in a rush of beer-induced honesty: —I used to want to be a writer. When I was a kid, I mean.

He nods as if satisfied, not asking for more details.

The food comes out shortly: beautifully curved mountains of coconut rice and thinly sliced cabbage. A giant fried plantain, flattened like an ancient cowpat, takes up most of the plate.

—Delicious, Lalo says, leaning over with his knife and lifting the bones from your fish in one swift motion. I never ate food like this growing up. With everything so beautifully laid out. So well arranged. Back in the orphanage, they used to serve us leftovers all mixed together. Tuna, cucumber, chorizo, watermelon, white rice, the works. I'm not kidding! *What's this*, I'd sometimes ask, if I was feeling brave. But the answer was always the same: *You're going to eat it*, they'd say, *and you're going to be thankful.* So there we'd be, sadly scooping our spoons in and out, like builders forced to eat their own cement mix.

You can't help but laugh at how sheepish he looks, like a puckish small boy about to start trouble. —To me, you say, that's basically child abuse. If someone fucks with my food, they're done for.

He smiles with his mouth closed. —The orphanage was a wonderful place, he says. They took very good care of me. I'd have been lost without it. But it's funny how as a child everything is so mixed-up all the time, isn't it? You don't get any say in the matter. It's much better being an adult.

—I dunno. Taxes . . . groceries . . .

You don't say, *Some days I can barely do my laundry.* Or, *Let alone return overdue library books. Forget about responding to gently concerned emails.*

He takes a long swig of beer. —I suppose I can never show you my room now. You'll see my unmade bed and scream.

You smile back. —How long were you in the orphanage?

He shakes his head. —No, no. Please, you first: where did you grow up after you left Medellín? What happened? Where did you go?

So you tell him in more detail, third-date level sharing rather than speed dating: living in that English boarding school. Twenty years ago in a cold northern city. You didn't know how to use the microwave, you loathed the taste of tea with milk, you'd never made your own bed and plantain chips were nowhere to be seen. The other international students were from Mumbai and Hong Kong, Beijing and Singapore. A boy from Dubai nicknamed you Paula Escobar; the girls invented the rumour that your feet had dandruff, due to the smears of bicarbonate of soda still left in your shoes. One of the few physical traces of Medellín you'd managed to bring with you, all the way across the Atlantic Ocean. Apparently, in England, nobody's feet ever stank or grew sweaty.

But as the white traces in your shoes gradually faded, so did that initial feeling, in the following weeks, months, years (and this is the part you don't say to Lalo, your voice slowly trailing to a halt). Junior school, senior school, uni. Twenty years in England – can you *really* call yourself Colombian any more? Isn't it ultimately a bit pathetic, a bit petty, clinging to those first eight years as a desperate marker of – whatever it is? God knows where your Colombian passport is, if it ever existed at all. And then there's the weight of the money – your father's family money – fat in the bank account, heavier and more real than anything else. British money is solid; it's straightforward;

it makes things happen and makes things possible; while Colombia is a vague weightless ghost you occasionally invoke as a wispy spell that proves – what? In pubs, you've often talked about Colombia in a deeply amused voice, rattling off the blandly standard details from any upper-class Third World childhood (or were you technically middle-class, compared to the other children whose families owned islands and helicopters and horse farms?). How, as a child, you never rode in a bus or a taxi. You grew up with maids and security guards in the apartment. Instead of fire drills your school had kidnapping drills. Etc., etc.

Sometimes your audience have asked questions. Other times they've laughed uneasily. More often than not, they've sipped their drinks and eyed you. *Wow*, they've occasionally ventured. *You don't sound Colombian . . . like, at all.*

It was a long slow lesson, but you learned it eventually: how there's something undeniably a bit . . . off about you.

Something embarrassing.

Maybe you're just kind of privileged and oblivious. Maybe you're just plain sad. Whatever it is, it's definitely something to be ashamed of. Deep inside you, rotting away.

And if there's one thing ten years of boarding school, three years of uni and never-ending years of postgraduate studies have taught you, it's that there's nothing you can ever do to hide it.

But what you do end up telling Lalo is how awkward it was – back in boarding school, when you'd open the door and someone else would do the exact same thing across the hall, so you were left staring at each other. —Sometimes, you say, picking at your napkin, I would immediately turn to the wall and press my ear against it, like I'd heard an awful noise. Just to avoid making eye contact. Sometimes I'd even mutter to myself.

—Brilliant, he says, dropping a forkful of rice into his lap. If I'd seen that, I would have run back inside. You wouldn't have seen me for the rest of the term!

Speaking of eye contact, his is intense: unwavering, unblinking. Like two Jedi swords jabbing at you. Enlarged red bumps dot the side of his shaved skull, like buttons on a weapon suitable for space warfare.

It takes some getting used to, but in terms of dinner conversation, there's something enjoyable about Lalo's dazed flitting from one topic to another. —We've been doing very well at the Anthill in terms of attendance, he says, holding the plantain to his mouth like a harmonica. But we need to expand. Dance classes, music. Financial literacy for the mothers. It's very important that the Anthill continues to support the community, to establish the values the neighbourhood needs during these uncertain times. The country is going through an interesting transition at the moment, as I'm sure you know. Have you ever had a boyfriend?

—Sure, you say, not missing a beat. You tell him about Dan Crawley, second year of uni. Dan Crawley was famous for playing sports you never quite understood, mysterious activities like hockey and cricket. You asked him once if he could give you a 'love bite' (you say this in English awkwardly, not knowing the Spanish translation), because you'd seen so many girls sporting them in your creative writing workshops – it had seemed like a badge of pride at the time, some weird initiation ritual.

—'Love bite'? he says, repeating the English phrase.

—Like a bruise, you say, touching his neck, close to the collarbone. You give it to someone by sucking. I think it's also called a 'hickey'?

There's a flicker of a second where it could go a variety of ways: he could smile nervously. He could look confused. He could even recoil, thereby justifying the sudden tension coiling up in your stomach of *Oh fuck, I've gone and done it again.*

But what he does is laugh and clap his hands. —'Hickey', he says in English, in a surprisingly clear accent. I used to do that when I was a kid: make giant bruises on my arm. Here, here and here, he says, lightly touching the back of your wrist, the centre of your forearm, the crease of your elbow. I once made a really big one there, he says, placing his hand on your shoulder. It looked like Africa. When a schoolteacher saw it, he asked if the orphanage staff were beating me.

He laughs again.

—Did it hurt?

His gaze flickers briefly to a man walking by, selling bouquets of wilted roses. Your shoulder feels cold when he takes his hand away. —Only when I touched it.

By the fourth beer the food has long since been cleared from the table. Even the crumpled-up wrappers from the coconut candies are gone. You reach inside your handbag and touch your box of cigarettes, but it doesn't seem appropriate to whip one out and pronounce your identity as a smoker, not yet.

—Oh God, he says, his phone whistling like a bird. He turns it face down on the table. I'm so sorry; I have no control over that. This guy from Spain, he was an Anthill volunteer a few

14

months ago. He's always sending me pornography videos on WhatsApp. He's crazy!

—Pornography?

—Exactly. Exactly! His wife would go crazy if she knew! And it's not just to me, either – there's like nine other people in the chat group. Women, even! Gringas like you. God, we used to get so many volunteers from Europe. We haven't had one for ages. Gringos are much more interested in Colombia than Europeans, don't you think?

—I'm not from the US, you say. I'm not a gringa. But he picks up his phone and taps at the screen, like he hasn't heard.

—Can I ask you something? he says, slipping the phone back into his pocket. What did you call me, back there on the pavement? When you first saw me?

—Huh? You're suddenly aware of that popcorn kernel again, still stuck in your upper molar. Oh. I said 'Matty'. He's . . . It's what I called Mattías when we were kids.

—Did you? That's very interesting, he says, as if speaking to himself. And I'm sorry, what do you go by again?

You pick up your napkin. You've shredded it into pieces so ragged, they'd barely serve as mummy bandages. —My full name is Maria Carolina, you say, but everyone calls me Carolina. (In England, you're actually often referred to as *Caroline*, but you rarely bother to correct people.)

—So what should I call you, then?

He's leaning forward, pressing his torso against the table. Hands tensed like claws.

—You can call me whatever you want.

—I'll be honest with you, he says. With so many volunteers coming and going from the Anthill, it becomes hard for me to tell them apart. In my head they tend to all be the same – *the new volunteer.*

He laughs but his hands are still tensed, fingers stiff. His shirtsleeve has risen up, exposing those puckered-lip scars.

You scrunch the napkin into a tight ball. —If you like, you can call me Lina.

—What?

He says it so sharply, you can't help but sound defensive. —It's what Mattías used to call me! Or at least . . . that's what I remember.

He leans back into his chair. Away from the table, away from you. —He doesn't.

A motorcycle screeches to an abrupt stop behind you; your heart jumps against the bones of your chest, a startled caged animal. —Doesn't what?

—Remember. Lalo rises to his feet. Excuse me, with your permission.

He heads to the back of the restaurant. While he's gone, a woman with acne offers to sell you a plastic bag full of nuts, which you accept. A few tables away, an old man with a tiny black dog in his lap raises his glass and throws ice over his shoulder, scattering it all over the street.

—Let's go, Lalo says, appearing at your side. It's getting late.

—But the bill?

—I took care of it, don't worry. He touches you on the elbow as you stand up. Listen, I wanted to ask you something: did you really mean it earlier, what you said about teaching some classes?

He wraps his fingers around the beer bottles' slender necks, lining them up at the table's edge.

16

You don't recall saying you were willing to teach anything. But he keeps talking: —Because it would be a great help to us. We'd truly appreciate it. I know Mattías would too.

—What kind of classes?

—Whatever you want. English, if that's easiest.

You make a face.

He smacks his hand against his forehead, as if this reaction of yours is unbearable, intolerable. —No, forget that, forget I even suggested it! God, Lalo, so stupid of you! What an idiot! I know what you can do, he says, wagging a finger. You can run Leadership Club.

—Leadership? (It seems you've moved on from only expressing yourself via cheerleader-speak to high-pitched questions.)

—It'll be easy, he says. Trust me. We've chosen specific children to participate, the ones who'll benefit the most. Kids who are well behaved and get along with others.

—It all sounds a bit vague.

—That's because it is. Mattías runs it, you see.

When he says Mattías's name this time, you have to swallow hard: rising warm liquid, the taste in your mouth you get when you're carsick.

Lalo says quickly, —But he'll be much happier if you run it instead! Especially if doing it makes *you* happy.

—Is that true?

Lalo nods fervently.

Mattías: happy that you're happy.

—Okay, you say. Sure. Leadership Club it is. I'm not good with kids, though.

He lines up the last beer bottle, clinking its belly against its companions. —But I thought you were a writer?

—Pardon?

—Teacher! He smacks his forehead again. Sorry, sorry. Lalo, you dummy, ugh! I meant to say: you're a teacher, correct?

You think about it: the first-year undergrads you taught last term. Sixty-plus essays about Roland Barthes. You submitted your marks three days late and never responded to any of the module leader's increasingly frenzied emails. Your student evaluations contained comments like *The tutor did not seem to know what she was doing* and *This class was more of a book club than a seminar.*

—Yeah, you say. I'm a teacher. Sure.

—'Piece of cake', he says in English, surprising you again with his perfect accent. You can pay the volunteer fee tomorrow. We ask everyone for a one-time contribution, the equivalent of sixty US dollars. I'll take you to the cash machine first thing, no problem. Shall we go to the bar?

You look at the row of beer bottles: it would be so easy, saying *Yes.* But instead you say (in an untypical demonstration of non-alcoholic restraint), —I should probably go to bed.

—Of course, he says. I didn't mean to pressure you.

—No, no. Next time, I promise.

He claps his hands, as if sealing the deal.

On the walk back, the two of you pass a Virgin Mary statue on a squat cement block, her hands broken off. —A paramilitary victim, Lalo says, pointing at her granite stumps, but you don't laugh. A flying cockroach buzzes past, brushing your arm.

—Jesus, you say, stopping in your tracks. Isn't that lovely.

He turns and karate-kicks the roach against the cement. You can't help but scream in surprise at how fast he's moved, the explosion of noise, the roach's little brown body smashed against the statue's base.

—That's how you do it, he says, straightening his shirt. That's how you clean this place up.

You glance over your shoulder as you walk away. The roach has left a dark smear under the Virgin's feet.

—You need to be careful in this city, he says, resting his hand briefly on a telephone pole. Especially you, with skin like that. I wouldn't carry your iPhone around if I were you. And forget about putting in earbuds.

He starts crossing the street in long strides, his sweatpants swishing. You follow, your enormous suitcase squeaking behind you, which he didn't offer to take this time.

—Medellín has changed a lot in the past few years, he says. As I'm sure you know. Oh, it's safer now, for sure. It's a bit of a tired narrative, to be honest, about how the city has transformed and all that. Everybody loves a nice renewal story, no? But war is not something good; on that we can all agree. And there's nothing better than having a quiet life with your family and living in peace. Who wouldn't want that, right? But to me (he says, quickening his stride), if this country knew the truth of what's going on – about what happened to its neighbourhoods, what's still happening – the truth would make it fall apart. So when you're walking around this city (he says, not looking at you as he speaks), when you're looking at this person or that one, you won't be able to recognise who was once a guerrilla or who was once a paramilitary. Who was bad or who was good. It's like when you put something in the trash: it instantly becomes garbage. And it doesn't matter if it used to be this thing or that thing, for the kitchen or the bathroom, used once and discarded or held on to for years and genuinely loved by someone, genuinely adored. Once they put you in the trash (he says, staring straight ahead, as though his eyesight is an intense beacon you both need to light the path ahead), you're rotten. That's just the way it is.

As the two of you approach the Anthill headquarters, he pulls a ring of silvery keys out of his pocket.

—Don't kill me, he says, but I had them all along. I should have checked my pockets more carefully. What a dummy I am, right?

—Ha, you say. You clutch the handle of your suitcase, looking vaguely around. More trash bags have been brought out, propped against the trees like freshly laid eggs. There's a bottle of duty-free whisky in your suitcase – should you invite him into your room to keep drinking? Would that be weird? Would it be even weirder (not to mention somewhat pathetic) if you just kept the party going by yourself?

The keys rattle in his hands as he raises them towards the lock. —I have something else to tell you, he says, but you have to promise not to kill me. Promise?

—What? you say. It feels like the conversation is getting away from you, escaping, like a balloon sputtering around the room. Maybe the jetlag is kicking in but you suddenly feel very, very tired. Okay, you say. I promise.

—It's Mattías, he says. It's me.

(Lina – is that you? I'm here!)

A HUNDRED THOUSAND YEARS
INTO THE FUTURE

At some point, I will wander through the abandoned building that was once our home. The orange plastic of my radiation suit will squeak with every step I take. I may or may not have a drone assistant, buzzing anxiously beside me, monitoring my vital signs amidst the deadly radiation. There I'll go, pulling along my cart of supplies: tinned food. Geiger counter. Plastic ziplock bags.

Inside the empty structure that was once our home, I'll step carefully over shards of broken glass. Glowing, highly evolved mushrooms will sprout out of what remains of the wall; wallpaper will peel away like sunburnt skin. I'll look around, eyes protected by rubber goggles. The drone will blinkingly inform me that safety readings are clear; advance investigations are a go.

And then, if I want to, I'll be able to superimpose what used to be here – like those colouring books with transparent paper, where you could lay one image on top of the other, changing what's underneath. I'll put the desk there, the window here, the bookshelf way over yonder. There are the brooms propped up on the couch. That's where the water streamed in, under the balcony door. And here's the door where your mother ran out, down the stairs, into the street.

But no matter how long and hard I'll look, I won't be able to place you. Or me. The two of us, together.

I'll keep looking, though: despite my drone's nervous murmurs that it'll probably be a good idea for us to go soon, that there's danger in lingering. Using my top-secret code name, it'll beam the message to me, the voice loud and clear:

Come in, Arctic Fox. Arctic Fox, do you read me.

But I won't give up. Wherever you are, I will find you. No matter how far ahead into the future. No matter how far back into the past.

PART II

THE NEW VOLUNTEER

THE ANTHILL

It's the faded pink building down the road from the grocery store. An hour by bus from the Metrocable stop. Telephone wires cross the sky, chickens cluck from a nearby balcony, a dog with enormous testicles flees uphill. 1 p.m. Here they come.

Chattering busily, streaming through the propped-open door. Ponytails bouncing, shirts untucked and speckled with dust from Tocineta and De Todito crisps. Some are in school uniforms, white socks pulled up to their knees. Most are in shorts and flimsy flip-flops, thin vest straps verging on uneasily inappropriate. Sweaters are tied tight over belly buttons or draped over shoulders. They're never that many, and the majority are regulars.

The new volunteer's first day.

—Hello, what's your name? Donaldo. Hello, Donaldo, nice to meet you! And yours? Hello, Julián. Nice to meet you, Dulce. Margarita – what a beautiful name. No running, please. What's your name, sorry? Becca? Betina? Sorry, Betina. Sorry, sorry. Thank you for standing in line, Dulce.

Five minutes in and she's sweating.

The Anthill has been running after-school programmes in this neighbourhood for over three years now (is that right? Is Mattías going to give her an introductory talk, a tour of the premises?). One p.m. to three thirty. Five days a week. The children arrive by foot, mainly from local neighbourhood schools, sometimes further. They hitch rides with uncles and brothers on the backs of motorbikes. They weave through traffic jams of stalled cars and honking trucks. They hop over puddles and stroll past piles of cement blocks and ladders propped against unfinished buildings, homes that look more like construction sites.

The Anthill children, arriving. They come with crusty nostrils and reddish-purple bruises under their eyeballs. U-shaped scratches on their foreheads and cheekbones. They come with lips split open from Lord knows what: grandmothers smacking them, wrestling matches in the schoolyard. After barely ten minutes, the new volunteer is already taken aback by the consistent presence of injuries: the cut-open knuckles, the beetle-shell-shaped scabs, eyes so swollen they can only peer out at the world through thin dark slits.

Assembly is only just getting started, on the flattened dirt round the back that doubles as the football field. Thirty-something children sitting in three messy lines, calling out to friends. She makes her way through the sea of collared shirts and muddy trousers. Her assigned position this week is the line of little ones, kindergarteners to first-graders (ages five to seven). She already likes this age group – for the most part they seem well behaved, respectful of authority, easy to deal with. She doesn't dare cast a glance in the direction of the older kids (ages eleven to thirteen), as though eye contact alone can be deadly. Girls with colourful beaded bracelets, stubby tongue piercings that only show when they talk. Boys with crucifixes and Nike logos shaved into their bristly skulls. They lean against each other and giggle, legs sticking out instead of crossed.

She's perfectly happy working with the young ones for now, thanks.

It's Maryluz who supervises the older ones. Maryluz: caked-on eyeshadow and tight white jeans. Silver piercings in her nose and eyebrows; hoops in her earlobes and lip. The tiny heart-shaped jewels sewn on her pockets match the studs on her sandals, and her hair hangs down in a ponytail so long it needs two fat scrunchies to tie it back. Maryluz is, as they would say in England, a total babe, but the coldly efficient way she supervises the older kids (rapping the boys' heads with her ringed knuckles, sternly intoning *Keep your hands to yourself, please!*) – it's both awe-inspiring and intimidating.

Eight to ten-year-olds, that's Shauna's watch: cheerfully North American (Montana? Wisconsin? One of those sad weird middle states), shockingly blonde-white hair (potentially dyed?), a Roberto Bolaño quote tattooed on her inner wrist in typewriter font. She gives the new volunteer the sunniest of smiles; the new volunteer smiles tightly back. If Shauna is a warm bubble of sunshine, Maryluz is a gritty, glittery rock. She makes accidental eye contact with Maryluz, who raises her floss-thin eyebrows and mouths a single word, piercings flashing in the sunlight:

Mattías?

The new volunteer shakes her head. More like a twitch. Where could he be; when is he arriving; is he coming or not? But then a few children start shouting. Pointing like sailors who've just spotted land, their chants growing louder and louder: *Mattías, Mattías, Mattías!*

Here he comes, dashing up the dirt road. Sweat stains on his long-sleeved shirt, a fully inflated football tucked under his armpit (is that where he ran off to? Where would he have

29

found a pump around here?). He's giving high-fives, he's calling out greetings, hugging children and calling them by name, hey Jordy, hey Nanci, I haven't seen you in ages, Francisco, where have you been? He's distributing fist-bumps, he's racing to the front. He comes to a stop by the wall mural: stick figures holding hands, the Colombian flag with a heart in the middle, a floating blue peace sign. And then there are the squat words in streaky paint, the Anthill's motto:

ALL WELCOME!
BE SAFE
BE RESPECTFUL
BE KIND

He raises his hands, conductor style, ushering everyone into respectful silence.

—Good afternoon, boys and girls!

The reply is right on cue, a messy chorus: —Goooooooood aaaaafternooooooooon, Mister Mattías! Picking at shoelaces, wiggling fingers into ears, pinching their friends.

———

—I'm sorry, I'm sorry!

That's what he said to her, standing outside the volunteer headquarters. Laughing, grabbing her by the elbows, as she stood on the pavement and stared. Her hands had gone weak and floppy; her suitcase toppled over with a heavy crash, like the felled monument of a dictator after a war.

—I shouldn't have done that, he said. I know, I know. Come here.

He pulled her close into a hug, but she couldn't raise her arms. She just stood there numbly, smelling the salty muskiness behind his ears. A grown man's scent.

When he let go and stepped away, she said in English, — What the fuck?

—I'm sorry, he repeated, more serious now. But please understand my position. I haven't seen you in twenty years. I wanted to see what you were like. How you behaved.

—Jesus Christ. Her hands shook as she bent down and pulled her suitcase back up. The metal handle knocked against her hip in a painful way, but she didn't cry out. Instead she said, Why would you do that? You couldn't, like, not lie?

—I know, I know. Listen. He put both hands on her shoulders and looked her straight in the eye, a very deep and uncomfortable stare. It's been so long. I want to spend time with you and catch up. I want to get to know you. That's very important to me. I'm so happy you emailed me, that you were able to come.

—You've totally fucked with my head!

—It's okay, though. It's okay. Please, let's go inside and I'll show you your room.

The volunteer headquarters was essentially a ground-floor apartment: kitchen, living room, the basics. There was an empty bookcase by the wall and a tree stump by the window, and a couch covered in long white scratches, yellow stuffing vomiting out. It was all terribly sparse, as though decorated by monks from *The Name of the Rose*. He crossed the room in a few quick strides and opened the door to a bedroom, which smelled so strongly of paint her eyes immediately watered.

—Off you go, he said, addressing three black cats curled up

on a fleece blanket. They lifted their heads, blinking their large yellow eyes at him. Go on, get. I put in new sheets for you, he said, lifting the cats up one at a time and tossing them gently outside. My room's in the back, behind the kitchen, but you won't see much of me here. I'm very busy.

—How long have you lived here? She sank down on the mattress, which rested on stacks of dusty wooden planks.

—Two years. I rent both this building and the Anthill, which you'll see tomorrow. It's a Metrocable ride to get there and then the bus, so be sure to bring change. There's no charge for the rent, only the one-time volunteer fee. But I do ask that when I'm not here, you please stay out of my room.

—Of course!

—There's no lock on it, you see. It's very important that I have privacy, a space for no one else but me. Does that sound fair?

—Of course, she repeated. I understand.

They looked at each other.

—Well, he said. Goodnight.

———

—I hope, Mattías shouts, that you're all having a good day!

—Yeeeeeeeeeeeeeeeeeees! comes the cry.

Near where the new volunteer is standing, a girl with dark eyebrows thick as caterpillars is repeatedly punching the boy sitting in front of her. The boy doesn't even turn around, like he can't be bothered to notice her abuse.

The new volunteer taps the girl on the shoulder. —No hitting, please, she says, arranging her face into what is hopefully a stern yet kindly frown.

The girl stares back, still punching the boy with her clenched fist. The boy's head slumps forward, but otherwise he doesn't move.

The new volunteer sighs.

Thankfully Mattías gets straight to it, pointing at one volunteer after another, like a knight jabbing them with an invisible lance. —Today! We have! Art with Maryluz! Football outside with me! Homework in the Education Corner with Shauna! And Leadership Club students, please line up with our brand-new volunteer, Carolina! Rotations at two, Free Time at two thirty! Have fun, boys and girls, be SAFE, RESPECTFUL and KIND, and don't forget to make good choices!

And that's it for assembly. The children rise in a huge wave, swarming towards the staff member they want to be with, some of them obeying Maryluz's shrill cries of *Walk, please,* most of them not. The girl with thick eyebrows stands up, twisting the ear of the boy in front of her as she does so. He cries out, hands flying towards his face.

—Bye, gringa! the girl says, waving sassily in the new volunteer's direction.

—Hey, the new volunteer says. I'm not a gringa.

But the girl is already dashing towards Shauna, not looking back. The boy trails after her, pulling his arms into his sweater so that only his elbows stick out. From behind he looks like an amputee.

The new volunteer crosses and uncrosses her arms as she follows them into the building. Maryluz's kids are already sitting obediently in a circle, watching her intensely as she hands out folded wads of toilet paper and brightly coloured straws. Shauna is getting her kids settled at the battered plastic tables, helping notebooks out of bags, pencils out of cases, distributing photocopied worksheets in a very important-looking and professional manner. And behind her, outside, Mattías is leading his enormous group of football players, setting down orange plastic cones to use as goalposts while giving three girls a piggyback ride at once.

He doesn't even give her a backward glance.

There's something awful about seeing him older like this. Inappropriate, almost. Like the time she stalked the Gómez twins on Facebook. Those eight-year-old boys she had sung next to in the school Christmas choir performance, they were now tanned muscular hunks, floating in Jacuzzis, bloated faces grinning at selfie sticks as they raised Martini glasses. Or Emma Green's last text message, sending out her new number: *lost my phone at my own wedding, just my luck amirite* (the reference to the missing phone had made the new volunteer swallow, hard). And then there was Emma's brazen request, asking if she knew a Hackney-based coke dealer (*pretty forward of me, haha, but you've lived here so long I figured you would know!*). The girl who had played Mary in the school nativity play; the one who had accompanied her and Mattías every Sunday to the evangelical church; the only person in her third-grade classroom who had been able to make a paper plane correctly the first time. She left Emma's text with two blue ticks next to it, not replying.

She's not an idiot – she didn't expect anything different. But wasn't there something a tiny bit traumatising about it? How things changed?

But this (she reminds herself, with the sternness of a teacher shaking a finger at a child) is what she wanted. What she came for. She wanted to come back. And here she is. She curls fingers into fists (she's been picking at her nails again, but thankfully they don't look too red, not bad enough to be noticed). Takes a deep breath. Walks up to Maryluz and waits for a pause during her instructions.

—Five squares each, Maryluz is saying, passing out the last wad of toilet paper. And if you rip it up on purpose, eat it, throw it away or do anything else that's stupid or uncalled for, you don't get any extras. We want to be good to the planet and not create extra trash. We need to take care of Planet Earth, the one thing we all share. Alma, is there a reason you're not sitting with your bottom on the floor?

—Maryluz? the new volunteer says.

Maryluz looks up with her Bambi eyelashes. The new volunteer swallows, conscious of the sweaty pores on her nose.

—I'm sorry to interrupt. I'm running Leadership Club today, but none of my students lined up with me. And since I don't know who any of them are, I can't find them.

Maryluz blinks. —That's not good.

—I should have learned their names earlier and matched them to their faces before assembly. I'm sorry.

—No, don't be silly. How could you be expected to know that?

Maryluz sets her plastic bag down on the ground, shirt rising high up her back. Her unhesitant dismissal of any potential guilt or shame makes the new volunteer weak with gratitude.

—Rebecca, Maryluz barks. Dafne.

Two girls look up from the toilet-paper flowers they're carefully twisting into shape.

—Can you be good helpers and clear off a table for Leadership Club? You're both in it today. Alma, Maryluz continues, you're in charge until I get back.

Alma nods with all the seriousness of a newly appointed commander. She has an enormous dark burn across her face, crinkling into her eyes – it's hard to tell where it ends and her mouth begins. Rebecca and Dafne immediately head to the closest table and begin unstacking the upside-down chairs.

—Let's get the others, Maryluz says. God, we're like cattle herders, aren't we? Alma will be good, though – she's one of the best ones.

They stroll towards Shauna's homework group in the Education Corner. Maryluz's wooden heels make clopping sounds like a show pony on the Anthill's cement floor.

—What happened to her face? the new volunteer says, just to fill the silence.

—Alma's? Her mother's ex-boyfriend threw acid on her. But wait. Maryluz tugs her ponytail over her shoulder. Why didn't Mattías set this up for you? On your first day and everything. Honestly, he's so useless. What an asshole.

She says it bluntly, like it's a fact that everyone knows.

—Yeah, definitely, the new volunteer says, a bit too quickly: why yes, she also knows Mattías, all too well!

—How did you hear about the Anthill? I hope it wasn't that pathetic website. Maryluz stops to flatten a *RECYCLE REDUCE REUSE* poster that's falling off the wall. I'm so embarrassed by that WordPress shit. Shauna's husband started building it but never finished. Did you find us on Facebook?

—No. Yes. I mean – I found the website, but I emailed Mattías directly.

Maryluz frowns. —Directly?

The poster immediately unsticks from the wall again, flopping forward in a weary bow.

—Yes, the new volunteer says. I got his email from a friend. A mutual friend. Did – has Mattías not said anything? She pauses. About me?

—Mattías never says anything about anybody. Maryluz rips the poster off and sets it on a nearby table. But he did say you'd be joining us from England. Which is a ton of information coming from him, believe me.

—It is?

—Oh yeah. Maryluz turns the poster so that it's face down. Our dear old jefe's a locked door. But he said you wrote books, or something. That you're a very creative person.

—Study. I study books. I'm a teacher.

—Me too! I teach art. Now it's Maryluz who pauses. The new volunteer eyes her, and Maryluz eyes her right back. Is she being . . . examined? But eventually Maryluz smiles and says, How lovely that you and Mattías are old friends. I'd love to hear all about it.

—Of course.

Clip-clop, clip-clop, go Maryluz's chunky heels on the floor. The new volunteer follows, a duckling once more.

Shauna looks up from a Days of the Week worksheet, smiling brightly. —Hello, ladies, she says in accented Spanish.

Maryluz explains the situation, while the new volunteer tries not to stare at Shauna's Bolaño tattoo: *El amor nunca trae nada bueno; el amor siempre trae algo mejor.* Love never brings anything good; love always brings something better. Dark font against skin.

And suddenly she's there: sitting in the back of the chauffeured car, her mother muttering away in the front seat as they crawled through stalled traffic (a university protest? A police roadblock?). The air smelled like exhaust fumes and French bread. And then the car inched past a group of men at a traffic light, their arms and collarbones dark with ink.

Criminals, her mother hissed, twisting around to watch them, while the chauffeur stared straight ahead. *Sicarios. Look, María – tattoos are how you identify them: the gang members, the assassins, the men for hire.* Her forehead pressed against the windowpane as she stared.

Was Mattías in the car with them? Slumped beside her in the back seat? Where were they going? Where had they been?

Focusing on the crayon drawings taped to the walls is a far more stabilising experience: suns with googly eyes, stick figures holding hands, a giant poster that simply says *PEACE*.

—Oh gosh, Shauna says when Maryluz finishes. But wait, why didn't you pull them out during assembly?

—I didn't know who they were, the new volunteer says, trying not to feel embarrassment like a badge on her chest, bleating out her basic incompetence to the world.

Shauna stands up, smoothing down her pink volunteer shirt. —Gabriela! she calls out. Tomás! You're in Leadership Club today! Go follow Carolina!

She points at the new volunteer, Uncle Sam style, *I WANT YOU*.

The new volunteer opens her mouth to speak but abruptly shuts it: better for her to step back, let the established volunteers lead the way for now. A few children look up curiously from their schoolbooks, but nobody moves.

—I'm doing my homework, one girl says abruptly, her head bowed low over the page she's scribbling on. I have a lot of it.

—I can help you later, Shauna says. But remember what Mattías said: it's very special that Carolina has travelled all this way to help run Leadership Club. And it's very, very special that you and Tomás were invited to be in it.

—What about the other boy? the girl says. Can he come too?

Shauna frowns. —What boy?

The girl still doesn't look up. —The dirty one, she says. What about him?

Her marker keeps scrawling back and forth.

—I don't know who you're talking about, Shauna says, still frowning. But if Mattías didn't specifically invite him, then no, he's not allowed.

The girl stays seated. The marker presses down hard on whatever it is she's drawing.

—Gabriela, Maryluz says. What do we ask of Anthill students?

Still not looking up, the girl says immediately, —To welcome everyone. To be safe, respectful and kind.

—And what else?

The marker pauses. —To make good choices.

—Exactly. No one here is going to tell you what to do. No one's going to force you to do anything. Here at the Anthill, we want you to be responsible for your actions. We want everybody here to have a choice, and no one else can make it but you. Mattías nominated you for Leadership Club, out of all the other students who come here every afternoon, because he thought Leadership Club was something you would benefit from. So if you don't want to attend, that's fine. But I recommend that you think a bit harder before making your final decision.

The girl still doesn't look up. But she snaps the cap back on her marker. She stands up slowly, notebook clutched tight. The boy beside her leaps to his feet, knocking over his chair.

And when the new volunteer finally sees their faces side by side, the tightness in her chest curls in, and what's left of her fingernails press into her palms.

It's the girl and boy from assembly.

LEADERSHIP CLUB

Sometimes it's like her life is finally getting close to resembling something vaguely back on track: reconnecting with her homeland, the country she left behind! Meeting up again with her childhood BFF! If only somebody somewhere, ideally one of the invisible judges on the icily vocal committee that's continuously judging her life – if only they could bring down a giant stamp of approval on this moment. But then, yet again, she ends up feeling like she's just . . . kind of embarrassing.

—Right, the new volunteer says. Do you all know each other?

Tomás and Gabriela nod. Dafne and Rebecca shake their heads. The other two boys who were supposed to attend chose to keep playing football (or, as Maryluz bluntly informed her, *They didn't want to come*). The chair she's sitting on is so low her knees feel ridiculously high, an *Alice in Wonderland* giant.

—Okay. Well, why don't we start with that? Let's go around the table and, um, say our names. Gabriela opens her mouth to begin but the new volunteer hurries on, interrupting without meaning to: And a fact! Let's all share an interesting fact about ourselves. A unique, original fact.

Nobody says anything. Tomás puts his index finger into his mouth and starts nibbling it like a cob of corn.

—Okay, I'll go first. My name is Carolina, and an interesting fact about me . . . is . . . (*what constitutes an 'interesting'*

41

fact, exactly?) . . . I'm from England. Do you guys know where England is?

Three heads shake and one nods. Gabriela says, —It's in the United Kingdom.

—That's right, the new volunteer says, trying not to sound surprised. The United Kingdom. Though I used to live right here, in Medellín.

—We're not in Medellín, Gabriela says. Medellín's down there.

She jerks her head in the direction of the cable car wires, the rows of brick houses dotting the mountainside, down into the valley below.

Nobody says anything for a beat. Then the new volunteer says, —Dafne, do you want to go next?

The pleading tone of her voice must be painfully obvious, but thankfully Dafne puts her out of her misery and takes the bait. —My name is Dafne, she says in a soft voice, and my interesting fact is I'm from Chocó.

Rebecca says the exact same thing. Tomás says 'Ituango', a word she's never heard before. —Where's that? the new volunteer asks, and he mumbles, —Antioquia.

Gabriela says, —My interesting fact is I'm from Brooklyn. The new volunteer looks at her. Gabriela wiggles in her seat. My mother lives there, she continues. In the Hamptons.

The Hamptons and Brooklyn are two different places, the new volunteer thinks, but instead she says, —Okay, I guess our interesting fact is that we all come from . . . somewhere.

She hands out blank sheets of paper and asks them to write out their names, along with images that represent them and their lives, an activity that feels vaguely age-appropriate.

—Draw what best represents you, the new volunteer says, in the brightest voice she can, sunny Shauna style. So we can get to know each other!

—We already know each other, Gabriela says, but pulls the cap off a marker anyway.

As the children hunch over their name tags – scrawling out letters, scribbling in houses, drawing fat-bellied clouds and anorexic flowers – the new volunteer looks at her own blank sheet.

What about her?

Should she draw a book?

A laptop?

A lit-up phone screen?

If she is *really* going to get honest with her name tag here – the kind of honesty that would make her dissertation advisor's eyes widen and reach for the office phone, in order to contact the sectioning branch of the NHS – then her paper should be nothing more than a giant red question mark.

Or one internet tab on her browser after another. Hundreds of thousands of hours frittered away, lost, withered into God knows what. Nothing, basically. Nothing insightful, nothing useful, nothing helpful for society.

It doesn't matter. Whatever best represents FEAR.

Or, better yet, SHAME.

Or, best of all, I AM SO SORRY ABOUT MYSELF AND EVERYTHING I HAVE DONE AND WILL EVER DO, AND FOR WHAT I AM DOING THIS VERY MOMENT, I AM SORRY I'M SORRY I'M SORRY I'M SORRY.

And on and on.

BBC You'reAPieceOfShit Radio.

The channel in her head she can never turn off. Always there, humming in the background. Like the noise made by the refrigerator in the Anthill kitchen.

And lurking at the very bottom of the hum are questions. Faintly whispering, in the deepest darkest part of her:

But what precisely am I sorry for? And to whom, exactly, am I apologising?

For now, though, the most recent thing she needs to feel sorry for is her apparent lack of foresight, as it's taken the children five minutes to finish their name tags as opposed to the thirty she'd originally planned for. Tomás is the only one still working, carefully colouring in a single giant 'T' on his paper with the quiet meticulousness of a tax accountant that makes her love him, just a little. When Gabriela asks where the trash is, the new volunteer tells her without thinking twice. But then Gabriela turns the plastic bin upside down and starts digging through the scrunched-up bits of paper and bits of broken crayon, picking up empty juice boxes and smashing them between her hands.

—I'm looking for my pencil, Gabriela says. Where's my pencil? Somebody threw away my pencil.

—Ugh, Gabi, Dafne says, yanking the markers to her side of the table. You're making a mess!

Rebecca taps the new volunteer's elbow. —Look, Missis, she whispers, holding up her name tag.

—Very nice, the new volunteer says blandly. Can you fill in this white space? She touches the upper corner. Maybe with a pretty sun, or some happy clouds?

When she withdraws her hand, she's left behind a tiny red dot on the paper. Gleaming and shiny. She and Rebecca stare at it.

—What's that? Rebecca says.

The new volunteer looks down at her fingers. There's a streak of liquid red skin on her thumb, where she's scratched herself raw without realising it. Blood.

—God, she says in English before she can help it. She tries to wipe the blood off Rebecca's paper, but it leaves behind a dark-brown smear.

—What's wrong with your nails? Dafne says. She lets out a tiny screeching laugh, as if delighted. Do you eat them?

The new volunteer crosses her hands behind her back, like she's waiting to be arrested. —No.

—But they're so tiny! Dafne's eyes are wide. Rebecca is still looking at the brown bloody smear, rotating the page.

—I have a disease, the new volunteer lies. I have a genetic disease that makes my nails very small. I'm very, very sick. Why don't we go ahead and finish up? Make sure there are no empty spaces! We want our name tags to be as full and as beautiful-looking as possible!

Dafne pulls a marker cap off with her teeth. Rebecca lowers herself into her seat, gingerly holding her name tag by the furthest corner possible.

The best thing is that this doesn't even compete with her very worst moment. Not even close. So many others in the running! Screaming and pushing each other out of the way, heaving themselves towards the #1 spot with the intensity of Olympic runners. Which to choose? The time she burst into tears during the conference presentation, and everyone stared as liquid dripped from her nose on to her blouse, and all she could think was *Stop Crying. Stop Crying. Stop Crying*? The New Year's Eve she threw up on the pub bathroom floor, and when she returned to her table, laughing and joking about ordering more shots, the bartender approached her and icily requested that she leave? The time her advisor silently passed back the draft of her dissertation, the passages she'd plagiarised highlighted with a blaring yellow marker?

—I'm a knight! Gabriela shouts. She's turned the bin upside down on her head, waving her arms around. I'm an astronaut!

Some of the children in Maryluz's group glance over, and Maryluz says in a loud voice, —Let's keep focused on our own work, boys and girls. Don't get distracted by Anthill students who don't know how to be respectful.

—Now, now, the new volunteer says, taking the bin off Gabriela's head and putting it back on the floor. Let's make good decisions.

The tiredness that seizes her. The heaviness in her limbs as Gabriela immediately picks the bin back up and puts it on her head again. And then Tomás abruptly lowers his marker and starts tearing his name tag into strips, which he then rips into confetti, which he then sprinkles on the concrete floor. A weariness that would be a tired grey, if it had a colour, and would be shaped like the cloud of dirt that always followed that one Charlie Brown character, the disgusting one who was always dirty.

There's no hiding it: this off-putting, awkward just-plain-wrongness about her. It can never be picked away and will always be noticed by others: exposed and bloody and raw.

—Tomás! Gabriela says, lifting the bin up so that her eyes peer out. Why did you do that? You've gone and ruined it.

—It was already ruined, Tomás mumbles. He puts his head down on the table and closes his eyes, like he's been shot in the back by a hidden assassin.

In her corner, Shauna is standing up and clapping. —Rotations are over, she's calling out. Please go to your next rotation!

Anthill children immediately begin pouring past, running outside for Free Time or to sign up for a fifteen-minute shift on the computer. Rebecca and Dafne look anxiously at the new volunteer, and she stares blankly back before remembering, oh yeah, they're not allowed to leave until she gives them permission. —You can go, she says, and they shoot off like rockets, racing towards Maryluz so quickly Dafne stumbles over her battered Crocs. Come on, she says to Gabriela and Tomás. We better go too.

Gabriela removes the bin from her head and sets it on the floor. Then she squats by the shredded bits of Tomás's name tag and picks them up one at a time, licking her fingers so the paper will stick.

—Thank you, Gabriela, the new volunteer says, and just for a second the tiredness lifts. She starts putting the markers away: two caps are missing, which she is already starting to see as an inevitable law of working with children, that something will always end up a tiny bit fucked. Tomás's name tag is basically garbage, Dafne's is an enormous flower and the brown smear of blood still floats in Rebecca's sky, a harrowing comet from hell.

And then there's Gabriela's. She brings Gabriela's name tag close to her face, rotating it this way and that.

It looks . . . familiar.

—Gabriela, she manages to say, in the most even tone she can muster. What's this?

Gabriela stands up, brushing her hands on her shorts. Tomás slides out his seat too, knocking the table with his hip. The cup of markers wobbles but doesn't tip over.

47

—Why did you draw this? What is it?

(Familiar of what? What does it remind her of? What is she trying to remember?)

—I was drawing it earlier, Gabriela says. In the Education Corner.

Tomás tucks his hands into his opposite shirtsleeves, an amputee once more. They're walking away from her, but for every step they take she takes one too, using her torso as a barrier. —What is it? she repeats, her voice rising. What is this supposed to be?

Gabriela shakes her head. Her eyes have suddenly gone very narrow.

—Is it a drawing of Medellín? I mean, of here?

Gabriela doesn't say anything. Tomás begins puffing like a steam engine, as though the pain of being kept away from Shauna's computer sign-up sheet is absolutely agonising.

—Well, the new volunteer says, you did the assignment wrong, then. You were supposed to draw something that represents you and your life.

She steps aside. Tomás shoots forward, the loose soles of his shoes flapping.

—Walk, Tomás! Maryluz shouts, not even looking up from tidying away what remains of art class.

—Go on, the new volunteer says to Gabriela. Go and play.

—I didn't.

—Didn't what?

Gabriela raises her chin. There's a scar there she hasn't noticed before – a thin white line on her throat. As though a sharp claw was traced into her skin, a fish-hook-shaped mark that never fully faded. —I didn't do it wrong, she says.

48

—Gabriela! Tomás wails, glancing anxiously over his shoulder as he stands in line, hopping up and down on one foot. All the spots are almost gone!

When she's able to speak, the new volunteer says, —Gabriela, your name tag is supposed to represent you and who you are. This . . . has nothing to do with anything.

Gabriela finally looks away. She skips over to Tomás. Wraps her arms around his waist and pulls him into a hug that is also a wrestle. —Why are you so weird, she says. And for the first time that day Tomás smiles, a huge toothy grin.

But the new volunteer looks down at Gabriela's name tag. Jagged black lines. White blotchy eyes. The marker scribbled furiously, uncontrollably, darkness spreading to the edge of the page.

But there, unmistakable: the triangle-shaped teeth. Opening and shutting, the great and terrible jaws.

(I warned you, Lina! Here I come!)

A HUNDRED THOUSAND YEARS
INTO THE PAST

It's dark and quiet – here, in this place where I'm waiting. I've been waiting here a very long time. Sometimes children wander in and I bite and scratch their necks until they run out screaming. Don't leave, stay here, keep me company! Most of the time, lately, to amuse myself, I watch her, observe what she's doing – this person who may or may not be you. I thought she was – is she? Your father calls you *Mary* over the phone; your English friends call you *Caroline* in that strange English lilt. Mostly, though, I close my eyes and follow you around. There you are, scratching your hand. Fumbling around in your suitcase for the duty-free whisky, riding the bus down from the airport. But now that you're back, ever so close to me (and only getting closer), I can see and hear you anytime I want, inside and out, then and now. I know it all, better than you know yourself.

But the question remains, even with you – her? – here. *The new volunteer* – this person who may or may not be you. For the time being, I suppose that's how I'll have to think of her, until I'm certain that she and you are one and the same – if she's the person I used to know. I'll have to wait and see, before I can know for sure.

But that's okay. If there's one thing I am, it's patient. To make time go by faster, I think about the time we spent together, you and me and your mother together.

The dinner parties.

The zoo.

Her fun little living room game.

And when that grows tiresome, I make up silly stories in my head. Make-believe ones, things that aren't true and could never happen. I prefer fantasising to remembering, invention over memory – don't you? A hundred thousand years ago, I climbed over mountains. I fought dinosaurs. I *was* a dinosaur. Blood dripped from my jaws. Lava poured out and preserved me for generations. I was a hunter. I was a warrior. I basically invented religion. I crossed continents; I migrated across the world. I knew how to find medicinal plants, the most magic of mushrooms. I was the first storyteller, crouching before a fire. I was the first cannibal. I was the first shaman. I nurtured a matriarchal society. I invented war. I crawled out of the ocean with a single gelatinous eye and a stumpy leg that took millennia to evolve into four. I ate algae and plankton; I lived at the bottom of a pond and was blind. I was a jellyfish, floating in the middle of the ocean without any brains. I was a cell that failed to develop mitochondria. All that, so that you could become you, and I could become me, and stay by your side. You and me.

But you didn't want me around any more. Lina – why?

COLOURING TIME

—What do you think of her boobs, Shauna says. The cable car buzzes, lifting them into the air like C-3PO and R2-D2 shot free from their spacecraft.

—What?

—Maryluz's. They're so fake, right? She bites into her pear. A bit of juice drips on to her pink Anthill T-shirt. Swallowing, she says, Her butt too, probably. And her eyelashes for sure.

The new volunteer looks out the window. A pregnant woman is sitting across from them, texting rapidly. An old man with a wilted face and elegant brown shoes is staring down at his hands. The *other* two volunteers – even newer than her, first-timers, a Welsh girl and a German guy – are riding in the Metrocable ahead with Mattías, who's currently giving them his welcome-to-the-Anthill spiel (the one she has yet to hear herself). The mountains around them are dotted with red-brick houses; the streets under their feet are clothes lines and construction materials and wet plastic bags tangled in gutters like the grossest shower hair ever. And behind and in front of them, the cable cars climb and fall, the furthest one rising away into the trees at the mountains' highest point.

The new volunteer says, —To each their own, I suppose.

Shauna wipes a droplet of pear juice off her chin. —The prevalence of plastic surgery in this country freaked me out so much when I first moved here. So depressing.

A moment, flashing: her mother pinching the flesh above her hips. Weepily shouting, *I need to get this removed!* Whispered rumours on the playground (Emma Green? The Gómez twins?): somebody's cousin or maid, they had just died, passed away in their sleep, due to cheap silicone that was really cement injected into their thighs.

If only she had something more coherent, more linear. A photograph glued in an album, part of a chronological sequence. Not these mixed-up flashes, scattered every which way, emerging at random moments all higgledy-piggledy.

She blinks rapidly to refocus. —How long have you lived in Medellín, Shauna?

—Eight months. Shauna takes another enormous bite of her pear, teeth creeping closer to the stalk. We were in Thailand before this. Now *that's* a depressing country. You think that people are being friendly, but really they're taking advantage of you. We kept meeting people on the street who'd take us out for cocktails, and then we'd just get overcharged! People are much friendlier here.

—I guess everyone has to make a living.

The cable car grinds to a halt through a station. The pregnant woman gets off and a young man in a football shirt gets on. The new volunteer moves as if to get off too, but Shauna shakes her head to indicate *Not yet; not this stop.*

—I thought Medellín was going to be more like Barcelona, Shauna says, carefully tucking away what remains of her pear into a plastic bag inside her backpack. Once my husband finishes his book, we'll probably move there.

—Your husband is writing a book?

Shauna nods. —About Medellín. He's from Barcelona

originally, but grew up in Los Angeles. The preschools in Barcelona will be way better for our son. I'll definitely miss how affordable everything is here, though. She laughs sunnily. What about you?

The new volunteer leans over, trying to glimpse Mattías in the cable car ahead. But all she sees is the Welsh girl's enormous black leather handbag, squashed against the glass.

—I might stay here for a while, she says. I'm taking a break, I think. And by 'break' I mean apocalyptically imploding.

She laughs too, but Shauna just stares back. It's an expression the new volunteer recognises from her university peers: that day she drank too much coffee in Caffè Nero and rambled about going to the hairdresser to get the wad of matted hair cut off her head, because it'd been so long since she'd combed it. *You'd think a hairdresser would have dealt with a rat's nest before, haha!* She'd meant to be funny, but instead everyone just sipped their lattes uneasily and changed the topic back to fellowship applications and graduation day outfits.

—I'm joking! she says, so loudly the young man in the football shirt glances over. Only joking! Of course I want to continue improving and advancing my academic career while I'm here. Of course.

Shauna zips her backpack shut and doesn't say anything.

The cable car grinds to yet another halt. In this station, the turnstiles go right up to the platform, so that the new volunteer can see the conveyer belt of people shuffling in and out. Street-sweepers with their orange uniforms and carts full of brooms. Schoolgirls wearing backpacks in front of their stomachs. Old men with every shirt button done up, walking with tiny shuffling steps that delay everyone behind them, but no one seems to be getting impatient or huffing irritably like they would on the Tube; no one is smiling, but no one seems annoyed either. She thinks of the sign that greeted her at the airport, squat letters before a backdrop of white-sand beaches and palm trees. *THE COUNTRY OF SMILES: THE ONLY DANGER IS THAT YOU'LL NEVER WANT TO LEAVE.*

—I think the car in front has some empty seats, she says, scooting over so that a woman in a fast-food worker's uniform can sit next to her. Should we join the others?

Shauna waves a hand dismissively. —You go; he's just giving his welcoming talk. Ugh, I've heard it so many times I could probably give it myself!

So the new volunteer clambers on to the platform, apologising automatically as she brushes against people's arms and legs (how long will it take both her body and her brain to accept that she's not in England any more, that she doesn't have to issue a constant verbal alert of *I'm sorry* and *Excuse me*?). She squeezes in by the Welsh girl, who accommodatingly moves her bag into her lap. Neither she nor the German guy look at her, their eyes fixed with great intensity on Mattías. He's wearing a long-sleeved shirt again, with small red specks on his chest (some kind of sauce?). The cable car creaks beneath them as it climbs higher.

—I've made so many mistakes with the Anthill, Mattías is saying, massaging his kneecap roughly with his fingertips. She can see the bone of his knee moving around beneath the thin fabric of his sweatpants, like a mountain shifting during a violent earthquake. So many mistakes! I can't even begin to get into all the mistakes I've made! Have either Shauna or Maryluz told you about the early Anthill days, how I wouldn't serve the kids any sugar? That didn't last long, let me tell you . . .

(What a shock it is to hear him speak English again! The way it streams out of him, with no hitch or hesitation! Like the DVD playing the current scene of her life is scratched, skipping to dialogue she last heard years ago, at the beginning of the movie.)

—Well, I think it's wonderful, the Welsh girl says, crossing her legs at the ankles. I looked into loads of volunteer opportunities in Medellín, and yours was the only one that looked good. I wanted to do something that genuinely helped the local community.

—Same here, the German guy says. Also, the Facebook page was in English.

Both he and the Welsh girl laugh. The new volunteer looks at the woman sitting with her daughter by the window. The woman is pointing at something, while the daughter presses her face against the glass, making binocular-shapes with her hands.

—Thank you very much, Mattías says. I'm very grateful to hear that.

—Is it okay that I don't speak any Spanish? the Welsh girl says, fiddling with the zip on her bag. Do the children there speak English?

—No, the new volunteer says before she can stop herself. Why would they? But then she remembers Gabriela: *My mother lives in the Hamptons.*

The Welsh girl and German guy shift their attention to her ever so slightly, a bemused undercurrent in their body language. *Wait, who's she?*

—That's right, they don't, Mattías says with a brisk crispness. But Carolina here can help translate.

The new volunteer smiles in what she hopes is a friendly and open manner, the smile of a successful, stable and productive person, as opposed to someone who didn't comb their hair for nine months and had to get a giant knot hacked from the back of their head. The Welsh girl smiles back and passes around some chewing gum, which everyone accepts but Mattías. The new volunteer nudges the Welsh girl, trying to indicate with her head that she should offer gum to the mother and child as well, but the Welsh girl puts the packet away in her bag.

—So tell us about the nunnery, the Welsh girl says, settling back. And the orphanage! How long did you live there? How old were you when you left?

—Oh no, Mattías says. You don't want to hear about that. It's boring.

—No, please continue, the German guy says. It's amazing – I can't believe they made you beg with a fake plaster on your arm. You could write a book about your life, man. Seriously.

—I don't even remember what I was saying.

—Go on, Mattías, the new volunteer says. She can feel the edge of the seat pressing into the backs of her thighs. It's definitely going to leave a mark. Tell us about the nunnery. Pretty please.

He's shaking his head and smiling, but his eyes look alarmed, the startled expression of a cat who's just heard a loud noise in the room. If he had ears on the top of his head, they'd be twisting backwards.

After getting out of the cable car, the five of them walk

uphill to the bakery, where they'll wait for the bus. They pass landmarks the new volunteer has already come to recognise, even on her second day. The food stand that sells fried intestines. The phone booth covered in peeling advertisements for PRÉSTAMOS. Street vendors call out prices of balloons, bags of dried herbs, cups of fresh fruit. The bustling life of the city, huge balls of phlegm on the pavement glistening like newborn aliens she has to carefully step over.

(Is this what it feels like to return? What is she returning to? Is this her country, her city? What is she doing here?)

At the bakery, Mattías points at the scratched-up chairs and tables. —Wait here, I'll be right back. The Welsh girl buys something enormous and cream-filled, the German guy buys something greasy and ham-filled, and Shauna buys a pastry dusty with white sugar, pressing her phone into her cheek as she talks intensely to her husband in a Spanglish jumble: *It's on the counter, I tell you! By the little china dolphin thing!* The German guy, also looking at his phone, remarks in awe that this bakery has no reviews; it's not even listed on Google Maps. The new volunteer sits on her hands and looks at the plastic buckets and shovels for sale across the street. This particular street seems to consist entirely of small businesses: cement and fabric, paint and mattresses. Little restaurants serving the menu of the day, the inevitable piece of leathery meat and white rice, salty soup and fruit juice. There's even a pet shop with a plastic tub in the window, filled with dozens of dirty-grey chicks.

And standing on the side of the road are the men. Skinny and casually dressed in jeans and polo shirts. Standing with their hands in their pockets, but looking sharply around, carefully observing every person walking by.

Lookouts. Guards.

Mattías walks straight up to them. He bumps fists and gestures towards the bakery, a broad smile on his face. She watches their lips move. The men laugh and slap Mattías on the shoulder.

—So how long have you been volunteering here? the German guy asks, pastry flakes scattering over his lap.

—Two days, she says, reluctantly looking away. But I'm from here originally. Medellín, I mean.

The way it comes out, she sounds defensive. But the German guy seems impressed anyway. —From *here*, he repeats, shaking his head, as if amazed. You grew up *here*? But I thought you were English! You sound English!

The Welsh girl takes out her GoPro camera and holds it up high to make sure that everyone's included, asking everyone to smile.

The new volunteer tells the German guy she's staying at the volunteer headquarters; both he and the Welsh girl are staying in Airbnbs in the same neighbourhood. The Welsh girl is a digital strategist (her words), the German guy a venture capitalist consultant (his). They both agree it's wonderful they were able to get time off to travel and do something like this; with so many troubles in the world, it's great that they're able to help; Medellín is absolutely gorgeous, except for the Venezuelan street beggars on every corner. The German guy asks the new volunteer how she got to the Metro station. —I took an Uber, he says, not waiting for her answer. Have you noticed the cabs here don't have air conditioning? And that a lot of them are really dirty? He frowns, shaking his head, as if just the memory is enough to disgust him. Some of them don't even have locks on the door.

The Welsh girl heads to the bathroom and returns promptly, reporting that there is neither toilet paper nor hand soap. The new volunteer offers her a crumpled white napkin to use, but the Welsh girl shakes her head quickly, like Seinfeld's girlfriend in that one episode where he keeps insistently trying to feed her a piece of pie.

—So what did Mattías say, the new volunteer says, gently touching the Welsh girl on the elbow, about the nunnery?

—Oh gosh, the Welsh girl says, brightening up, as if relieved by the opportunity to excitedly chat away. It sounded so mental. So he was an orphan raised by nuns until he was, like, fifteen. They made him live in a dark room all by himself, and he didn't learn to read or write until he was a teenager. And they put him to work in the laundry room, sweeping detergent foam down the gutter. Imagine doing that every day of your life for fifteen years! He even has scars on his arms from getting scalded by the hot water!

—Wow.

—I know, right? And then he started working as an assistant teacher at a local primary school. He taught himself English by watching Hollywood movies and reading DVD subtitles. But he got into a fight with the school director. And then (dropping her voice to a low, dramatic whisper) he told us he made a *deal* with the *paramilitaries* to get permission to found and run the Anthill.

—Did he, now.

—Yes! Apparently, paramilitaries used to completely control the neighbourhood back then. But they're gone now, 'cause the war's over.

—No, the new volunteer says, it's not. But the German guy

is leaning towards them, brushing crumbs from his trousers. —But how did you hear about the Anthill? he asks, tapping the table to get her attention, as though her conversation with the Welsh girl should automatically cease now that he's participating. Do you follow the Facebook group?

The new volunteer looks down at her hands. Forces herself to keep her fingers flat on the table, no picking or squeezing allowed. She says, —I heard about the Anthill because Mattías and I grew up together.

The Welsh girl's eyes widen. —You were in the nunnery too?

—No.

—The orphanage?

—No. No nunnery. No orphanage.

But before she can say anything else, the German guy is jumping to his feet. Mattías has reappeared, Mattías is here, with a see-through plastic bag filled with bread rolls slung over his shoulder. Shauna whips her phone away; the Welsh girl springs up too. Eager and ready to serve.

—Let's go, Mattías says, sliding coins across the counter towards the woman who served them, who gives him a crooked smile. Time to catch the bus.

Crossing the street feels like a video game as they plunge through a tiny gap in the traffic, ducking men on motos and dusty cars. The bus in question has pulled over on the far side of the road, well away from the honking traffic jam of cement trucks and beat-up taxis. As they board the bus, the driver holds the turnstile with his hands so that the new volunteer can't push it with her hips, and he slips the money she passes him directly into his pocket. As Shauna plops down across the aisle, she says under her breath, —That's a shame.

—What? Did he just steal our fare?

—No, gang taxes. If you see a driver *not* do that around here, though, they're asking for trouble.

The Welsh girl and the new volunteer sit together – counting the ride down from the airport and yesterday's journeys, today is the fourth time in her life that she's ridden on a Colombian bus. Mattías and the German guy stand in the aisle, hands pressed against the ceiling to prevent themselves from swaying.

—I love feeling like I'm in danger, the Welsh girl tells her as they rattle up the hill. When I was in Brazil and went into the favelas, I've never felt more alive. There were guys walking around with guns everywhere. Guns, tucked down the front of their underpants! And in plain sight! And the view was beautiful, the Welsh girl continues, nodding at the window, not able to gesture due to her tight grip on the seat cushion. Mountainside views, she says. Isn't it crazy how anywhere else in the world, this view would be prime real estate? Like Los Angeles. I moved to LA last year but what I really want to do is travel. Europe is so boring, she says, as the bus groans its way past two rusty metal dumpsters. Through the grimy bus window, the new volunteer catches a glimpse of a wizened old woman, picking through the trash with a stick. The people aren't alive there, the Welsh girl says. Not like here. Everything in Europe is so well arranged. So overprotected. If I can travel for the rest of my life, I'll be happy.

A pregnant woman pushes her way past the man carrying two buckets, and Mattías steps towards the bus door to give her space. He's now riding with his body half in, half out of the vehicle. As the bus scrapes past a dying bush, its long brown strands scratching his face, the German volunteer starts laughing. —I wish I could take a photo, the German volunteer says, as Mattías ducks his head to avoid hitting a rock jutting out of the mountainside. No one would believe this! No one would believe this crazy bus!

—It's a romanticised view, the new volunteer says carefully, as the Welsh girl unscrews the cap of her water bottle and takes a long sip. Isn't it? The idea that it's our unique experiences that define us. Like those tubercular poets tramping around the Alps and Italy in the nineteenth century. *The Magic Mountain.* Isabel Archer.

—Who? The Welsh girl spills some water on her jeans as the bus bounces over a particularly deep pothole.

—This Henry James character. *Portrait of a Lady.*

It feels dumb to be talking about *The Magic Mountain* and Henry James on a bus while outside grandmas are picking through garbage in search of food. It feels, pretty much, like the worst thing in the world.

—Sorry, she says, I'm rambling. But it's an idealised concept, isn't it? The idea that, if we have enough special, authentic experiences, that those experiences will make us exceptional, singular individuals. And that's to be valued above all else.

—I couldn't agree with that more, the Welsh girl says. She asks the new volunteer to take a photo of how her knees are crammed in by the seat in front of her. This bus is absolutely insane, she says. No one in my family would believe this. This bus is so crazy.

The new volunteer has to take the photo several times in order to get the angle the Welsh girl wants. It's hard to keep the phone stable with the bus rattling. —Hang on a sec, she says, tapping on the 'Square' option.

Has this phone followed the Welsh girl all over the world? The favelas of Brazil, the hair salons of Los Angeles? If there was a Google Maps line of blue dots following the Welsh girl around, where else would it go, tracing her movements? Through the other desirable Southern countries, maybe: Thailand and Cambodia. Meditation centres in India, yoga retreats in Indonesia. And apparently here is Colombia, joining the list of shiny, appealing destinations.

Her own dotted blue line: from Medellín to Heathrow and back again.

What about Mattías? A simple blue dot, hovering in Medellín, unmoving?

And Gabriela's – to New York and back again?

But the Welsh girl, the German guy (and her? Does she count?) – the North to South flow of people, as opposed to vice versa. She can see them coming, clear as anything, as she raises the phone and taps the red button. Digital strategists and venture capitalists, dozens of them, countless. Pressing their faces eagerly against the walls of the countries they want to enter, rattling the doorknobs in their desperate enthusiasm – how desirable it all was! The dirty, filthy energy of these countries and their shitty buses! How authentic! For them, the doors opened. For them, entrance was permissible. Here they came, were coming, had already come: admitted effortlessly, unhesitatingly.

—Oo, the Welsh girl says, nodding in approval as the new volunteer hands the phone back. That's a good one.

They get off the bus in a terrible rush (did the driver miss the stop?), Mattías shouting *Go, go, go* like a SWAT team leader as they stumble their way through the turnstile. Blinking in the sunlight, stepping over piles of wet garbage and flies, hurrying to keep up with Mattías's brisk pace. Fridays, like today, are different at the Anthill: as it's closed for the weekend, he instead opens the building to host Community Meal. Bag of bread still slung over his shoulder, gesturing enthusiastically, he tells the Welsh girl and German guy about how he's started hiring single mothers from the neighbourhood to cook and clean for Community Meal.

—Their ages range from fourteen to forty, he says, leaping out of the way of a speeding motorcycle. Watch it, you son of a bitch! You're going to get someone killed! That's what your volunteer salary is contributing towards, he continues, not missing a beat as the Welsh girl and German guy laugh nervously. The salaries for the single mothers. We appreciate it so much. And, of course, the food they cook is amazing! I can't wait for you to try it!

On the opposite side of the road, a man in a sleeveless white shirt is playing with a dusty dog. The dog's teeth are clamped down on a plank of wood, which the man swings around in circles, the dog's paws leaving the ground (the Welsh girl has to jump sideways at one point, to avoid being hit). The new volunteer looks at Mattías (will a similar 'watch it' outburst follow?), but instead he and the man bump fists.

—There's one thing, though, Mattías says, that I would like you to keep in mind. The man claps him on the shoulder and whispers something in his ear. Mattías nods, his expression unchanging. Two things, he continues. Three. It's something I ask of all volunteers, not specifically you guys, so no need to take it personally. First of all, no religion. No discussion of it, no mention of it. None whatsoever.

He crouches down and picks up a crumpled candy wrapper, tucking it in his pocket.

—It's important to keep the planet clean, he explains. Since it's the one thing we all share. Number two: no politics. Religion and politics have no place at the Anthill. And number three – and this is probably the most important – please don't accept any contact information from the students. No Facebook, no email, no phone numbers, no nothing. Don't follow them when they leave, don't ask where they live, do not – I repeat, do *not* – go into their homes. Respect their privacy, their personal space. You especially, he says, turning towards the German guy. Please don't flirt with the students. Female *and* male. Don't invite them on dates outside of the Anthill, and so forth.

—Of course not, the German guy says, blinking. The Welsh girl is gazing around. She takes a photo of a scraggly rooster on a balcony. The new volunteer watches the man and the dog stroll downhill, away from them. Neither of them look back.

—I only bring it up, Mattías says, because it's been an issue in the past. This one time, there was this Australian guy . . . He stops at the Anthill door and pulls out the jangly metal keys. Can't be too careful, he says. Long story short, I caught him with an eleven-year-old in the bathroom.

As he tugs the Anthill door open, a black dog with a single milky white eye rushes out.

—Motherfucker, Mattías says, jerking back.

The dog jumps up and down, its tail wagging frantically. The new volunteer bends down to scratch under its chin. It snuffles her hand with an anxious dry nose.

—Motherfucking son of a bitch, Mattías says.

Inside the Anthill, there's black liquid smeared all over the floor. It's thick like grease and the smell is sweetly foul, like the juice that gets left behind at the bottom of a bin. The new volunteer turns towards the mop but Shauna darts forward and grabs it first. The German guy runs his hands through his hair, asking worriedly if the substance is 'poop'. The Welsh girl coos over the dogs: —Come here, precious blackie, that's a good girl!

—She must have been locked in overnight, Shauna says, briskly unstacking the buckets.

—Then what's this? The new volunteer gestures at the broken glass by the door. A single pane in the window is broken.

Mattías shuts his eyes. He presses a clenched fist against his forehead, as if praying for strength. —Oh God, he says, eyes still closed. The supply closet.

This time, the new volunteer is able to hurl her body up the staircase, racing to the Anthill's first floor, beating Shauna to it.

Mattías follows close behind. —Please not the supply closet, he keeps repeating, like he can't help himself. Anything but that.

The supply closet is locked. The door doesn't even rattle as she tugs on the handle. The fridge, however, has been left open, and the air is filled with the same sweet rotten scent as downstairs. Without waiting for anybody to tell her to, the new volunteer starts taking packages of limp vegetables and chicken drumsticks out of the fridge, dumping them in the garbage.

—Don't! Mattías shouts. He grabs a packet of chicken and gives it a good long sniff. This will still work, he says, putting it back inside. I'll just ask the mothers to cook it at a really high temperature.

68

—Sounds good, the new volunteer says, trying not to look flustered (is there anything she can do here that doesn't consist of getting in the way?). Worst-case scenario, we'll all be sick together!

He gives no sign that he's heard, shutting the fridge door as the Welsh girl and German guy tramp upstairs. Scratching her thumb with her opposite fingers, the new volunteer trails behind Mattías as he immediately begins giving the others the tour he never gave her.

—Welcome to the Anthill, he says. As you can see, here is the kitchen. Here are the ESL tables. And over there are the sewing class materials – sewing class is on Monday afternoons, also for single mothers only. If you have any clothes you need mended, they can do it for you for free! Such good experience for them! And such a great deal for you!

—What's this? the Welsh girl says, standing by the supply closet. She tugs at the handle but, like before, it doesn't budge.

—Please don't touch, Mattías says smoothly, with all the grace of an English butler. No one has keys for the supply closet but me. No one ever (he says, rattling the keys in his hands for emphasis) has access to any of the Anthill keys but me.

—Has this place ever been robbed? the German guy asks, hands in pockets as he looks around nervously.

—Of course not! I'm not going to let people get away with that! There's nothing I wouldn't do for the Anthill.

He picks up an enormous bag of dog food off a nearby shelf and pours orange bits of kibble all over the floor.

—If you don't know that about me, he says, you don't know me at all.

Four dogs appear out of nowhere, rushing up the stairs and wagging their shaggy tails. They hoover up the food like frantic vacuum cleaners before the scattered kibble has even stopped bouncing.

—I know I shouldn't feed them, he says, putting the bag back on the shelf and punching it hard so that it crumples down. I know that they'll keep coming back. But I can't help it. No one else will take care of them, see.

Back downstairs, Shauna has already scrubbed the floor clean and is now sitting at a table, correcting what looks like English homework. Shauna is busy, Shauna has her hands full, Shauna knows exactly how everything works around here and can't afford to waste a single second. The single mothers have also magically arrived, as though the sound of Mattías unlocking the door has instantaneously summoned them. They're a group of ten, whispering and giggling amongst themselves, carrying transparent bags filled with onions, celery, potatoes.

—Good morning ladies, Mattías says in Spanish. The women grin cheekily, call out various replies (*Jefe, how embarrassing for you! We almost beat you here!*), but he's already turned back to the volunteers. They're wonderful women, he's saying, switching back to English. Very inspiring. Very strong. If only I could tell you their stories and what they've been through. So much! The people of Colombia have suffered so much! The scars of this country, you can't even imagine. Do either of you speak any Spanish?

The Welsh girl shakes her head, and the German man holds up his index finger and thumb, indicating a tiny space of air. —My girlfriend's Colombian, he says. She's taught me a little.

70

—Good afternoon, the new volunteer says to the women. They nod and smile and say it back in a chorus. A few of them are wearing faded pink Anthill volunteer T-shirts, just like Shauna's, with the Anthill logo written on the front in fat letters:

ALL WELCOME!
BE SAFE
BE RESPECTFUL
BE KIND

—What's on today's menu? the new volunteer asks.

—Soup, says a young woman with a scraggly ponytail, smiling shyly as if embarrassed.

—Perfect, the volunteer says. A popular choice. Can't go wrong with that.

—I would hope not! says an older woman with half the hair on her head missing. The group laughs a cackling raucous laugh. The German guy and Welsh girl eye them, smiling uncertainly.

—How much does a shirt cost? the Welsh girl asks, turning abruptly towards Mattías. She reaches into her bulky handbag.

—Only thirty thousand pesos, Mattías says. They're in a box by the computers. Here, let me show you; you can also keep your personal possessions there – it will all be perfectly safe, I promise, not a single volunteer has ever been robbed, not once in the entire history of the Anthill . . .

As he leads them away, the new volunteer is learning the single mothers' names: Leidy, Nanci, Manuelita, Mireya, Vicky, Carol (*My name is Carolina too!* she says, sounding more excited than she means to, but Carol just grins and raises her eyebrows), Elena, Lucha, Carmen and Piedrahita. She then impresses them with her ability to point at them and recite their names perfectly, one at a time, going around in a circle first one way and then the other.

—I'm a teacher, she explains, as Nanci applauds and Manuelita mouths a quiet *Wow*. In England.

—England! Elena says. She has a mole on her upper lip and wears tiny white shorts so dirty they look grey. We've had volunteers from England before.

—Do you remember from where? I live in London.

—Yes! Elena says, nodding firmly. London! That really tall guy came.

—Him! Mireya says as a few others nod, murmuring their recognition. Poor guy, his head was always hitting the ceiling. She ducks her head in imitation.

—Prince William with hair! Carmen cries out, and there it is again, the explosive cackle of gleeful laughter.

Piedrahita touches her gently on the arm. She has a gaudy tattoo of an eagle on the back of her unbelievably thin wrist. —What do you write about? The new volunteer's expression must have changed, because Piedrahita immediately withdraws her hand. You said you were a writer? In England.

The new volunteer looks at her. Then she says, —I said I was a *teacher*. Not a writer.

—Oh! Piedrahita says. I thought you said something else.

The new volunteer presses her nails into her skin. —Are you all from Medellín? she asks, addressing the whole group. Heads shake. Only Leidy nods.

—I've lived here my whole life, she says. It's changed, though. Lord knows.

—It *has* changed, hasn't it? the new volunteer says, an eager note in her voice, but Vicky has picked up a rag and is hurrying upstairs, calling out over her shoulder to hurry up, ladies, the soup won't cook itself and they've got a lot of mouths to feed. She steps aside to let Leidy follow, reluctantly turning away. Behind her, she can still hear the women chatting as they head upstairs, murmuring busily.

She heads to the main section of the Anthill, the Free Time area that doubles as the Education Corner: grimy plastic tables, metal closet filled with battered games, shelves of tatty books. This is where the children are expected to come and wait for Community Meal, while the adults stand in line. Maryluz is there by the propped-open Anthill door, sitting cross-legged on a precariously high stool (how does she not fall off?), handing out sheets of paper for the children to colour. Today she's wearing a tight jean skirt and a halter-neck that exposes the entirety of her bare back. When she sees the new volunteer, she stands up in that skilful manner of young women who know how to move without flashing their underwear.

—Want to watch these ones for me? She points at the children with her lips. It's Colouring Time. Pre-Community Meal, it's *always* Colouring Time. And after Colouring Time is Dancing Time. No matter what the kids say, don't let them dance until *after* colouring. Not even if they beg, not even if they burst into tears. It's important for them to have routine.

The new volunteer gives a thumbs-up, but Maryluz has already stuck her head deep into the art cupboard. The children are sitting quietly, colouring away. Apart from Tomás, there's only girls in attendance. —Hello, Sara, the new volunteer says, awkwardly letting herself be hugged. Hello, Diana. Hello,

hello, hello. There's only one spare chair left (Maryluz's stool is definitely not an option), so that's where she sits. Hello, Gabriela, she says. Hello, Tomás.

They look up from their drawings. Gabriela rises and kisses her on the cheek, pressing her sticky hands against the new volunteer's face. She smells like a summer barbecue, or beach bonfire. Smoke and ash.

—Good afternoon, she says in her raspy voice.

The new volunteer feels oddly touched, though this was absolutely the last thing she wanted: the poverty porn of small children clambering all over her.

—Do we have Leadership Club today? Gabriela asks, sitting back down.

—Not today. Fridays are different, since we have Community Meal. But we'll do Leadership Club again on Monday.

Gabriela nods as if satisfied, picking up her coloured pencil.

—What a lovely drawing, the new volunteer says, touching Tomás's paper. What nice birds. And is that a rabbit?

—It's a lion, he says, scribbling an orange mane around its buck-toothed face.

—And what's that, Gabriela?

Her drawing is a brown rectangle, thickly outlined, with different-coloured circles and triangles and squares inside.

—A picnic basket, Gabriela says in English, her chair squeaking as she shifts around.

—You know what a picnic basket is?

Gabriela nods, reaching for the blue pencil. —Mattías taught us in Leadership Club. And my mother, who lives in New York.

—How long did Mattías run Leadership Club?

74

Gabriela shrugs. —Until you got here.

Tomás slides his paper over before the new volunteer can respond. —Draw me a motorcycle!

With the yellow pencil, the new volunteer draws what looks more like a bicycle, with big clumsy wheels.

—It's not very good, she says apologetically, but Tomás seems unfazed.

—The smoke! he says. Draw the smoke!

She draws the exhaust fume spewing out the back, a pudgy cloud that hopefully even Bob Ross would call 'happy'.

—So how old are you guys? she says, as Tomás rotates his paper this way and that, attentive as an art critic. These are the reliable conversation-starters she uses with small children, like the opening routine of a Las Vegas comedian that hasn't changed in decades: *how old are you, do you have any brothers or sisters, what's your favourite subject at school.*

—I'm seven, says Tomás.

—Eight. That man sells marijuana. Gabriela says this last part in a whisper, nodding towards the street. The new volunteer starts to turn in her seat, but Gabriela hisses, Don't look! Don't look! She hastily turns back: a man in a sleeveless shirt, a dog trotting beside him – is that the same man from earlier? The one who whispered into Mattías's ear?

The men of this city: always there. Always watching.

—So stupid, right, Gabriela says, adding what looks like a purple apple to her picnic basket. What a stupid thing to do for a living. Such stupidity!

—I agree, the new volunteer says. Selling marijuana is a stupid thing to do. I hope the two of you focus on learning English and going to school instead of doing something like that. What are your favourite subjects at school?

—Spanish, says Tomás.

—Mathematics, says Gabriela.

Tomás passes over his paper again and asks the new volunteer to write the phrases I LOVE YOU, I LOVE EVERYBODY and FRIENDSHIP FOREVER. —And write Gabriela's name. With yours too, pretty please.

She writes GABRIELA in capital letters. —You know what, Gabriela, she says, tapping the page to get her attention. You share a name with a very famous Colombian writer. One of the most famous and best writers in the world!

—Who? Gabriela looks up from her picnic basket.

—Gabriel García Márquez! She starts laughing nervously at Gabriela's blank expression, has to stop herself. You haven't heard of him?

Gabriela just stares at her. Tomás tugs on her shirtsleeve. —Miss, do yours now!

She almost writes her full name, MARÍA CAROLINA, but hesitates. Her pencil moves slowly across the paper, forming an 'L'. She immediately scribbles it out and turns it into what Tomás will hopefully interpret as an ugly palm tree. She writes CAROLINA instead. —Do you guys have any brothers or sisters? she asks, using the brown pencil to draw her hair in a U-flip at the shoulders.

—I have one brother, Tomás says. Five sisters. And a cousin in the US.

—Are you the baby or the oldest?

She starts writing the letters of I LOVE YOU in bubble handwriting. Tomás doesn't answer, watching the pencil move, as if hypnotised by the fat letters she's creating.

—He's the third one, Gabriela says. Number three.

—Ah. And what about you?

—I have sisters, Gabriela says. But they're dead. The paras killed them.

—The guerrillas killed my dad! Tomás says, reaching for the blue pencil. He joined them and then they killed him!

—I hid in the house, Gabriela says, snatching the blue pencil before Tomás can touch it. When they were raping them. And then they set the house on fire and I ran outside and hid. I hid for hours.

She draws another chubby cloud, and some raindrops that look like marks made on a prison wall to keep track of the days.

The new volunteer says, as carefully as she can, —That sounds really scary.

—It was. I was really very very very scared. But I hid in the jungle and they didn't find me.

Sometimes, Gabriela talks too fast. In that low mumbling tone of hers, it's hard to understand what she's saying. The new volunteer has to lean in close, pressing her knees against the miniature table.

—They threw my grandmother in the hole too, Gabriela is saying. But then she lived. She crawled out into the jungle and found me. She has a limp now because they never got the bullet out. She still walks around with it inside her.

—My father was shot too! Tomás says, almost shouting. He also had a bullet inside!

—Do you live with your grandmother now, Gabriela?

—Yes, she says, drawing birds like upside-down 'W's in her sky. But she doesn't walk very well so she can't leave the house. She works as a hairdresser.

77

—No, she doesn't! Tomás says, still with alarming intensity. She does not!

—She does too, Gabriela says calmly. Her wigs are all over the furniture. She can't take the bus to the hospital to get medicine for the baby.

—Your grandmother has a baby? Whose baby?

—Hers. She cuts hair but it's not enough money. But Mattías helps pay the rent.

—Rent?

She's struggling to catch every word – those slippery phrases coming out of Gabriela's mouth in that urgent yet casual rush. Does Gabriela tell this story to everyone? Is this just an everyday encounter for her, a bland exchange, or is what's happening something deeper, more meaningful, a life-changing moment of trust?

—Yes, Gabriela says. He brings groceries for us too.

The new volunteer swallows. She says the next part with deliberate steadiness: —I'm sorry that happened to you, Gabriela.

Gabriela frowns. She lolls her head around, as if stretching her neck. The new volunteer catches a glimpse of the same scar she saw yesterday, that thin white line, shaped like a fish-hook.

—Gabriela? You can talk about it with me, if you'd like. If you think it'd make you feel better.

Gabriela lets her chin flop forward into her chest.

—It can be good to talk about the past with other people. It's helpful.

Gabriela leans forward, tapping her finger on Tomás's piece of paper. —Tomás, you forgot to write your name.

She leans forward with the black pencil, writing something

down in careful squat letters. The new volunteer and Tomás stare at the cramped-up handwriting. Tomás's lips move as he reads it out loud: —*Tomás . . . Shithead.*

He lets out a wail and bursts into tears, covering his face with his hands.

—That's what you are, Gabriela says calmly, underlining the word 'Shit' with three dramatic strokes. And your father too.

—Gabriela. Let's be kind and respectful. Let's be nice to our friends.

(Why do words feel like useless fingers in a broken dam sometimes? Trying to hold back the surge of raging water on the other side?)

—He's not my friend. Gabriela slams the pencil down on the table. His father is a FARC shithead.

—But they kidnapped him! Tomás screams, pulling his hands away. The skin under his nose is shiny with snot. He didn't want to go!

—And not only that, Gabriela says, her voice dropping to a whisper that's really more of a hiss. His mother is a *crackhead.* They live on the *street.* They sleep on a pile of cardboard, 'cause they don't even have a bed—

—You're a liar! LIAR. LIAR. LIAR—

The new volunteer opens her mouth, but nothing comes out. But Maryluz is at her side; at the sound of Tomás's wailing Maryluz has rushed over. —Oh, Gabriela, Maryluz says, sighing as Tomás tearfully buries his face into her jean skirt. Gabriela slips her feet out of her flip-flops and hugs her knees into her chest.

When the new volunteer shows Maryluz what Gabriela wrote, Maryluz just shakes her head.

—This one's trouble, Maryluz says, trying to pat Gabriela's shoulder, but Gabriela ducks away. She doesn't mean to be, Maryluz continues, but she is. Gabriela, am I going to have to tell Mattías about this?

Gabriela presses her chin into her knees. —My mother's in the Hamptons, she mumbles.

Maryluz starts picking up the coloured pencils and putting them back in the plastic cup. —Guys, let's be careful about keeping the pencils in their proper place, okay? She passes Gabriela a fresh sheet of paper. One for you, she says, handing one to Tomás, who immediately pulls his face away from her skirt. One for you. And one for—

She stops, looking out at the street, past the propped-open Anthill door.

—Where'd he go?

—Who?

—The little boy.

—No, the new volunteer says, shaking her head. Tomás was the only boy when I got here.

Maryluz shakes her head too. Frown lines are starting to appear on her forehead. —He was sitting there, she says. In that chair.

She points with her lips at where the new volunteer is sitting.

—You can't have missed him. He was absolutely filthy. I've never seen him at the Anthill before.

—There was nobody here when I arrived, the new volunteer says, louder this time.

Maryluz raises her eyebrows. —Hmm, okay. I guess he must have left in a hurry. Believe me, you would have remembered. She raps on the table to get the children's attention. Kids, where'd that little boy go? The skinny one?

Gabriela shrugs exaggeratedly, her shoulders jamming into her ears. —I dunno, she says, still mumbling.

Tomás says, abruptly looking up from his paper, —He stank! He pinches his nose and waves the air in front of his face, as if to demonstrate the strength of the stench. Like garbage!

—I know, buddy. Maryluz sighs. He sure did.

—He grabbed my shirt, Gabriela says suddenly, twisting around to show them. He's always bothering me!

Maryluz and the new volunteer look. Sticky black liquid, that sweet garbage smell. It's pretty much a perfect handprint.

But those little curves at the end – the sharp lines – pointy – razor-thin.

As though the nails have been filed.

—Gabriela, Maryluz says. What direction did he walk in? I'd have liked to get his name.

—There was nobody walking away, Maryluz, the new volunteer says before Gabriela can speak. And there was nobody sitting here. I said that already.

Maryluz opens her mouth to speak but the Welsh girl has strolled up, camera in hand. —What a pretty picture! the Welsh girl says, leaning over Tomás's paper, as though his drawing is a lighthouse beacon, luring in eager volunteers from far and wide. Is that me? the Welsh girl asks, tapping the stick figure drawn by the new volunteer, the U-flip hair and triangle skirt. So nice, the Welsh girl says in broken Spanish. Is it fin? Finito?

—Yeah, the new volunteer says, as Maryluz moves to the doorway, looking up and down the street. We're finished here.

DANCING TIME

It's been a full hour and the kids are still at it. She's sitting on the dirty floor, sweaty and red-faced, arms sore from swinging Rebecca and spinning Dafne. Justin Bieber croons away in Spanish on the widescreen TV, connected to an ancient laptop playing the videos. And all around her the children are dancing, hands on hips, swivelling, swaying and bouncing and leaping and laughing.

This one, play this one! The children beg, tug at her shirt-sleeves, linger as close to the dirty laptop screen as they dare. Her preferred choices are 'Gangnam Style', 'Harlem Shake' and 'Mambo No. 5', since they lack the distressingly sexy choruses and gyrating dance moves of 'Macarena' and 'La Bomba'. *This one*, they plead. *Play this one next. Not that one, it's bad, ugh, not that one again, why do you always play her choice and not mine?*

Their running monologues! The way they clamber and climb over her, like she's a tree. I want this, I want that, he's a cheater, she's unfair, I like Tina, I hate Roberto, I have a bicycle, I like chicken, I don't like pasta or potato or carrots in my soup so I'm going to pick every individual piece out and leave it in a sticky puddle on the table, where's Mattías, where's Maryluz, where are you from, I don't like my school uniform, when is English class, when is art class, are you a Christian, my favourite colour is red, did you hear about the baby that was thrown into the ravine and found there three days later with her head split open and flies and worms moving around inside, when they rescued her she was still breathing, she was still alive, poor thing, and they took her to the hospital where she lived for three more days but then she died, her mother threw her there because she didn't want another baby girl, have you been to the ravine, have you seen it? It's just around the corner. If I found a baby girl there I would keep her, I wouldn't have thrown her away. She didn't die, stupid, they sold her to the narcos, the ones who work with the Mexicans, they kept her alive and filed her teeth and her nails, when she opens her mouth now it looks like the mouth of an animal, all fangs. I have a dog, I have a bird, I have three sisters, I have five brothers, my father lives on the coast, my stepfather works in the mine, my uncle works in construction, my mother works in the factory. I'm from Miami, my brother's in Houston, my sister's still in Caracas. Can you pick me up so that I can touch the ceiling? Can I hold your hand so that I can slide underneath your legs and back up again? Can I play with the stringless guitar? Can I climb up to the very top of these stacked chairs? Can I eat the ham in my sandwich but not the bread? Did you hear about my cousin? He was interrogated by the paras, they tore off his fingernails, they poured gasoline over his arms and set him on fire, his skin was burned, it's all lumpy and scarred now. My other cousin? She was pregnant? Her ex-boyfriend broke into the house? And cut her throat? She used to cook here? But doesn't any more. The boyfriend didn't go to jail, he still walks the streets, he's a bad man.

—Yes, is all the new volunteer can say. No. Nodding and nodding, shaking and shaking her head. Yes and no and no and yes.

Community Meal began over an hour ago, but the line is still creeping out of the building: grandmas holding the hands of toddlers, mothers cradling babies, solitary men. As the tables began to fill up, Mattías and the German guy disappeared upstairs, returning with the flat-screen TV. The new volunteer helped connect it to the laptop (similarly summoned from the depths of who knows what part of the supply closet, which seemed to possess powers similar to Mary Poppins's handbag). And then Mattías reached out, placing three fingers on her inner wrist, as if checking for a pulse.

—Don't let anyone else touch this, he said gravely. It was his most direct address to her all day. Holding her breath, it took her a second to realise he meant the electronics. And keep the children dancing till we call them over, he continued. It's important to let senior citizens eat first.

She nodded furtively. A soldier called to serve, unquestioning.

So here she is, playing DJ. The German guy and Welsh girl are currently nowhere to be seen – perhaps they're in the kitchen, helping with the dishes (though Mattías repeatedly stated that there was no need; *that's what we're paying the mothers for; you're here to focus on the kids!*). Or maybe they're outside taking photos, showing the kids what they'd look like with googly eyes and emoji faces. It's probably okay for her to take a break too, isn't it? It seems about time to let them eat anyway. Snapping the laptop shut (the children cry out as the TV screen goes black), she tells the children firmly (over their cries and moans of disappointment) that they should go and line up now, run along, get in line to eat, hurry hurry!

Off they go, dashing and skipping, whooping and whispering about the cake, did you see it, the rainbow frosting, will there be enough slices for everyone, I want a big one!

She sinks into the nearest available seat, next to an old woman with a beautifully ruffled pink shirt and a little girl fiddling with her napkin.

—Good afternoon, the new volunteer says, introducing herself. The old woman's name is Josefina, and the little girl, her granddaughter, is Sonya. Have you had anything to eat yet?

Sonya points shyly at her napkin, where a few cake crumbs and a gluey wedge of rainbow frosting remain.

—Lucky you! Getting to eat dessert first. I suppose there are worse things in life.

Josefina nods and clucks her tongue. —Indeed there are, girlie, God willing.

The new volunteer asks where they're from, and Josefina says, —Córdoba, but I've lived here fifty years. Too long! Too old! When did I become such an old woman? She grins toothily and the new volunteer smiles back. She asks what kind of work she does or used to do, and Josefina says, Harvesting yucca, but I don't do it any more. Too tired, too old, as you can see.

—I can imagine, the new volunteer says. I work as a teacher. I'm only twenty-eight but I already feel tired most of the time. I shouldn't complain, though!

The old woman chuckles. —Teaching is a good job to have, girlie. That's good, so good of you to do it.

The new volunteer tells her that she likes her shirt, such a lovely pink colour. —Pink is a good colour for summer, isn't it?

Josefina touches her on the arm and says, —God bless you, girlie. Are you here next week? Bring me another one if you can. Or a dress for the little one here. Bring me some towels.

She winks. Sonya has started eating the remaining crumbs on her napkin, shaking them on to her tongue.

—Of course, the new volunteer says. I'll talk to Mattías. I'm sure he'll be able to sort something out.

—Or you could give money. Do you have money, girlie?

She pokes her hand into the new volunteer's shoulder, palm turned upwards. The tips of her fingers are cold, like they've been kept in the fridge.

—I don't have any change on me, the new volunteer says, regretting the words as soon as they leave her mouth.

—You can go to the shop and break the bill, Josefina says, her hand now tapping the new volunteer's shoulder with a single index finger, the way you would type one-handed on a keyboard. Do you understand what I'm saying, girlie?

One of the single mothers appears with a tray of pasta-rice soup. As Sonya accepts her bowl, she knocks her mug of fluorescent red juice all over the floor.

—I'll get a mop, the new volunteer says, rising quickly (too eagerly?) to her feet. Her seat is immediately taken by a boy with a wide patch of dried skin peeling under his nose.

—No worries, no worries, Josefina says, reaching for her napkin. Sonya seems similarly unperturbed, slurping down a gloopy spoonful of pasta.

—Shauna, she says, inching towards the table where Shauna is trying to open a box with child-size scissors. There's been an accident.

—Tell Mattías, Shauna says without looking up, ripping the cardboard with supernatural strength. He needs to tell the single moms to do it.

—I can do it myself, the new volunteer says, but Shauna doesn't answer, busily pulling out baby clothes, smoothing them out on the table.

He's standing in the doorway, leaning against the frame.

—Mattías?

He holds up a single index finger. He's talking to two women in the food line, both middle-aged. One is wearing bright-green eye make-up that the new volunteer finds incredibly beautiful, similar to bioluminescent jellyfish. The line for Community Meal is still so long it trails off into the street.

—We currently don't offer health or fitness classes, he's saying to the women. But that doesn't mean that we won't in the future. We do have our sewing lessons on Monday – free, of course. We're hoping to start up manicure and pedicure classes in a few weeks. For International Women's Day we'll be hosting female professionals from Medellín; they'll be giving a talk on legal rights. And in terms of employment, the cooks I hire for Community Meal are single mothers only, but I'm hoping to create additional employment opportunities . . .

The German guy and Welsh girl walk past, each carrying yet another cardboard box. Her eyes follow them to the corner, towards Shauna's table, which is now surrounded by mothers and their infants. Shauna is holding up a variety of outfits, pressing them against each baby's body to see if they fit.

Clothes for babies. Food for all. After-school classes for kids and employment for single mothers. International Women's Day. Manicures and pedicures.

It's quite a place Mattías has made for himself here, isn't it?

—Thank you, the woman is saying to Mattías. That's useful to know and I appreciate it.

Mattías nods, his face expressionless.

Dare she even think it?

Now, of all moments?

The quietest, darkest, most awful thought?

—We'll come by for the community garden shift tomorrow, the woman is saying. Mattías nods again.

The feeling inside her. Hard at the centre, like a popcorn kernel. A cracked yellow shard.

The graciousness with which he turns to person after person. The intensity of discussing future plans.

Like he's showing off a basket of groceries. Gabriela's picnic basket, holding up one item after another. Joy, fulfilment, empathy, compassion. Meaningful work. A meaningful life.

(Is this what her mother had been looking for? All those years ago, wandering the streets with her Baptist church?)

As if he's saying to her privately, a secret whisper:

Look at this.

Look at what I have made of my life.

Look at what I've done. My connection to this country. While all you did was run away. You left. Left.

And what about you? What have you been up to all these years?

—Thanks for waiting, Mattías says, finally turning to face her. A little girl with taped-together glasses runs up and hugs his leg; he pats her on the head. Great to see you, Veronica, I'm so glad you're feeling better. What's up, Carolina?

—I need a mop, she says. There's been a mess.

—Don't worry about it, he says. The mothers will take care of it.

—I don't mind – I want to help.

—Don't worry, he repeats. Just have a good time with the children. Have fun; enjoy yourself! That's what you're here for!

I'm not a tourist, she thinks. *Don't talk to me like that.* But what she says instead is, —Actually, there's something else I wanted to discuss with you.

He catches the eye of one of the single mothers. He points in the direction of the spill, mouthing frantically, *Mop, please.*

—Sorry, I know you're busy—

He laughs, or maybe it's just a cough. —When am I not?

A small boy tugs hard on the end of Mattías's long-sleeved shirt. As the fabric springs up, she catches a glimpse of what she's seen before, a sight she hasn't thought about since that moment, when they stood together with her suitcase between them: on the back of his hand, lumpy scar tissue. Puckered and wrinkled, like the mountain ranges on a spinning class-room globe.

Mattías quickly pulls his sleeve back down. —Yes, Romano?

Romano stands on his tiptoes and whispers something she can't hear.

Mattías smacks his hand against his forehead. —Romano, you are absolutely right! Forgive my tardiness, please. Everyone! Listen up!

(Heads swivelling, chairs shuffling. The entire room, attentive. Mattías is speaking! Everybody listen!)

—Thank you for coming. We very much appreciate your presence here. It is now . . . (eyes darting around the room) . . . time . . . (lips pulling into a smile) . . . for the raffle! Shauna (turning towards her, steady and confident, Churchill in the war room, Lincoln at Gettysburg), do you have the jar?

89

—Yes! Shauna shouts from her corner with the baby outfits, holding up an empty coffee tin like she's displaying a prize on a game show. Everyone, do you have your tickets?

There's rustling and stirring as hands reach into pockets and bags. Small bits of paper are pulled out, with numbers written on them in hurried black ink. Josefina in the pink ruffled shirt looks around worriedly.

—Wait, the new volunteer says, just as Mattías is taking a deep breath to bellow out further instructions. Are there any extra tickets?

Shauna hands them over with a slightly miffed expression.

The new volunteer quickly heads to the table she was sitting at earlier, presses the tickets into Josefina's palm. —Good luck, she whispers. I'll keep my fingers crossed for you.

The old woman raises her hand like she's waving goodbye. Sonya is already wiggling around, peering eagerly to see what numbers they have.

As Shauna begins to shout out instructions (*Please be careful with your ticket! If your number gets called but you don't have your ticket, I'm afraid you cannot claim your prize*), she tries again. There he is, near the line for the toilets, tying the lace on Tomás's tatty shoe.

—Mattías? There's something I wanted to ask you—

She touches his arm and his reaction is immediate. He jerks away, accidentally smacking his skull into Tomás's chin. Tomás's eyes widen, but he doesn't cry or make a sound.

—Oh Jesus, Mattías says, touching Tomás's cheek. I'm so sorry, Tomáso-man. Are you okay?

Tomás nods. A red mark on his chin is slowly growing darker. Over in her corner, Shauna is rattling the jar. —All right, everyone, she shouts, I hope you're ready, I hope you're listening closely for your number to be called!

—Mattías? she says. But he's moving away from her, towards the exit.

God. Is she that repulsive to him? The rest of the children start clapping their hands and chanting, a rising call: *Ra-ffle, ra-ffle, ra-ffle, ra-ffle . . .*

Three quick steps. She does it again, putting her fingers on his shirtsleeve. This time, he doesn't flinch. But he turns his head in a very slow and controlled manner, as if restraining himself.

—Yes, Carolina? he says. His eyelids look heavier than usual, more swollen. A face that she doesn't remember and didn't recognise, the eyes of a tired man. Because that's what he is, isn't he? That's what people become when twenty years go by, don't they?

—Look, she says. I know you're busy. I know things are crazy and that you have a lot going on. But (*get it out now, fast as possible, just say it!*) – do you want to have dinner together?

He blinks.

—We can go to the fish place again? And get a beer?

—Of course, he says. Whenever you want.

He moves away so that they're no longer touching.

—Thirteen! Shauna bellows. Who has number thirteen?

The children murmur and rustle, looking anxiously at each other, but no winner holds their hand up high.

—Tonight? she says, taking a step forward. Let's go out tonight.

—Oh, no. He shakes his head. Tonight's not good. Tonight

I'm going to Itagüí prison with the shoe delivery. The prison-
ers, their shoes keep getting stolen, see. Some never take them
off; they even sleep with them on. They wear their shoes till
they crumble to bits – you wouldn't believe the smell!

He starts waving his hand in front of his face, as if trying to
demonstrate the strength of the stench. But the new volunteer
doesn't smile.

—Tomorrow, then? How about tomorrow?

—Seventeen! Shauna is scanning the crowd, holding the
ticket close to her face. I repeat: seventeen, do we have a winner?

—Tomorrow? He taps a finger against his lips. Tomorrow's
no good either – I'm in Poblado all day, picking up next week's
raffle prizes.

Another step back. Another step forward.

—I just think it would be good, she says, if we could set a
specific day together. A specific time. So we can catch up! I've
been here two days and we haven't caught up yet!

—But we have caught up, he says, his shoulders brushing
against the doorway entrance, still backing away. Catching up
is something we've already done.

—Is it? She follows him outside, past the overflowing garbage bin, past the dog with swollen tits (the one Mattías
referred to earlier as 'Eight-Bras', sending a nearby crowd of
children into an explosion of squeaky laughter). But I want to
know more about you! And what you've been up to!

—What I've been *up* to? He repeats this in the style of an
incredulous Fox News anchor, eyebrows shooting up his
forehead.

—Like the orphanage, she says. I want to hear more about it.
He stares at her like she's a lunatic.

—Where they mixed all the food in the bowl? And made you eat it?

His expression doesn't change.

—It's just that . . . I have no idea what happened to you! It's been so long.

Tell me about Colombia, she could be saying. The invisible subtitles running beneath her words, bluntly spelling out what she wants. What she needs: *Tell me about you. What's happened. What's changed.*

His foot bumps against a rock jutting out of the dirt road.
—Carolina, he says. As I'm sure you've realised, the Anthill is going through a lot right now. The country is going through a rapid transformation at the moment and there's many opportunities to be taken advantage of. It's important that I be around. The sewing classes, the financial literacy programme, the community garden . . .

He gestures vaguely towards the building, the dirt road, the mountains beyond.

—I'll think about it, though.

—Think about what?

They both turn. Maryluz is leaning against the doorway, squinting at them.

—Are you guys making plans to hang out later?

—No, Mattías says.

—Yes, the new volunteer says.

Maryluz checks under her nails, as if to make sure they're still clean. Hers are long and perfect, of course. Not a chip in sight.

—Want to come along? the new volunteer says. Do you have something planned?

Maryluz's demeanour changes right away: beaming like a model, albeit with shockingly crooked teeth. —Funny you should ask! You can come to my art show – here, Carolina, give me your phone. Mattías never bothers to text me back, the jerk.

She whips the phone from the new volunteer's hand and busily begins tapping away. Mattías's expression cannot be described as anything other than severely pained.

—What kind of art show? the new volunteer asks.

Maryluz's nails tap against the screen. —Well, it's technically not my show, it's a friend's. But my paintings will be on display.

—Paintings? Mattías sounds completely mystified, like she's speaking a foreign language.

—Yes, you asshole! The way that she says it, though, she sounds happy. My paintings! Listen to this guy. Four years. Four years working with him and he acts like it's breaking news!

Four years? Wasn't the Anthill founded three years ago?

How well did these two know each other, exactly?

—Perfect, the new volunteer says, somewhat icily. Just tell us when and where.

Maryluz passes the phone back. —You'll be coming together?

The new volunteer looks at Mattías. He's crossed his arms behind his back and is looking vaguely around, like a sailor in a crow's nest searching for dry land.

—Yes, she says. Together.

Maryluz briskly flicks her ponytail back over her shoulder. The Anthill children are now pouring out of the door. Whooping and calling, hollering and shouting, holding their raffle prizes to their chests: a rubber ball, a fuzzy fleece blanket, a plastic packet of white socks. Most of the adults remain outside, eating the last of the cake, the ham and bread, chatting and laughing. But Mattías is walking away, back into the building. —Hey, jefe! Maryluz calls out. Don't you want to know when and where? But he doesn't turn around. He doesn't look back.

I'LL FOLLOW YOU INTO
THE FUTURE

Instead of following her around (this person that could be you, but probably isn't), maybe it'd be far better for me to spend my time fantasising. Healthier, even. After all, why should all my attention be focused on her? (Is she you? Are you her?)

It's so lonely here sometimes. A child came in the other day, but I snapped at her face and grabbed at her shirt, clawing and scratching. I chased her outside, where I opened the fridge doors so that the food inside would rot. I vomited black liquid all over the floor, smeared it everywhere with my feet. I broke the window and brought the dog inside so that it could keep me company, so that I wouldn't be alone, at least for a while. I can't help myself; I get so impatient and excited knowing that you're here, that you might be getting close. Lina, when are you coming; when will you get here; when are you going to find me?

But should I really be wasting my time this way? Pestering children and waiting for you? Perhaps I should go back to my earlier fantasy – that fun little story about me and my drone assistant, exploring the ruins of your mother's house. Perhaps that would be a better way for me to spend my time:

Come, drone assistant, I can say. *Let us depart from this pointless and shameful location.* Buzzing cheerfully, the drone will oblige. His engines will whirr as I strap myself in. My anti-radiation suit will handily transform into an astronaut's, the drone into a rocket ship. I'll blast off into the sky, leaving behind faint vapour trails. I'll transcend space and time. I'll *become* time. I'll stumble over moon craters. I'll gasp as I inhale the burning, gassy air of Jupiter and Venus. I'll work on a clean-up crew, gathering the debris spinning in thick clouds around various planets. Astronaut and space-shuttle trash. So many silvery packets of liquefied food. Countless broken-off bits of crushed satellites floating around. So many things can never be recycled into something else. Some things never get a second chance. I'll explore newborn stars. I'll investigate the abyss-like effects of black holes. I'll report all my findings back to the intergalactic government for a fee.

And then I'll use the money to come and find you. Money is real, money is heavy, money makes everything possible. So with money in hand I'll follow you to the very edge of the universe, where atoms are all smashing and burning into each other, like fairy lights on a Christmas tree on fire.

Hello, I'll say, as I take you by the hand. Together again, at long last. And finally, in person, I'll be able to say to you, face to face:

Have you forgotten? What it was like, the two of us together? Back then?

ART GALLERY PARTY

—Her name tag? he says. Really?

The two of them stand in the art gallery, beers in hand. They're supposed to meet Maryluz here in half an hour, so that she can take them to *another* art gallery, the one where the party is actually taking place. The new volunteer is picking at the label on her bottle – its logo is an ancient pre-Columbian symbol, half-man, half-animal. The window is open and if she strains her neck she can see past the metal bars, see the lights of the city and traffic outside, the flocks of roosting parakeets and pigeons, the surging of people in the crowded plaza below. A tree covered in so many bougainvillea vines it looks like serpents trying to drag it back down to hell. University students dressed in black, swigging rum from plastic cups. And then there are the clusters of foreigners, dreadlocked backpackers, shorts and sandals, smoking cigarettes and looking around. Enjoying their experience, the thrill of journeying in a newly peaceful country. A trendy country, safe and clean, one that has left all its darkness behind.

—Yeah, she says. It had these . . . teeth?

It comes out as a question, but he's already nodding. —Yeah, that sounds like Gabriela.

He moves towards the next piece of art: like most of the photographs here, it's of a naked woman. Crouching in a field of coffee beans with her back to the camera.

—She's one to watch out for, he says. You can't really blame her, though. Like most Anthill children she's been through a lot.

—She said some other kid had been bothering her. A 'dirty' kid.

She puts 'dirty' in quotation marks with bunny-ear fingers.

Something strange flickers across his face, but it's so brief, so quick, it's hard to tell if it actually happened, or if it's something she's imagined. But then he's shaking his head: —I don't know anything about that.

He takes a long sip of beer. She stands there, watching him.

—Gabriela is a handful, he says. She doesn't mean to be, but she is.

He takes a step towards another piece of art.

—You know what children are like, he continues. They get carried away. They start playing games, invent something silly in their head – pretend to be someone they're not – and before you know it they think it's real.

—Like the Arctic Fox.

She says it quietly. The naked woman in the next photograph stares intensely out at them. Her faded grey eyes are so washed-out they're almost white. Her arms are crossed over her breasts, like she's trying to hide them.

—I guess I like this one, he says, taking another swig of beer. I think she's some famous underwear model.

She says it again, louder: —Like the Arctic Fox.

This time he looks at her, his face showing what looks like genuine surprise.

—The what?

—You know. That game we used to play when we were kids?

She plucks at something invisible from the sleeve of her cardigan sweater. It's too warm this evening to be wearing it, really.

—Remember? she says. It was the end of the world after everything had exploded, or something. The Arctic Fox was my bodyguard – you had this radiation suit—

—I don't.

—Don't what?

—Remember.

He looks her straight in the eyes and she looks back, but as usual what she sees there isn't familiar. She's been searching his face for little traces, signs that might give it away – the boy she can barely remember – a gesture or phrase that would build a bridge between then and now, provide an undeniable link. Instead he just looks tired. An extremely tired grown-up man, holding a nearly empty beer bottle, with puffy skin under his eyes.

He says, —We better think of something to say about these photographs, because I guarantee Maryluz is going to ask us some boring complicated question about them.

—That's sad that you don't.

—That I don't what?

—Remember.

—Why?

He moves on to the next frame: a map of Colombia, with thick lines drawn over the terrain. White lines made of Liquid Paper, yellow lines made with gluey glitter. They criss-cross over mountain ranges and surrounding oceans, representing the different historical trading paths of cocaine and salt, bananas and gold. Green globs for emeralds; brown smudges for coffee. Cattle and chocolate; oil and rubber. What an enormous country it is! Mountains, beaches, jungle, forest, cold weather, hot weather, all the extremes jumbled together, higgledy-piggledy. The complete opposite of a united kingdom.

—I don't know much about art, he says, sighing, but this one seems a bit broad.

—I don't believe it either. That you don't remember *anything*.

—I didn't say that I don't remember anything. You were the one who said that, weren't you? *I have a really bad memory . . . I was only eight when I left.*

He's looking at her with wide, attentive eyes.

—But it's true, she says, gesturing helplessly towards her skull. Everything's all . . . She struggles to choose the right word. Mixed-up, she tries.

—Well, you seem to remember quite a bit, for someone who claims otherwise.

Oh, she feels nervous having this conversation! Why is she so nervous? She takes a long sip of her beer, liquid courage.

—Of course I remember, he says, not waiting for her to respond. I have very happy memories of our time together. It was a wonderful opportunity that your family gave me. Your father, of course, but your mother especially. May she rest in peace.

He touches his hand to his forehead, as if about to make the sign of the cross. Her fingers tighten around the neck of her beer bottle, as if strangling it.

—I'll always be very grateful to them. I *am* grateful. I was able to go to an excellent school and learn English. I'd never have been able to do that without them, as I'm sure you know. I think back on that time with nothing but fondness. It was a lovely childhood. And we played lots of silly games together, didn't we?

His tone of voice is very friendly and kind and open, but his eyes don't move from the map of Colombia before him, slashed up with thick crusts of Liquid Paper and glitter. His eyeballs stay very rigid and still, like buttons sewn on the face of a stuffed animal.

—We had fun. Lots of fun. And it was all a very long time ago.

She nods vehemently. —It was fun, wasn't it?

—Yes, he says, waving towards the art gallery owner, who's just emerged from the kitchen, holding a freshly uncorked bottle of wine and two glasses. It was fun. And it's fun being here now. Perhaps it would be best if we both focused on that.

The bottle she's holding suddenly feels very heavy. —Sorry, I didn't mean—

—You don't have to apologise. You apologise a lot, don't you? It makes you sound very unconfident.

He bends down and sets his empty beer on the ground with a clink.

—Look, he says as he stands back up, switching to English, as if he doesn't want the nearby collage of Bolívar and Santander to hear, a collage stylised as the *Goodfellas* movie poster, with both Bolívar and Santander carrying shotguns and wearing dark sunglasses. I'm likely coming off as rude. But it's best if we're direct with each other, isn't it? So let's be direct: the past is past and I don't want to talk about it. To be blunt, I didn't depart from your family on the best of terms. As I'm sure you know. But your father has been a great friend of the Anthill – like I said to you before, if it weren't for your father's donations the Anthill wouldn't exist.

She takes another swig, longer this time.

—I was so happy when you emailed me. Surprised, of course, it goes without saying. He laughs so quickly it sounds more like choking. It made me glad, genuinely so, reading those things you wrote – how you wanted to come back and find out for yourself what it's like here, how it's changed. Because it has changed, hasn't it? It's a country looking to start again, a fresh page, a new beginning – and that isn't too much to ask for, is it?

—No. She tugs her black cardigan closed. Liquid courage, here it comes: But I feel really shitty that . . . that I didn't stay in touch with you. I feel terrible that we didn't speak for so long.

—But I don't. I don't feel shitty at all. Not for a second.

—He never told me that he contacted you, she says, and there's something new in her voice now, a hardness that makes him look away. He didn't tell me you'd been in touch.

—I told him not to.

She presses her lips together.

—It was for the best, he says, waving again at the gallery owner, indicating that he should come over with more alcohol. Trust me. I wanted to protect you. It wasn't safe here for a very long time, you know.

—I know that. Of course I know that!

—So why does it matter? You're here now.

—You never wrote to me, she says, speaking English herself now as the gallery owner approaches, beamingly pouring a glass of wine. You wrote to goddamn Emma Green before you wrote to me.

He raises his eyebrows. —You met up with Emma?

—She invited me to her wedding.

Shrugging, he passes her the glass, filled to the brim. —If it wasn't for Emma's contribution, we wouldn't have been able to fund the Christmas party. He takes his own glass from the gallery owner, raising it in a half-mocking toast. Switching back to Spanish, he says, My advice to you, Maria Carolina, is to focus on the experiences you're having in the present moment, in the here and now. Move on – that's what everyone else in this country is trying to do. Don't get dragged down by a bunch of dead fossil memories that . . . He hesitates. That aren't relevant.

María Carolina. The formality of it.

She turns to the gallery owner and asks him where the bathroom is. He smiles smuttily, pencil-thin moustache stretching across his face. —One moment, please, he says, giggling as he holds up a single index finger. For a beautiful girl like you, I need to run back there and turn on the camera!

He keeps giggling, as if deeply pleased with himself.

She closes and opens her eyes. —Did you really just say that? she says. Seriously?

Her handbag swings as she walks away. Behind her, the two men are silent. It's only when she ducks through the bathroom door that the murmuring of Mattías's voice begins, low but urgent.

On the toilet, she sits with her elbows on her legs, fists pressing into her forehead. Her middle finger keeps scraping at her thumb, reddening the skin, until forcibly, consciously, she makes it stop.

When she comes back out, Mattías is waiting right by the

bathroom door. Reaching for her glass of wine (did he down his that quickly?), he then takes her by the arm, like a formal escort at a nineteenth-century ball. He says, —Time to go.

—But Maryluz?

—I texted her already; she'll meet us at the party. Come on.

As they walk through the gallery, she catches a glimpse of the owner, standing with his back pressed against the wall. His eyes are wide and dilated. His forehead slick with sweat. Torso shaking.

—Have a good night, Mattías says, heading for the exit, not looking back.

The new volunteer cranes her head to look back. The gallery owner is slinking away, sliding along the wall, like he's trying to stay as far away from them as possible.

—Jesus, she says, following Mattías down the stairs. What did you say to him?

He doesn't answer. On the pavement outside, he chugs the rest of her wine and crams the glass into a nearby bin, one that's already overflowing with empty glass bottles of aguardiente and cracked plastic cups. She makes eye contact with a man in a wheelchair on the pavement, selling tiny models of boats on a camo-patterned towel. He raises his eyebrows at her, as if to say *IDK what his problem is either.*

—Do you make these yourself, sir? she asks, stepping away from a nearby pile of wet paper covered in chicken bones and flies.

The man holds a boat up to show her. It's surprisingly light when she takes it: a battleship, the kind that wouldn't be out of place in a book of Second World War photographs. She rotates it around in her hands.

—How long does it take you to make one?

He holds up two hands: seven fingers. Days, weeks, hours?

—How old were you when you first made a ship?

He grins wheezily, exposing a mouthful of grey gums. But then there's a scuffling sound behind her, a yelling voice, and she turns to look: two teenage boys are running, fleeing, ducking past the telephone poles, weaving around taxis and trucks. As she stares after them, she accidentally makes eye contact with a little girl across the street. The little girl is staring at her. She's standing at a traffic light, holding up laminated postcards of saints to sell. The new volunteer blinks.

—Gabriela?

She says it to herself, rather than calling out. The little girl turns and scurries away into the darkness of the alley, leaping over a stack of flattened cardboard. The sandals on her feet flap like anxious tongues.

—You like talking to strangers, don't you? Mattías is at her side again, wiping his hands on his shirt.

She shrugs, still straining to see into the alley. But the little girl is gone, disappeared into the shadows.

—Sellers, he says. It takes her a second to understand who he's referring to: the teenage boys, both already long gone. On someone else's territory, he continues. And that's asking for trouble. I would know, believe me. They were lucky to get away when they did. He slaps the man selling battleships on the shoulders. Good to see you again, brother. I hope you've been taking care of yourself.

The man nods, bowing his head. —Good to see you too, Paco, he says in a raspy voice.

She looks at the alley one more time, but the little girl is still gone, her vendor's spot by the traffic light now occupied by a juggler. As they cross the street, a newspaper blows against her bare leg. She has to speak loudly in order to be heard over reggae blasting from a nearby bar: —So. Did Paco volunteer at the same time as Lalo?

He smiles and puts his arm around her waist. —What was that phrase your mother made me write down all the time? *I will not be cheeky?*

She can't speak.

He rubs the part of her cardigan that covers her hipbone. —We better get a move on.

———

The bathroom at Maryluz's art gallery party has posters and advertisements in English on the walls. A tour of street graffiti, a documentary film festival. Invitations to join a hiking group, a flyer for the Pablo Escobar Museum. She looks at them with her phone pressed against her ear, listening to the ringing. She calls twice in order to give him enough time to turn over couch cushions, look under chairs for the sound's source.

A rustling sound as he picks up. She says in English, — Hello, Papa.

—Yes, hello?

His voice is clipped, terse. It's going to be a short conversation – she can tell.

—Hi, she says again. It's María Carolina.

She puts her fingers in her mouth and starts scraping her nails with her teeth, before immediately pulling them out again.

—Oh yes, he says in his faint British accent. His voice isn't slurring – a good sign. Hello, Mary.

—Just calling to say hi. How are you?

She listens, but there's no sound of the TV in the background. Is he in the office?

—Well, you know. It's all good here.

He takes a deep sucking breath – smoking? Is he smoking inside again?

—How was work?

—Oh, I'm on leave for the next few weeks. Company request, ha.

Another deep sucking breath – definitely smoking.

—Great, she says. Well. I'm really tired, I guess. My supervisor wants another chapter from me soon.

—Wonderful.

A faint clinking sound. Ice in a glass?

—Yeah, if things go according to plan my submission date will be in September. I've been writing pretty much non-stop. Ha.

—Wonderful, he repeats. That's wonderful, Mary.

The toilet behind her starts making a strange sound, like a choir singing, and she presses the phone harder against her ear.

He says, —What was that?

—Nothing. Sorry, the signal here is rubbish. Well, I better let you go; I don't want to take up too much of your time.

—Yes, he says. Thank you for calling, Mary.

—Bye.

—Bye.

She has to tap the red button several times to make sure it's hung up properly. She accidentally throws the wad of paper into the toilet instead of the wastepaper basket, but flushes it anyway – a horrible gurgling sound is decidedly not promising. As Mattías would say, *Time to go.*

Washing her hands at the sink, it's easy to get distracted by the ads in English. Juice cleanses, reiki retreats. *A WARM, BEAUTIFUL, SAFE APARTMENT IN POBLADO, RIGHT IN THE CENTER OF MEDELLÍN ACTION.* (Surely this doesn't mean the Medellín action from the news headlines of her childhood!) Shaking her hands up and down to dry them, it flickers across her mind. A VHS-esque memory, shimmering into view:

Five years old (four? three?). In the indigenous market town, high up in the mountains. Her parents, they must have taken her and Mattías there one Christmas (what year was it? Before travel by road became too hazardous?). Hazy images, random and disconnected like all of her memories, the raw fragments left of the first eight years of her life. A guinea pig dressed in tiny blue overalls. Mattías eating her peanuts, and her swatting him. A table covered in cassette tapes. Her mother bought them cups of sugar-cane juice; her father was God knows where (drinking beer in a bar?). And then, when a couple of street performers started playing music on a CD player, preparing for some sort of performance, her mother kicked off her ballet flats. She grabbed the musicians by the wrists, shouting and laughing. She wanted to join in, why wasn't everyone else dancing, dammit, what was wrong with them, didn't everyone need more dancing in life?

Her mother, twirling barefoot in a circle, long hair flying.

She and Mattías hovered alone by the sugar-cane stand, watching.

And then, out of the corner of her eye, she saw dreadlocks. She saw blonde. She swivelled away from her mother. *Matty,* she said, tugging at his arm. *Matty, look.* He turned instantly, obeying her command. And there, wearing a backpack the size of a small child, was a big-booted tourist. Dark boots, leather ones, the kind she'd previously only ever seen on the feet of army officers. The tourist was trudging around, German or Swiss or who knows from where, somewhere deeply exotic and foreign. Calmly taking photos of the tiny clay pots for sale, the mountainous scenery, the indigenous vendors in their black bowler hats.

How she and Mattías had wordlessly stared!

The strangeness of seeing a tourist!

And here she is, twenty years later, in a bathroom with English written all over it.

It's not that she hadn't expected things to change. But to have changed this much!

A tourist – someone whose presence automatically transforms the background into a backdrop, a brochure. Is that what the Anthill children think when they see her? *Gringa* – that's what Gabriela called her, the very first day. Wandering around, looking for thrills. Looking to consume.

But if that's not who she is, what else could she possibly be?

When she comes back outdoors, Mattías is nowhere to be seen. Christmas lights hang over the courtyard, giving it a fairy-tale feel. She makes her way to the bar, where she pays for another beer (thank God the bartender has change for her 50,000 peso bill!). As he hands over the money, coins clinking in her hand, she can't help but remember Josefina at the Anthill, prodding her with her upturned palm: *You can break it at the store.*

She drinks pretty much half the beer straight away. A trance remix of Echo and the Bunnymen is playing. She looks at one face and then another. Young people in jeans and shirts and leather jackets, smoking unfiltered cigarettes, talking and laughing.

—It's the craziest show, one woman is saying, gesturing enthusiastically with her arms. Victims and perpetrators, coming together. Sometimes at the end they even hug! It's hosted by a man who worked in both Rwanda and South Africa.

—That's beautiful, her friend says, touching her hand to her heart. What time is it on?

—Carolina!

Maryluz in the corner, waving. She's sitting in one of the few chairs pushed against the wall. The new volunteer tries not to bolt over, a grateful horse fleeing to a somewhat familiar pasture. Maryluz's eyelashes look extra-long tonight. She's wearing a tight white shirt that shows off her belly button, nineties pop star style. Are those scars on her stomach or stretch marks?

—It's so nice to see you. Maryluz kisses her cheek and clinks their beer bottles together. Are you having a good time? Where's the jefe?

—He wandered off. So much for being my party buddy.

—Typical. Maryluz snorts.

—Yes, the new volunteer says, a bit too quickly. Typical! That's . . . exactly what he's like.

Sipping her beer, Maryluz asks the new volunteer how long she's going to be in Colombia, what she plans on doing while she's here. —If you want to volunteer somewhere else, she says, my friend runs a crocodile farm. These poor little abandoned narco crocodiles. A few are descended from Escobar's ranch. God, so sad! One of them is brain-damaged from being force-fed too much ecstasy and marijuana. Can you believe it?

She presses her fist under her eye, like an actor in an ancient tragedy.

—You'll have to excuse me, Maryluz says. I get very emotional about animals. I used to be vegetarian.

—Like Mattías, the new volunteer says, her stomach twisting, but Maryluz is busily taking a pack of cigarettes out of her handbag. It looks strange with no pictures of bloodied lungs or yellowed toenails on the carton, as in England.

—Do I want a cigarette? Maryluz says, as if talking to herself. She shoves the pack deep back inside. I only smoke when I'm nervous. And I'm not nervous right now. I'm happy! This is a happy day.

—Me too, the new volunteer says, only realising that it's true when it comes out. Standing here in this city, speaking Spanish and drinking beer. What else could be better? Why can't she get a PhD in this? Raising the bottle to her lips, she says, So am I.

She and Mattías made a pact, Maryluz explains, leaning against the wall, while the new volunteer watches the crowd: the carefully crafted man-buns, a hoverboard propped up by a potted palm tree (there's even an e-cigarette or two). Their pact, Maryluz tells her, as the sweet smell of pot whiffs over, was that they wouldn't touch a bite of meat (or, in his case, any animal products whatsoever). And that they wouldn't smoke cigarettes either. If either of them failed, if either of them caved in either category, they had to pay the other the equivalent of an Anthill volunteer's donation. In *cash*.

—He's so intense, Maryluz says, shaking her head. It always has to be so extreme with him! All or nothing.

—Right, the new volunteer says, widening her eyes, as if that will make it seem like she knows exactly what Maryluz is talking about: *Haha, that Mattías, I couldn't agree more!*

—But naturally, Maryluz says, he and I had to – hmm, how to put this . . . *renegotiate* the terms.

She touches her mouth briefly, as if to make sure it's still sticky with lip gloss.

—I'm only human, unfortunately – not like our good friend Mr Terminator here. I need a little smoke every once in a while, just for courage. But we're nothing if not good at negotiating in this country!

She laughs and takes a long drink.

The new volunteer thinks, *'Our' good friend?*

—You and Mattías have known each other a long time, she says, in as even a tone as she can muster.

Maryluz nods, suddenly serious. —He's the best person I know.

The new volunteer looks down at the ground, at nothing in particular.

—My God, Maryluz says. I wouldn't know where to start! The time the woman with Aids came in all cut up from her husband and he got covered in her blood? The time the house next door to Virginia's caught fire because of a candle and he ran into the building to save the baby formula? The time some delinquents came with pool cues to rob the Anthill and he jabbed them in the eye? She shakes her head. But it's there: the fondness that only comes from knowing someone so genuinely. So thoroughly.

(Is this Maryluz's Medellín? Man-buns and marijuana? And is that Maryluz's Mattías? Covered in Aids blood? Running into burning buildings? And for her, the city and the man both: unfamiliar, unrecognisable.)

—There's a line between responsible and irresponsible, Maryluz is saying, reaching into her handbag like she wants to touch her cigarettes for comfort. And our dear jefe crossed it a long time ago.

She sets her bottle on the ground with a clink.

—Excuse me, I have to change my tampon. She touches the arm of a bespectacled man. Esteban, have you met my co-worker Carolina? She just started at the Anthill yesterday.

Esteban is good-natured enough to turn in their direction. He asks the usual opening questions, standard conversational stuff (*nice to meet you, where are you from, how long will you be in Medellín for?*). She opens her mouth, closes it. Opens it again.

—I'm from England, she says. I was born in England.

—You're English? he says, eyes widening. Wow! Your Spanish is excellent! You barely have an accent!

—Thank you, she says modestly, and just for a second it feels good, like a genuine achievement. I studied really hard, she adds. For years!

(What a wonderful version of herself that would be! *Mary Caroline*. Working hard in university, learning a new language from scratch! Such a simple story about herself: so easy to narrate, so straightforward! Instead of . . . whatever she is. Whoever she is.)

He asks about her plans in Colombia and she talks enthusiastically about how fun it's been getting to know the city, randomly listing activities she's seen on flyers. The graffiti tours, gosh, so fascinating. The House of Memory Museum: very powerful and affecting. Such a sad history, such a tragic past. She hasn't done any of the Escobar shit because she thinks it's exactly that: vomit-inducing shit, not to mention gross and insulting.

—Really? he says, his expression immediately changing. I disagree.

—You don't think Escobar tourism is stupid?

He shakes his head. —I prefer it to a museum, he says. Museums have always felt like coffins to me.

He holds his bottle up high, as if to check how much beer is left in it.

—In my opinion, he says, suddenly sounding formal, like he's cautiously making a speech, it makes me happy that visitors are coming with a genuine desire to learn. It creates a lot of safety and income for locals – the tourist industry, I mean. And it's good to have tourists like you, coming with an authentic curiosity about the country, and what it's been through during the war.

She lifts the bottle to her mouth for a long sip, but there's nothing in it, so she has to do a fake swallow.

—There's no point in hiding it, he says. There's no point in trying to pretend it didn't happen.

She doesn't say anything. When he asks if she wants another drink, she nods.

Standing in line at the bar (which is basically a plastic table with a sweaty man in an apron behind it), Esteban talks about his job teaching psychology in the university (*I'm a teacher too*, she almost says, then presses her lips together at the last

115

second – can you really call yourself a teacher if you've basically gone AWOL from your university?). But his real passion is being a cuentero, a professional storyteller.

—Do you get stage fright doing that?

—Not really. He hands her another beer, shaking his head at her offer to pay. Like anything, storytelling is one of those things where your nerves disappear once you do it enough.

—What's one of your favourite stories to tell?

As the music in the background changes to Buena Vista Social Club, he tells her his version of the Gemini story. The twin brothers, their lives and deaths. It's hard to hear him over the music and chatter of the partygoers (the fact that she's constantly scanning the crowd for Mattías's stubbly head also makes her a little less mindful than she should be). But from what she can gather, one of the twins ends up dead. His brother is forced to carry the dead body around with him for years, dragging the heavy weight from place to place (are they Centaurs? Siamese? It's never quite clear). Finally, the living brother goes to his father, Zeus, begging for help. *Please help me*, he says. *Please bring my brother back to life; make him like he used to be. So that we can always be together, the same way we always were.*

Esteban pulls a cigarette out of a packet and offers it to her. She accepts, even though it has no filter.

—So what did Zeus do?

—Well, he says, flicking the lighter for her, Zeus couldn't bring him back to life. No god could do that. Even in the world of the gods, once something is dead, it's gone. Some things can't ever be returned.

He watches her inhale.

—The crowd always cries at the end of that one, he says, lighting his own cigarette. They love it.

—What's it supposed to mean?

It comes out sounding blunter than she intends it to. She takes another deep sucking breath from the cigarette.

—It can mean whatever you want. I tell it different ways at different times. He smiles. But I suppose for most people it's a story of acceptance.

—Is it, though? She blows out a big cloud, trying not to cough. Maybe there was a big plot twist that she missed.

He watches her flick the ash. —Do you have a boyfriend?

—Oh my, she says, reaching for the phone in her handbag, fumbling for it. I'm so sorry, I have to take this call. Hello? Can you hear me? She presses it hard against her ear, furrowing her brow in fake intense concentration. Yes, yes, she says as she turns away, waving her fingers at Esteban, but he seems unperturbed, turning good-naturedly towards another group of people. Uh-huh. Wow. Wait, you're breaking up.

A hand on her lower back makes her jump.

—Hello, Mattías says gravely, standing under the flickering Christmas-tree lights. In the half-lit shadows, if she didn't look closely, he could be a perfect stranger. Who are you talking to?

She lets her hand flop away from her face. It feels easier to tell the truth. —I was just pretending.

—Like in boarding school?

She can't help but smile. He smiles back. She notes the two beers he's carrying, one in each hand, both empty. —Where did you go? You disappeared!

—But you don't need me, he says. You're so good at making

conversation with strangers. You were always the friendly one.

—I was?

—Of course. Listen, he says. There's something important I want to discuss with you. Actually, could we sit somewhere and talk for a bit? Somewhere private?

He leads her away from the main crowd, towards the front room where most of the art is hanging. Standing by a portrait of two astronauts in a womb, he looks around, as if to check that no one is listening.

—Okay, he says. So there's something I've been thinking about.

He reaches into his pocket and pulls out his phone, tapping on the screen.

—It's been weighing on my mind quite a bit, to be honest. It's really been stressing me out and making me quite unhappy.

—What is it?

That coiled ball of tension inside her. Here it comes: he's going to let it out. All of it. Everything about their past – her mother, the evangelical church, the works. It's going to come rushing out of him, everything she deserves, everything she has coming to her, an unstoppable surging force—

He says, —There's been a fire.

He brings his phone close to her face.

—In Moravia. The former rubbish dump.

She stares at the screen: orange flames and black smoke. Women in pyjamas fleeing a squat wooden building. Firemen standing by traffic lights.

—Eight thousand square metres burnt, he says, scrolling rapidly with his thumb. A hundred families left without homes. Unfortunately, Moravia is quite inconvenient to get to.

But this guy I know – we can hire a van from him. He owes me a favour. We've worked with him before, the time we took the kids to the zoo—

—Wait. What?

That hummingbird flitting around, darting from one thought to the next. It's like being with so-called Lalo all over again. Or has she been with Lalo the whole time after all, and she just hasn't noticed?

—The neighbourhood's been burned to the ground, he says, like he's patiently explaining a maths problem to her, a complicated yet essential equation she's failing to understand. The people living there, they've lost *everything*. What they worked to earn, what they slaved to save. So. He takes a long, shaky breath. We could rent a van. Organise a trip there, bring them food, water, clothing, blankets . . .

—You want to drive there?

—You're right, he says, eyes widening. I'm being silly. We could probably host at least one family at the volunteer headquarters. Two families! We can fit three people in my room and four in yours, easily. They can use the couches. They can use the floor. The Italian girl left her yoga mat behind, somebody could use that . . .

It's frightening her: the speed with which the words are coming out of him. So fast he's almost stuttering.

—Look, he's saying, spreading his fingers on the phone to zoom in. Look! People had been living there for years. Their entire lives, generations. Twelve dead. Three dogs and a cat. Can you imagine how awful that would be? What would it be like, getting burned alive? Losing everything you own, your home, where you've lived your entire life?

119

The shakiness of his voice, the rising tone. —Mattías, she says. That's a lovely idea. It's very kind and considerate of you.

—I try to be, he says. He presses his fingers under his eyes. I try to be good.

—You are. She pauses. And you know I can help with the price of blankets and food, or whatever. But do you honestly think it's a good idea, inviting a bunch of strangers into our – your home?

—You're right, he says. You're exactly right.

He shoves his phone away and heads towards the gallery entrance, pushing his way ruthlessly through the crowd, his running shoes making no sound on the tiled floor. By the time she's able to hustle over there too, he's already hunched over the notepad, the one where people are supposed to sign up for the email newsletter. He's picked up a pen and is scribbling rapidly.

—Here, he says, eyes fixed on the page. This is much better, isn't it?

She looks at the jittery handwriting: GOFUNDME CAMPAIGN – PLEDGE TO HELP MORAVIA FAMILIES DISPLACED FROM THE FIRE.

—Much better, he says. We can go from to person to person. Yes. That Swiss girl from four months ago, I can forward her the link and she can send it to her church . . .

He puts the pen down and wipes his fingers on his shirt. His hands are shaking.

—You were right. So silly of me. So stupid! Of course it wouldn't make any sense to host people in the volunteer headquarters. What a crazy idea. God, Mattías, you dummy. You idiot. Totally bonkers. It's the no-sugar rule all over again.

He tucks and untucks his shirt, as if he can't decide which is better. She watches him, not speaking.

—But still, he says. You know what I'm like. I get carried away. I get all kinds of crazy ideas. Oh, Carolina, I've made so many mistakes! I can't even begin to get into all the mistakes I've made! Have either Shauna or Maryluz told you about it? The time I tried to organise a protest against the forced shanty-town evictions? Or the 5k race to fundraise for the garbage-pickers? Or when I banned sugar from the Anthill premises?

—I don't, she says.

—Don't what?

—Know what you're like.

He just stands there for a second. Just looking.

—Jefe, Maryluz says, touching his waist as she approaches. He immediately leaps away.

—Maryluz! he says, putting his hands in his armpits, as though his fingers have just become very cold. As you can see, I made it. So now you can't complain about me ever again.

Maryluz raises her eyebrows, but she's smiling. —This guy, she says, seemingly addressing the new volunteer, but her eyes don't leave him, not for a second. Listen to him. What a joker he is. What an asshole.

She watches Maryluz fiddle with her hair, which is hanging soft and loose over her shoulders. There it is, another thought clogging her throat, sickly and thick: *And how long have you had a crush on him, Maryluz?*

But Maryluz stands there without touching him, one hand in her hair, the other holding a white plastic cup filled to the brim with wine.

—What a good influence you are on him, Maryluz is now

saying. Less than forty-eight hours here and look at the influence you've had! I can't even tell you, Maryluz says, reaching out and touching the new volunteer's wrist, with her impossibly long and bejewelled nails. You wouldn't believe how many times I've invited him to come out. Always an excuse: a haemorrhaging child, the red-light district outreach, board games with the glue sniffers under the bridge . . . He's harder to get a hold of than the Pope.

—That's how I like it, Mattías says. That's exactly how I intend it to be.

He reaches out and puts his hand on the new volunteer's neck. She freezes, just in case his fingers are trying to flick away a bug, but instead his hand kind of just . . . sits there.

Maryluz brings her cup to her lips but doesn't drink. Her fingernails are also still on the new volunteer's hand. She feels like a toy that two kids on a preschool playground are reaching for – is there going to be a fight?

But Maryluz just smiles and says, —So many times I've invited him. And do you know how many times he's come?

She finally withdraws her nails, and the new volunteer immediately steps closer to Mattías.

—Not once, Maryluz says. That's how many times.

—Haha, the new volunteer says, officially winning the award for the fakest laugh ever. Haemorrhaging children is a pretty good excuse, though.

Maryluz doesn't react. Instead she says, —Man of mystery. That's who you are.

—That's how I like it, he repeats. That's exactly what I want to be.

His fingers are still on the new volunteer's neck. It suddenly seems a bit sad that Maryluz is standing off to the side, all by herself. While she and Mattías are together. But then there's that old familiar feeling, spreading like prickles over her skin:

The two of them together is like feeling completely safe. Her protector at her side again, at long last.

—Well, Maryluz says. She laughs but it's a stiff noise, jarring. Did you see my paintings?

—No, he says. I'm afraid we were just about to leave.

The new volunteer opens her mouth, but nothing comes out. When Maryluz looks at her, all she does is nod.

It's pouring outside as they both walk to the corner to wave down a taxi. Fat-bellied rain, water that feels warm on her bare skin, not chilly like in England. She shakes her head when Mattías offers her his jacket.

—Well, he says, holding it over her head anyway, I did promise your mother I'd take care of you, or else she'd never forgive me.

—But I thought the country was all about forgiveness now.

He smiles and bows a bit, as if to say *Touché*. —Should we get one more drink?

They choose a street vendor with umbrella-covered seats. She gets steak and arepa, while Mattías buys beer from a near-by shop. Or rather: she gets steak; Mattías gets arepa with no cheese or butter. —So tasty, she murmurs wondrously as she saws away with the puny plastic utensils. One of her fork prongs has already snapped off. So cheap, she says with her mouth full of meat. Do you know how much steak this good would cost in England?

—No, he says. Currency exchange has never been my strong point, I'm afraid.

He holds the arepa the same way he held the plantain during their first meal, like a harmonica. She can feel the juice from the steak trickling down her index finger, down her arm, speeding towards the tip of her elbow.

—Are you vegan, Mattías?

He blinks.

—It means you don't eat cheese or—

—I know what it means. He breaks the arepa in half and takes a big bite. With his mouth full, he says, I don't like labels. I'm just . . . me.

He smiles at her with crumb-covered lips. And in that moment, it's like she can maybe . . . sort of? See him? The little boy?

She says, —So how much did Emma donate?

—Enough, believe me. He wipes his mouth with the back of his hand. Where did you see her?

She tells him about it: Emma's wedding in London and the reception dinner afterwards – her first contact in twenty years with a figure from childhood. Distant people, half-forgotten names. Emma Green and the Gómez twins. Lala Pereira and Eduardo something. Foggy faces from primary school, as mythological and hazy as movies watched on VHS tapes. He finds them on Facebook, he tells her. The school alumni list, Instagram and Twitter. He isn't embarrassed! He has no shame! And why should he? There's nothing, he informs her, that he wouldn't do for the Anthill. The internet has made fundraising so much easier, a total game changer. It was rough going at first, but thank goodness international volunteer work is becoming more fashionable these days; all the San Francisco CEOs are interested; everyone wants sections on their start-up websites about the value of being a 'change agent'. But for donations (he says, shaking a fist with growing intensity, like a lawyer during a climactic courtroom scene), it's absolutely key to solicit people with a personal connection to the country. Most foreigners don't care about Colombia, see. Have no interest. And why should they? What with everything else going on in the world. North Korea, etc. He doesn't blame them.

—There's an advantage to that, though, she says, reaching for the plastic cup of ají sauce. No one's going to nuclear-bomb the Anthill.

He nods and picks at his napkin. In the silence that follows, maybe they're both picturing it: the world around them in flames, burning up, blistered. The Anthill reigning above it all, surviving.

—But what about you? he says abruptly, leaning forward. Tell me what you've been up to.

She tells him, lips burning from the ají's spice. The undergraduate degree in creative writing. Her PhD in British literature, specifically Gothic horror. Books filled with scratching sounds coming from upstairs, thumps in the closet, creepy sex cults and half-animal children with furry arms. She was supposed to have submitted last year. Her current date of submission is . . . to be determined (she doesn't mention that she hasn't checked her university email since arriving here). He keeps nodding, she keeps going. The boarding school childhood, the summers spent at different friends' houses, all painfully, charitably kind (they all seemed to be named after flowers, Roses and Irises and Lilys, with equally bland benevolent personalities). Giant chilly farmhouses on the margins of Bath and Somerset and Hampshire. Rooms so icy and frigid she got goosebumps in July, only wore shorts three days out of the year. Her father followed her to England eventually, abandoning Colombia like a Civil War general fleeing the charred smoking remains on a battlefield, the stinking corpse of the semi-bohemian life he'd tried to build there. He moved back into his ancestral family home, the estate that was his inheritance, his right. He didn't work for a long time – he's doing some consulting now, sort of (or so she's heard). They have lunch once a year on her birthday (not recently, though, the commute was tiring for them both). And she calls him on the phone regularly – why, she just spoke with him earlier tonight!

—I always wondered if he looked for you, she says as he brings back another two beers. I always wanted—

—But what happened then? he interrupts, opening her can and passing it to her. What did you do next? Where did you go?

The moments that make up a life. How to tell it? Can you fit a life into a few sentences? The on-and-off depressive, the failed academic, the sort-of Colombian – was that sufficient? Her first summer out of university, waiting to begin her PhD in the autumn. That was the summer she spent interning at the literary magazine, the one where she passed out in the editor's office after a heavy night drinking and woke up to him fingering her, but she never mentioned it and he didn't either. She lived with freegans, she explains to Mattías, as he licks his finger and picks up the last crumbs of arepa from his aluminium foil, like a junkie scrabbling around for the last desperate bits of crack. Vegans who collected all their food for free from dumpsters behind Waitrose and Sainsbury. These freegans, they grew all kinds of mysterious plants in the kitchen. Bean sprouts. Alfalfa.

It looked like, she tells him, Dr Frankenstein's laboratory. They dumpster-dived bread from bins. They went to summer music festivals (how horrified, how incredulous they were to learn that she'd never been to one! *How can you call yourself British, when you've never been to a festival?*). The rent was under £150 a month and she slept in a bunk bed in a sleeping bag. One day, she got in a terrible fight with Freegan Dreadlock Girl about using non-organic detergent in the dishwasher. Freegan Dreadlock Girl went crazy, absolutely mental, ending up destroying the raised garden beds, the ones built out of empty suitcases. Later, she found out it was all because Freegan Dreadlock Girl had stopped taking her lithium.

—You've lived quite a life, Mattías says when she finally stops to take a breath. With stories like that, you could write a book.

She shakes her head. What she can't seem to put into words is that it *was* a good summer. Things had felt good. *She* had felt good. Twenty-one and walking down the street in her tiny white miniskirt, the kind Colombians would call a puti-falda, a prostitute's skirt, because in those days she was still on medication and awesomely thin – the kind of thin where everyone constantly complimented her on how 'great' she looked, despite the yellowish jaundice tint in her hands, the constant tremors and teeth-grinding, the fact that she ate one piece of cantaloupe for breakfast and exercised for two hours a day, one Jillian Michaels video after another. She had felt so *Alive* and *Ready* and *Confident*. A PhD programme that autumn! She was really going to make something of herself, wasn't she? She was really going to Be Someone and Do Something! She did poppers in dimly lit pubs and pulled off a bearded Dutchman in the bathroom, but that kind of thing hadn't felt shameful, not back then, it had just felt . . . alive. Like another experience, in a life that was going to be full of them, gloriously so. Her phone didn't connect to the internet and she read Charles Dickens on the Tube and she never, ever worried about applying sunscreen to avoid wrinkles on her face. She was so full of potential. So full of hope.

And now? What is she now?

Mattías begins waving his hand around exaggeratedly.

—Not now, brother, he's saying. Addressing someone behind her. Catch me tomorrow. I go to the laundromat on Saturdays.

She turns around, shifting in the rickety metal chair. A man with dirty bare feet is shaking Mattías's hand. —But Paco, the man is saying. What about today? What about now?

—Not today, brother. But come find me tomorrow, I promise.

He reaches for her leftover steak and passes it to him. She opens her mouth but shuts it quickly. The man bumps fists with Mattías before walking away.

As Mattías scrunches up the aluminium foil she says, —We should have given him a knife and fork.

—He has other things on his mind, Carolina. He says it gently, as if explaining something painfully obvious.

—I know that, she says sharply, but he just tosses the aluminium foil ball into the nearby bin.

—I usually give him something, he explains. After doing my laundry. A shirt. Shorts. Boxers. You know.

—You give him your clothes?

—Only when he tracks me down.

—Does he ask around for Paco?

He eyes her. Not answering.

—What's up with that? she says. Why do you go by different names with different people?

He takes a pen out of his pocket. —Are you using your napkin?

She hands it over, meat juice stains and all.

—Now. He takes a deep breath. Kickstarter is the one where you offer prizes depending on how much people contribute. Is that correct? Uff, there's so many of these platforms now, I can't tell them apart!

He tries to tap the pen against his cheek, but it whizzes past his ear instead. —Shit, he says, and it's only then that she realises how drunk he is, how drunk *she* is, the two of them together. Is this how her mother and father met, all those years ago? Drinking beers and eating arepa under a darkening sky (or was it sausage roll? Did they meet here or there?). The native and the foreigner – is she both at the same time?

—Anthill T-shirts, he mutters. And suddenly it's like she's no longer there, as if she's faded into the background of his life, irrelevant. Framed drawings from the kids. Home-baked goods from the single mothers . . .

—Wait, she says.

His eyes flick towards her.

—What about you? She scoots her chair closer, the metal leg scraping against the pavement. I want to hear more about you. What you've been up to.

His face goes very still. Watchful. A guard on the castle parapet, on the lookout for enemies.

—I want to know, she says, but her voice sounds small.

He shakes his head. A short, terse movement. —No, he says.
You don't.

She doesn't say anything.

—It's getting late, he says. We better go home.

And there's nothing left for her to do but agree.

I FOLLOWED YOU
INTO THE PAST

In the centuries I lived without you, I wandered the scorched earth. I zipped my radiation suit up as far as it would go. I was careful to avoid the highways, the marauding bands. I wandered into abandoned houses and scavenged cupboards for dusty tins of food. I befriended feral packs of miserable dogs, closed the eyelids of the dead as gestures of respect. If I found starving cats, gaunt-eyed and growling, I fed them. If I encountered wounded or injured birds, I put them out of their misery. Smoke rose high in the sky as the land burned. The squeaks of my cart and the buzz of my drone assistant were the lullabies that sang me to sleep. I only ever dreamt standing up.

How did I live all that time without you? Where did I go; what did I do? Should I tell the truth or is it more truthful to lie? In the years I lived alone, I shook hands with tattooed cannibals. I made deals with female-only environmentalists. I was tortured by the snarling vigilantes but didn't speak a word. Some things should never be said out loud. I joined the top-secret militia, helped guard the one patch of green by the river, the only place in miles that wasn't a belching mess of tar and slick oil and burning garbage. And whenever I encountered a child – dirty, alone, wide-eyed but solemn, in the way that only children at the very end of the world are – I let them follow me. I didn't leave them alone. Nobody else would take care of them, see.

Blessed are the children that no one gives a shit about. Blessed are the wanderers and the caged. Because inside us, still and silent, there's something that's hot. There's something that's burning. There's something that's very much alive.

I'm waiting for you, Lina. Are you going to find me?

THE ANTHILL MONTAGE

Araceli and Romano. Santiago and Valentina. Nanci and Anna Maria with their juice-stained dresses; Orlando and Salvador with their faded green Atlético Nacional jerseys. Bethlehem and Fatima from Venezuela. Noah with his gap-toothed smile and shockingly yellow Crocs. Even though the new volunteer has been working at the Anthill for three weeks now, every afternoon (without fail) Fatima will dash towards her at full speed, crying out *I need my Carolina!* Embracing her in what the new volunteer has now come to recognise as the universal Anthill hug, the child's legs wrapped around the volunteer's knee. When the new volunteer takes a step, Fatima hangs on.

—Take me with you! Fatima squeaks. Don't let go!

Nata and Nubia from Tolima. Carlos with his droopy eyelid. Brisa from Puerto Berrío, with the scars all over her face from when she fell off a motorcycle. If the blue dots of Google Maps could trace where the Anthill children come from, it'd be a thick scrawl of journeys, comings and goings and many more journeys to come. The Anthill children, on the move.

Some of them make her nervous. Yes, better to come right out and say it bluntly. Some of them even make her afraid. Take Nestor, with owlish spectacles that wouldn't be out of place on Harry Potter himself. And yet the rage that comes out of him! That sputtering, volcanic anger that seemingly erupts from nowhere!

The day he threw a chair at her leg, screaming *You're a fucking bitch* when she wouldn't let him sign up to use the computers, because he pulled Rebecca's hair so hard she fell on to her knees.

Or the way he flipped the bird at Maryluz, waving both fingers back and forth at her, like an air traffic controller, laughing and cursing hysterically as Maryluz said (with the cold calm of a gangster issuing an order), *Go home, Nestor. You're not being kind. You're not being safe. And you're definitely not being respectful.*

Or that afternoon when Mattías had had to tackle – yes, tackle! – Nestor to the ground, because Nestor was standing by the wall and banging his head against it, smacking his forehead repeatedly into the bricks, because – because – someone had cut ahead of him in line? Bumped into him? Refused to let him join the bingo game? So many different options when it came to Nestor!

The new volunteer hasn't found out exactly what triggered Nestor that day, because he hasn't been back to the Anthill since. Nestor is five years old.

But despite it all – it's fun. It's draining. It's dirty. It's nasty. It's never-ending. And she can't get enough. Five days a week she strolls through the streets, past the panadería that sells cinnamon rolls. Past the dogs (Eight-Bras, Blackie, the one with the milky eye, the one with the gimpy leg). Past the little shop that she can now point out to the *other* new volunteers, ones even newer than her, ones she can tell proudly, *Over there, that's where you can break big bills to get change for the bus. Oh, they have the best tinto too!*

The Anthill volunteers: Australia and New Zealand. California and Miami. The Google employee who spoke excitedly about his desire to experience the 'real' Colombia. The Irish girl who asked repeatedly if it was okay to wash her hands at the Anthill sink, was the water hygienic, would it make her sick. And then there was the Dutch bitcoin investor, scouting Medellín for potential office locations: he talked enthusiastically the entire Metrocable ride about how the future for Medellín lay in imitating Amsterdam's tourism model, in terms of providing easy access to sex and drugs. *It's happening already, isn't it?* That's what he said, waving his hand at the window, at the laundry lines and brick houses below. A come-all, help-yourself gesture.

And then there's Leadership Club. The day they made *THANK YOU* cards for the Anthill staff (everyone wanted to make one for Mattías, shouting and snatching up crayons, *let me do it, me, me!* As a compromise, Mattías got one giant card that everyone had signed, with an enormous *I LOVE YOU* and *YOU'RE THE BEST* scrawled across it). The afternoon they made new recycling posters, and gave a presentation during assembly about how important it was to take care of the planet (*Don't be dirty pigs!* Gabriela screeched at the rows of seated children, glaring with her thick caterpillar eyebrows, as if daring them to defy her). The Friday they did Community Clean-Up, slipping on latex gloves provided by Maryluz (how excited Rebecca and Dafne had been to use theirs! Gabriela blew hers up like a balloon; Tomás burst into tears when it exploded). Pacing up and down the dirt road, picking up every tiny bit of trash they could find. Bottle caps, Styrofoam wedges, infinite orange cigarette stubs. So much of the world consisted of tiny broken-off things, didn't it? Discarded and forgotten. The children threw everything into a black garbage bag, filling it to the brim.

—Why are people so dirty? Gabriela asked at one point, crushing a piece of cardboard under her feet. So unhealthy! When I grow up I'm going to be a doctor. In the Hamptons.

The new volunteer couldn't resist: —Is that where you used to live? With your mother?

But Gabriela just unscrewed the cap from a dented Gatorade bottle, not replying.

Days at the Anthill. Days turning into one week, then another. The countless games of Memory and UNO, swallowing back yawns. The unbearable tedium of gazing around the room and waiting for Tomás to realise that, yes, it's finally his turn. The torturous boredom of Go Fish – there was that one Tuesday she purposefully allowed him to cheat, tilting her cards forward so that his eyes could flick gleefully downwards.

—Keep your cards *up*! Gabriela cried, urgently nudging the new volunteer's wrist. He saw everything!

—No, I didn't, Tomás said humbly. But sure enough, once his turn came around, his eyes widened with hunger: Carolina . . . give me . . . a *seven*.

—Cheater, Gabriela muttered as the new volunteer handed over her seven of clubs. Dirty cheater.

So much of working at the Anthill is like being a lifeguard, isn't it? Struggling to hold back yawns as the daily waves come in and out, only to be emotionally and mentally shattered by the unexpected tsunamis. Nestor's tantrums. The day Gabriela slapped Rebecca and called her a slut.

And then there was the afternoon a young woman appeared. Staggering inside, slumping against the Anthill door. Sobbing in a way that the new volunteer initially mistook for hysterical laughter. Her hands were pressed to her face, blood pulsing between her fingers. The entirety of the Anthill fell silent, even the children. Mattías ran over, touching her arm and whispering. The new volunteer wanted to keep staring but didn't (when was not looking respectful, as opposed to cowardly?). But then Mattías said her name:

—Carolina!

She came to him as fast as she could.

—Take the keys out of my pocket, he said. I don't want to get blood on them.

They rattled as she pulled them out.

—Take care of the Anthill, he said, leading the woman away, pressing his hands against hers, like they were trying to make a tourniquet. The woman was weeping quietly now, muffled whimpered sounds that were somehow worse than the screaming.

—What happened?

—He sliced her lips off. I'm taking her to the hospital. (Over his shoulder, twisting his neck to look back at her.) You're in charge, Carolina!

The standing there, the silence. The way Tomás and Gabriela looked down at their UNO cards, Gabriela's hand reaching to the deck to draw. Shauna's quiet retreat to the kitchen upstairs, to bring down the mop and bleach. But there was no mistaking the shaky way Maryluz turned away, busying herself with sorting the origami swans. The heaviness of the keys in the new volunteer's palm.

—Do you want these back?

That's what she asked him the next day. It was assembly, the lines of children wiggling and laughing. Yesterday – the screams and sobs, blood all over the floor – it was now seemingly forgotten, irrelevant to the present moment. It was so brutal, somehow, the way everyone just moved on.

He looked at her. —Would keeping them make you happy?

She shrugged. But it was hard to deny it: the unexpectedly sharp stab of pleasure. Her, the new volunteer, Mattías's chosen one!

—You keep them, he said. It was about time I trusted someone else with them anyway.

There was no mistaking it then, either: Shauna's frozen expression, Maryluz's incredulous frown.

But Mattías just clapped his hands, calling out the days' activities: —So! Today! In art! We continue with the origami theme! Dodgeball with me! Homework with Shauna! And Leadership Club students, you know who you are! Don't forget to make good choices, and to be SAFE, KIND and RESPECTFUL!

She keeps the keys hanging around her neck by the lanyard. They bounce against her heart with every step she takes.

Mattías, Mattías, Mattías. His shaky hands and sweaty face. His trembling voice, his rants about fundraisers for murdered Afro-Colombian environmentalists, about the need for financial literacy classes. The way he dashes from place to place. Running, sweating, the evolving collage of food stains on his shirt.

And then there was the time a man with a tiny skull tattooed under his eye came to the Anthill. He accepted a wrinkled yellow envelope from Mattías and immediately left, neither of them exchanging a word. His visit lasted less than seventy seconds, tops.

—What was that? the new volunteer asked, as soon as the man was out of hearing distance.

—Drug money, he said.

She stared at him. He started laughing, hard.

—Carolina, of course not! He's the sewing class teacher! He needs money for materials.

He wiped his eyes, even though there were no tears there.

—And, more importantly, there are much better places to sell drugs than here. Believe me, I would know.

And then he went off to organise an arm-wrestling contest.

Gang taxes – that's what Shauna had called it, on the bus.

Oh, he can be infuriating, can't he? In a way Maryluz was right. *You asshole*, she called him, swatting him with a paint-brush, but never without affection. That was the day she had to lead assembly herself. Mattías had arrived late, rushing in at the absolute last minute and sitting with the youngest Anthill children, who all giggled and squirmed with the thrill of his presence.

—And don't forget, Maryluz said, standing before them, her eyes hard as pool balls. Even though things have been sloppy here recently – a bit off-track – it's important to remember: no chaos. No disorder. And no mess.

—You hear that, children? Mattías jumped to his feet, racing to get the football. The children followed close behind, screeching and laughing.

—That goes for you too! Maryluz screamed. But he didn't look back.

The new volunteer fiddled with the keys. And when Maryluz made eye contact with her, as if seeking confirmation, all the new volunteer did was shrug and smile, raising her eyebrows as if to say: *That's Mattías.*

As if she knew him. Better than anybody.

Because in a way she does, doesn't she?

Because of what they've been through. The two of them, together. Even if she doesn't exactly remember their childhood. *A lovely childhood* – that's what he called it. Filled with silly games. A time to look back on with nothing but fondness. But whatever it was, they survived it, and that's something no one else will ever have or understand. Him and her.

Still. It felt terrible to say it to herself, there in that moment – so brusquely and openly, as the Leadership Club children swarmed around her and tugged at her hands.

The quietest, most secret, selfish thought.

(Squeezing the metal keys hard, pressing them into her palm.)

It had been a relief to not talk to him for so many years.

To have him be gone. Out of sight, out of mind.

And yet. This sort of thing happened to most people, didn't it? Why, you couldn't say in touch with *everyone*. It simply wouldn't be possible! Childhood friends drifted apart all the time. It wasn't terrible or unforgivable, it was just . . . something that happened. It was like (she told herself, the Anthill children leaping and running around her) the lifeboats in *Titanic*, floating on the surface of the freezing water. You couldn't reasonably expect them to let *everybody* in. Let them pull you under. Let yourself sink. Even Jack himself hadn't wanted to pull Rose down, drag her to the bottom of the icy ocean. There was no point in that whatsoever! You couldn't let yourself get swarmed and overwhelmed by the darkness of the world, the suffering of others. There was nothing wrong with focusing on yourself, doing what was best for you and moving on with your own life (nodding firmly, resolutely, as the Leadership Club children shouted and poked and pulled). Self-Care, not Selves-Care. That was how the world worked. That's just how it was.

CLEANING THE ANTHILL

But then there are special days at the Anthill. Different. Like today, right here and now. A day when Mattías has taped a sign to the Anthill door: *CLOSED FOR CLEANING*. Even though he told the kids at assembly days in advance, there are still several children who show up at 1 p.m., moaning piteously (*Closed?? Why??*) as they're shooed away by Maryluz, the most brutal of sentries.

Cleaning the Anthill. Outside, Mattías and Maryluz wash the windows with filthy mops and depressed-looking rags. Inside, it's the new volunteer and Shauna, tackling the Anthill's main space. They crawl around on their hands and knees, liberally using paper towels, scraping gum off the bottom of chairs and tables. Flat gum, grey gum, gum with fossilised tooth marks, gum with faint shades of colour (purple, blue, red). They pull the bookcase from the Education Corner wall, unearth a spot so thickly coated in dust it clearly hasn't been touched in ages, an ancient tomb of Anthill years gone by. The mould in the drinking fountain! The thick scummy layers in the sink drain! The dust! Oh God, the dust!

—It's like archaeology, she says to Shauna as they toss out shrivelled corpses of spiders, dried-up beetles, pins, paperclips, an infinite number of nasty hairbands.

—I know, Shauna says, sighing. It's a miracle we haven't killed a kid from dysentery yet.

It's mainly Shauna who talks as they clean – oh, how Shauna can talk! About anything and everything! The complete opposite of Mattías, with his tense Terminator jaw, and Maryluz, her rock-hard focus about now and now only. As they wipe, spray, sweep, Shauna talks, talks, talks. About her Fulbright project (domestic violence in Medellín's urban neighbourhoods) and how much Colombian men hate women (*This is the most sexist country I've ever lived in, and I've been living abroad for eight years now! I couldn't believe it when I first came here – how much the men hate women.*). About her childhood growing up in Montana. Her mentally ill mother, too schizophrenic to renew her food stamps, thus leaving Shauna and her sister to scavenge through their cabinets, crunching on dry ramen and shoplifting day-old bread (freegans, but not by choice). The time she crawled behind a bush during a party and passed out, thus inducing extreme panic in her friends, who worried she'd fallen into the lake and drowned.

—I was only trying to nap, Shauna says, wagging a finger knowingly at the new volunteer. Whenever I get really drunk, I get incredibly sleepy. That's how you know I'm wasted.

The new volunteer nods. 'Wasted' – such a North American word. She dips her rag into the bucket of soapy water.

Shauna dips her rag in too. —Did you drink in high school?

—Excuse me? She's caught off guard, but the way Shauna is smiling is politely insistent.

—In Medellín, I mean. Shauna wrings her rag out. The water splashes on the new volunteer's wrist. You said you were from here, right?

Speech Recitation time. —My mother was Colombian, the

new volunteer says. My father is British. I left Medellín when I was eight, and I live in London now.

But Shauna interrupts. —Oh wow, she says, and there's something in her tone that makes the new volunteer pause. Could it be . . . reverence? You only lived here eight years? But your Spanish is amazing!

The new volunteer shrugs. She can't explain it either.

But Shauna is talking again. She wants to know what year the new volunteer was born; what time period she was living here. —My God, you were living in Medellín *then*? What kind of work were your parents doing? Shit, I'm so sorry about your mother. Your father was a *lawyer*? What kind of law? She clearly finds the vague explanations unsatisfying, frowning as the new volunteer mumbles something about how she doesn't know, he was an international consultant for land reform lawsuits, something like that, but he doesn't ever talk about it, his former life and career, his hippy idealism, it makes him depressed (the understatement of the century – Shauna, of all people, doesn't need the gritty details). Her father's job didn't seem that important to her at the time; it was just something he did when he left the house during the day; it's not something he does any more; she didn't pay attention; she was just a child.

—He went out into the countryside to visit clients, the new volunteer says, raising her fingers to her lips, nibbling on a flap of loose skin. Until the roads got too dangerous . . .

She's about to explain about the motorways, the dangers of travelling. But Shauna has interrupted; Shauna wants to speak. Shauna knows all about that time period in Colombia. It was a very fascinating moment in Colombia's history, Shauna explains. She took a political science class in university and knows all about it. The course focused on the Unión Patriótica as a case group, the guerrilla leftist party established in the late eighties, whose members were deliberately assassinated by drug lords, paramilitaries and government forces alike. Exterminated! It was awful, such a horrible time, and the way Shauna's eyes widen, the way she squeezes her rag, it would be so easy to believe that she's lived through it herself; this pain, these scars, the weight of this incredibly traumatic past. —Can you imagine, Shauna says, if something like that were to take place in England or the US? If leftist candidates like Bernie Sanders or Jeremy Corbyn were basically *afraid* for their *lives*? That's why this post-peace-negotiation era is so fascinating. The extremity here could potentially parallel, God forbid, the developing extremity elsewhere. Freaking Charlottesville white supremacists. Self-armed lunatics in Eastern Oregon. Do you know how many human-rights workers have been assassinated in Colombia this year alone? (The new volunteer does, but Shauna tells her anyway.) Oh, how upset Shauna is! If only Colombians stopped taking the violence of their country for granted! If only they actually got angry at the assassination of their political figures, their social leaders, their journalists and activists; how horrible it is that the country can carry on as normal amidst such terror!

—Yes, the new volunteer says once Shauna pauses to take a breath. The Unión Patriótica was founded before I was born. It's a bit before my time . . .

But Shauna wants to tell her about Colombian political culture. Intensely this time, her face turning red from the force of her feelings, the rag forgotten as she puts her hands on her hips. It shocked her, Shauna informs the new volunteer, the extremity of the political and social divide here. The vehement hatred between right and left. How there could be such fabulously luxurious homes and fancy tourist resorts when there were Anthill children digging through the garbage. —They dig through it, you know, Shauna says. Every night, after we throw it out. Children, digging through the trash because they're hungry. Feudal! It's a feudal society! And the political culture doesn't help, Shauna announces. Such dishonesty. Such corruption. I'll never get over the cruelty here, the ruthlessness. Hypocrites. Such hypocrites.

The new volunteer cuts in. She says, —Shauna. I'm not trying to be rude. But Bernie Sanders and Jeremy Corbyn aren't corrupt because they don't have to be. They have choices.

Shauna takes a deep breath.

But the new volunteer doesn't stop. She says, more sharply than she means to, —For a lot of people here – and I mean normal people, everyday people, not politicians – it's not always a choice between taking the bribe or not. It's between taking the bribe or dying.

She rubs the rag hard against the table.

—Not to mention that neither of us know what we would do if we were in a similar situation. So probably we should just shut up about it and not judge.

—I don't agree with that at all, Shauna says forcefully. Not one bit. Don't you think silence and acceptance is part of the problem? In terms of complicity?

The new volunteer rubs the rag even harder. Still the mark won't come out. And in her head, the Welsh's girl's voice is chirping away: *and then he told us he made a* deal *with the* paramilitaries *to get permission to found and run the Anthill.*

—It's important to speak the truth, Shauna says. At whatever cost! It's important to hold people accountable. Public accountability: that's what the victims are trying to do now, post-peace negotiations. The rape victims, Carolina. Assault and disfigurement.

Shauna's voice is shaking. She keeps going.

—Staying silent makes you an accomplice. And quiet acceptance leads to impunity. That's exactly the problem with the political culture here. It's why people are dying!

The new volunteer lets her arm flop back down to her side. She must have sighed without realising it, because Shauna is now raising her hands in the air, don't-shoot style.

—Listen, she says, smiling, but her eyes are still flashing. I didn't mean to upset you.

—I'm not upset.

—I want to discuss this with you. I mean it! Mattías and Maryluz never want to talk about this kind of stuff with me; they always change the subject.

—But I agree with you, the new volunteer says. Pretty much.

The incredible weariness descending over her: a hot, heavy blanket. She glances at the windows. The mops are still bobbing up and down, scrubbing away at the glass. Mattías and Maryluz, working hard, together in their own little world. Shauna in hers. And her? Where does she belong?

—We should do dinner together, Shauna is saying. I want to discuss this with you. Actually, I'd love for you to read my master's dissertation and hear what you think. I can email you a PDF. Or, listen, I could even give you a physical copy. Yes! She claps her hands excitedly. —Carolina, you should come to my apartment! Come tonight! Oh my gosh, I can't believe we haven't done something like this earlier! I'll phone my husband now and tell him to start cooking something tasty – he deserves to pull his weight around the house, right?

The new volunteer finally tears her gaze from the windows. She looks Shauna directly in the eye.

—Yeah, she says. Sure. I'll come to dinner. She pauses, then says it loud and clear: On one condition.

———

As Shauna goes outside to deliver the news to Maryluz and Mattías, the new volunteer heads out the back to empty the bucket of sudsy water. The door knocks against something as she opens it.

—Eight-Bras, watch it! she says, turning towards a dark, hunched shape.

But it's only Gabriela, scooting away on her bottom.

—Hey, the new volunteer says, her knees cracking as she crouches beside her. You okay?

Gabriela shrugs. She's in the same clothes she's worn all week, which among Anthill children isn't particularly unusual.

—How long have you been here?

She shrugs again. She reaches up and absent-mindedly touches the scar on her neck. It looks red now rather than white, scabby like she's been picking at it.

The new volunteer's eyes flicker towards the bin. Shauna's voice: *They dig through it, every night.* —Are you waiting for Mattías?

Gabriela shakes her head. Still not speaking. Staring at the ground, as if upset.

—We're almost done cleaning. It's boring when the Anthill's closed, isn't it?

—Yes, Gabriela says in that croaky little voice of hers. It's boring and stupid and I don't like it.

—Want to help me finish?

Gabriela frowns. —Is Tomás here?

—No, unfortunately. But he'll definitely be here on Monday.

—What about *him*? she asks. The other boy?

—What other boy?

Gabriela sighs, but doesn't answer.

—Nobody's here but staff.

But Gabriela has leapt to her feet. She's running, she's slipped into the Anthill so fast it takes the new volunteer a second to realise what's happened. She struggles upwards, following Gabriela's quick darting figure. Through the Anthill, up the stairs, until they're standing before the supply closet.

—Come on, Gabriela, the new volunteer says, sounding terser than she means to. Mattías said it himself: no Anthill children allowed.

But Gabriela's already grabbed the supply closet handle. She's pulling hard, and just like that the door creaks open. — Helloooooo? she hollers, rushing inside. Are you still here?

—Gabriela!

The new volunteer follows. The closet is astonishingly large and pitch-dark – almost cave-like – completely unlit by the weak backdrop of light behind her. Her hand touches the door briefly for support. She pauses. Stares.

The inside of the door is covered in long scratches. Deep scratches. The metal flaky and splintering.

Like something's been trying to get out.

—There you are! That's what Gabriela is saying, in a sing-songy tone. Like she's talking to a baby, or someone much younger than her. Boy, you stink! Why didn't you take a bath like I told you?

The new volunteer runs her hand along the wall, searching for a light switch. Fumbling along the shelves. And then her fingers touch something wet and soft. Squishy, like damp newspaper.

—Gabriela?

There's a rustling sound. And then—

—Lina?

She screams. Her hand flies back. She turns. Her shoulder hits the door. She's running, running, past the ESL tables, past the computers. Behind her, Gabriela is standing in the supply closet doorway, hands against the frame. Gabriela is not moving, Gabriela is watching with wide and curious eyes as the new volunteer stumbles down the stairs, wiping her hand on her shorts repeatedly, panting hard, not glancing back.

But the voice

(his voice? *That* voice?)

THE ARCTIC FOX, RELEASED

There you are, Lina!
  I'm coming for you!
  Over and out!

STORY TIME

The new volunteer had forgotten that Shauna's husband is Spanish, but the food served at Shauna's dinner party is tapas style: sliced tortilla, rolled-up bits of ham, fried egg with chorizo and bread. As the maid brings out the tray of little plates, the new volunteer is already counting in her head how many she can have without seeming greedy. Maryluz shakes her head (*I ate after class, I'm full*); Shauna holds up a hand like a policeman directing traffic (*Later, I need to put Arturo to bed first*). The new volunteer hesitates, but still takes three.

—Thank you very much, she says to the maid. It looks absolutely delicious. Was the tortilla hard to prepare?

As she serves Mattías and Shauna's husband, the maid explains that, no, it's not as tricky as you'd think, the secret is to use lots of olive oil and to turn the pan upside down on a plate. The new volunteer asks if she can come to the kitchen later and have a look to see how she did it, but only if it's not too much trouble, and the maid nods, heading back to the kitchen to bring out the salad.

So there she is, on the tatty leather couch with Shauna's husband on her right, Maryluz to her left. Mattías sits on a child-size chair he insisted on taking, knees nearly reaching his chest, Gulliver on Lilliput furniture. On the armchair, Shauna fusses with her toddler son, who keeps turning towards his father with an anxious expression reminiscent of the very youngest Anthill children. Shauna keeps snapping her fingers in an attempt to get him to look at her phone.

—Arturo, Arturo, she keeps saying in English, making a clicking sound with her tongue. Look over here, love. Look at Mommy's camera.

The new volunteer holds up her glass of wine, so that Shauna's husband can fill it to the brim. —I'm sorry, I didn't catch your name when I came in?

He leans in for an air kiss, even though she already gave him one at the door. —Lalo, he says. Thank you again for coming.

When she feels capable of appearing calm, she looks at Mattías. The longest, slowest stare she can manage. But he's talking to Maryluz, rocking back and forth on his miniature chair, discussing the upcoming field trip to the botanical gardens. Maryluz's shorts are so tiny they end at the crotch.

—We can ask the Nazi with the van to drive us, he says, fiddling with a shoelace. He offered to do it before. Besides, he owes me a favour.

—That bald guy in the bodega? Maryluz takes a pack of cigarettes out of her tiny silver handbag. I don't like him. He keeps threatening to poison the dogs.

—But I only call him 'the Nazi' as a joke!

The new volunteer touches Maryluz on the wrist. —I thought you didn't smoke.

—I do tonight. Maryluz pulls out a purple lighter so fluorescent it could glow in the dark.

—Can I bum one off you? I'll give you some pesos.

—Don't be silly. Maryluz tugs one free and passes it over. Is that what they do in England? Charge you at parties?

156

—Feel free to light up in here, Lalo says. We'll put the kid to bed.

Shauna is already rising to her feet, lifting Arturo up by the armpits. —Beddy-bye, Arturo, she says, still speaking in English, now in a sing-songy voice. Say bye-bye!

Arturo opens and closes his mouth like a goldfish, but obediently lets himself be draped over his mother's shoulder. Maryluz is a woman on a mission, her lighter clicking before Shauna has even left the room.

—I'm nervous, she whispers to the new volunteer, passing the lighter over. I hope I don't do anything embarrassing.

—Me too, the new volunteer whispers back, feeling conspiratorial. And it's hard not to love Maryluz then, just a bit: for all her glamour and bluntness, the metal hardness of her piercings, she's still struggling.

As the new volunteer turns back to Lalo and Mattías, smoke rising between her fingers, Lalo is telling Mattías about a camping trip he took to the Pacific coast of Chocó. Maryluz is silent, sipping her wine, letting the men talk.

—I was on that beach, brother, Lalo is saying, in that shitty little tent for three weeks. I shit you not, it rained every – single – day. There were slugs inside my sleeping bag. I woke up with a leech in-between my toes. We talked about this last time, didn't we? But the good thing is I ate fish at every meal. Fish for breakfast, fish for dinner, fish for lunch. I couldn't get enough.

—Ocean fish, right? the new volunteer says. Never river.

Lalo finally glances at her, tilting his beer approvingly in her direction. —Hey, he says. This girl gets it! This girl knows my mantra.

He points his trigger finger at her cigarette, miming taking a drag. She passes it over.

—Trust me, the new volunteer says. Whenever you can, avoid fish from the river. No tilapia or carp ever.

She doesn't look at Mattías, but out of the corner of her eye she can sense him shifting around a bit, in his tiny child-size chair.

—That's what I always say, Lalo says, passing the cigarette back. Are you a mind-reader, honey?

—I just had a feeling.

Mattías clears his throat, as if preparing to speak. But the new volunteer turns away abruptly to ask Shauna, who has just returned, how old Arturo is (who would have thought that her standard conversation-starters for Anthill children would prove so versatile, in such varied social situations!). With the corkscrew sticking out of the wine bottle like a weird adult version of the Sword in the Stone, Shauna tells the new volunteer and Maryluz about Arturo: how he's two and a half years old; how he keeps getting into fights at the nursery, complaining that the other kids 'smell'; how he was definitely a bit of an unplanned accident, ha. Why, if someone had told Shauna at Burning Man three years ago that she'd be a *mother*, in *Colombia* (though technically Arturo was born in Seattle, where Shauna was waiting for Lalo to finish up his Cambodian contract), a mother at thirty-seven . . . Shauna doesn't finish her sentence, her voice trailing off, beginning again abruptly as she throws herself into the armchair, which releases a startled *whoosh* beneath her. —Sometimes it's like I'm waiting for someone to come up to me, Shauna says, playing with her coffee-bean bracelet. Somebody invisible, from I don't

know where. And have them tell me *You're doing a bad job.
You're just . . . crap.*

Red wine makes the new volunteer daring: —At being a
mother?

—At everything! Work, study . . . My online therapist
thinks I have executive function disorder.

She tries to smile, but her eyes look jittery, anxious.

—Shauna, Maryluz says, don't fuck with me: you're thirty-
nine? And all this time I thought you were my age.

Shauna smiles, all bright sunshine again, and the new volunteer can't help but beam back. Is this . . . bonding? Is this
what it feels like to initiate healthy adult female friendships?
She lifts her glass too quickly and sloshes wine on her wrist.

The evening goes on. Whenever she can, she tries listening
in on Lalo and Mattías, using her ears like secret spy satellites.
Lalo is talking about his hiking trip to Ciudad Perdida, up in
the Sierra Nevada. —Now that's a trip you need to take,
brother, he tells Mattías, handing him another beer. Three
days of hiking through mud and clay. We ran into some soldiers and they let us take photos with their guns. Those Bel-
gian tourists were freaking out, man. And this Italian woman's
backpack was so heavy with all her bullshit, she ended up hiring a mule to carry it for her. I'd never expect a woman's bag
not to be heavy, right?

Mattías just sits there listening, drinking his beer. Maybe
it's the miniature chair, but it's strangely sad to see him looking so small, in contrast with Lalo's expansive gestures, loud
voice, decisive head nods. Like a little boy, next to a man.

—That Ciudad Perdida is a freaking theme park, Lalo says,
taking a long swig. Believe me, they get away with shit that

wouldn't fly in America. I mean, swinging on vines across rivers? No safety regulations whatsoever! It's got to be good for the tourist economy, though. At least until someone gets killed.

—What do you do, Lalo? the new volunteer asks, unable to restrain herself. Like, for a job?

—Lalo's not working at the moment, Shauna says quickly.

—Shut up, honey! Lalo says, laughing. Listen to her, sheesh. She doesn't know what she's talking about. Do you, babe? I'm a freelance writer, he explains to the new volunteer, shifting in his seat to face her. I get paid to work when I want, doing what I want. I don't like having any boss other than me. That's just the kind of person I am. I have a website too; I'll give you my card later. You should check it out – I've written a ton of posts about Medellín. I have a piece coming out in the *Guardian* soon.

—Is that right?

—Yeah, I know Medellín really well; I've lived here for nine months. Crazy, right? You need to be careful in this city, though. Especially you, with skin like that. I wouldn't carry your iPhone around if I were you. And forget about putting in earbuds. That's what I tell Shauna all the time, but does she listen to me? Does she?

He reaches for the new volunteer's cigarette without asking permission and takes a long drag.

—That neighbourhood. I'm telling you, man, he says, now addressing Mattías. You're missing out on a seriously good opportunity, not inviting those evangelical church groups. Those Baptists! You're missing out on some extreme funding from them.

—The Anthill doesn't host groups from religiously affiliated organisations, Mattías says automatically. He's holding his beer in-between two hands, like a baby with a milk bottle. Or political, either. It's one of our core policies.

—Yeah, yeah, I've heard your little tour-group spiel. You'll take their money, though, won't you? For your fundraisers? I volunteered at the Anthill, see, he says to the new volunteer, taking another drag from her cigarette, which he still hasn't returned to her. I taught English there with Shauna. The things I do for love, right? I know you probably won't believe it, but Medellín used to be *really* unsafe. Like, *dangerously* unsafe.

—Was it?

—Hard to believe, huh? That's why Mr Big-Shot here likes to keep foreigners around the Anthill. For his own protection – pretty damn smart!

Lalo laughs. Mattías doesn't say anything. The new volunteer says, loudly, —That's not true.

—Honey, come on. It's obvious – isn't it, jefe? Having gringos nearby guarantees his personal safety. God knows what kind of crap he got himself into, back in the day. Hey, Mattías, I'm only joking! Using my wife as a freaking human shield—

Shauna coughs. Mattías still doesn't speak. Lalo touches the new volunteer on the arm.

—But any questions you have about the city – what to do, where to go – just ask. Where to go party and stuff. I used to work at a travel agency so I'm an expert.

—I can see that.

—Lalo, Maryluz says, blowing smoke from her two nostrils like a dragon. You know that she's from Medellín, right?

He flicks ash on the floor. —No, she's not. She's English.

161

—Maryluz is correct, the new volunteer says. I was born and grew up in Medellín. I moved to England when I was eight.

—There you go, he says, stubbing out the new volunteer's cigarette on a grease-stained plate. I was right: England. That's what I said.

The maid brings out another tray of tapas, slices of melon and fried potatoes in a red sauce. When the new volunteer asks Shauna to open another bottle of wine, Shauna says, —Red or white? Hmm, let's just do both!

The new volunteer's fondness for Shauna thus increases exponentially. Even more so when she refills all their glasses to the brim.

—You haven't eaten a single thing! Shauna says to Maryluz, who's lit another cigarette. No wonder you've lost weight! Carolina, look at how skinny she is! Look at her wrists!

—I ate before coming, Maryluz repeats. She takes a long drag of her cigarette.

—Everything is super-tasty, Shauna, Mattías calls out from his corner, where Lalo is discussing his intermittent fasting routine. The new volunteer keeps her eyes fixed on the smooth lake of wine in her glass.

—You want to know the secret? Shauna says, bracelets jangling as she takes a long sip. Maggi stock cubes. Beef, chicken, whatever. Gotta love all the sodium here!

The new volunteer takes the biggest glug she can. Back in England, people always commented on how much she salted her food. *Whoa, slow down there!* That's what a boyfriend once said (well, fuck-buddy, but whatever), watching her jiggle the salt shaker liberally all over her full English breakfast, even the baked beans. *You know that sodium causes you to retain a lot of water weight, right?*

Why did it take coming back here to realise that everything else she'd been eating up till now had no flavour to it?

As Shauna talks about how she and Lalo met in Lima, and Maryluz delicately reapplies pink lip gloss so thick and gloopy it verges on paint, the new volunteer is suddenly (randomly, inexplicably) reminded of the dream she had last night. It comes back to her in such a rush it takes her breath away, leaves her frozen in her seat. In the dream, Mattías was climbing into a spaceship, dressed in a silvery astronaut suit. The two of them, they were standing in the kitchen of her parents' apartment (what was the name of the neighbourhood where they lived? Was it this neighbourhood, where they both are right now? Could she be retracing her childhood steps without even realising it?). Her dream-self – she started tearing through the cupboards, searching for long-lasting food Mattías could take with him on his space voyage. The Nutella her mother only allowed them to eat after church on Sundays. Her father's tins of sardines in tomato sauce, posted to him from Britain. Food he'd need to live on, to survive.

Oh God, she said in the dream, holding up packets of ziplock bags. *Mattías, what are you going to drink on your space voyage? All this food is going to make you incredibly thirsty!*

Dream-Mattías nodded thoughtfully. She frantically tugged open the freezer door (oh, the way it always got stuck!) and took out the ice cube trays. *Can you take these?* she said, waving them around. *Can you suck on them in space? Can you hold one in your mouth until it melts, then spit it out till it refreezes? I don't want you to run out and die of thirst!*

In the dream, it had all felt so urgent and desperate: was it safe for him to undertake interstellar galactic travel? With only stale Nutella and tinned sardines to sustain himself? How could she help him prepare; how was he going to survive on his own? *Matty,* her dream-self said to him, *what are we going to do?*

About what?

And he pulled down the visor of his astronaut helmet, blocking her out, so that all she could see was her own reflection, staring back.

Just keep doing what you've been doing, he said behind the glass, his voice muffled and distorted, as if speaking through a broken microphone.

What? she said. *What have I been doing?*

Nothing, the voice said, twisting and crackling. *Nothing at all.*

—Carolina?

She looks up too quickly. The last of her wine spills on her shirt. The maid is lighting a citronella candle to keep the mosquitoes away, its thin smoke rising in wisps. Shauna is slumped in the armchair, staring vacantly at the wall. Maryluz is shaking her last cigarette into her palm. Lalo has stood up and is walking away, maybe to the bathroom, maybe the kitchen, maybe to check on his son. And Mattías is sitting there, looking at her very quietly and very seriously, still in his little boy's chair.

—It's been decided, he says. We're going to keep drinking.

———

On the street, Mattías strolls ahead. Lalo has stayed back, citing an early Skype call from London tomorrow: *It's a really exciting opportunity – I've been working on this book about Medellín, see, and these publishers are interested.* His book is about Medellín's incredible transformation from a war-torn city, the most dangerous city on earth, into an innovative twenty-first-century metropolis. It's about urban renewal, it's about change, it's about the promise and regenerative potential of hip-hop culture and street graffiti. *Shauna, you didn't tell them about my book?*

The new volunteer brings up the rear with Shauna and Maryluz. The regiment of soldiers, following their general. They take up the entire pavement, stepping over dusty rocks shaped like boiled potatoes and broken shards of glass that look sharp enough to pierce through Shauna's flimsy ballet flats. They stroll past palm trees and bars (wait, was that a Hooters?), Italian restaurants and coffee shops. It's cloudy tonight, and the mountains she can usually see surrounding the city are hidden, no small bright lights. It's strange to think that somewhere up there is the Metrocable, the dust-spewing buses, the Anthill beyond – an invisible backdrop to the trendy neighbourhood, looming over everything but completely out of sight.

(Was something invisible if it wasn't paid attention to? Did she look up at these very mountains, this exact same sight, as a child? What did she think about?)

They take a taxi into Centro, Mattías in the front seat and the three of them crammed in the back. Shauna and Maryluz gossip the whole time about former Anthill children: the Vallejo twins, whose mother was stabbed by their father; Filoberto, who was

run over by a milk truck and had to use a catheter and whose
genitals (Maryluz whispers) are now completely useless, poor
thing, at age thirteen, imagine. Clarabella, whose brother
dragged her out of the building by the hair; Luisa, set on fire on
the bus by her boyfriend. —Animals, Shauna sighs, but Maryluz shakes her head: —Compared to humans, Shauna, if someone were to call me an animal, I'd take it as a compliment.

They get out at the plaza with the Botero statues, near a
donkey pushing its face around in a tower of garbage. As Mattías pays the driver, a man with no shoes and an unbuttoned
shirt approaches them, hissing and clicking his tongue in
approval. —My queens, he says. My gorgeous dolls.

Maryluz says, —Mister, don't be gross.

He retreats behind a concrete pillar, but not without whistling one last time. Getting out of the taxi, Shauna trips over
her ballet flat, which flies off her foot and into the gutter.

—I've got it, the new volunteer says, quickly scooping it up.

She slides it back on to Shauna's foot, Cinderella style.
Shauna rests one arm on Maryluz's shoulders for balance.

—Do I seem drunk? Shauna says. Am I embarrassing
myself? Fuck, I'm so embarrassed. Fuck, fuck, fuck.

—You're fine, Shauna! Maryluz says.

Shauna drapes her other arm over the new volunteer's
shoulder. It feels heavy, like a bag of sand (could Shauna be
that drunk already? From four bottles of wine, split between
five people? Is she drunk herself?). The three of them follow
Mattías like that, half-dragging Shauna along, like soldiers
carrying their wounded captain away from the booming can-
nons, because no one deserves to be left to die alone on the
too-much-to-drink battlefield, not out here, not like this. It's

like the Anthill children when they help an injured teammate off the football field, their skinny arms wrapped in determined support around each other's waists. Why, they're just children themselves, aren't they? She and Mattías and all the rest – children watching over other children! Like her mother and father before her! How could she have not realised this earlier? —I've got you, the new volunteer says, as Shauna's fingers press into the flesh of her arm for support. I've got you.

Mattías takes them to a bar with picnic tables and ceramic ashtrays with surprisingly beautiful patterns, swirling blue flowers and yellow insects. A few feet away from their table, a shirtless man lies on his back on the pavement. He brings a paper bag to his glazed face and inhales deeply, but Mattías nudges her and whispers, —Don't stare. So she orders a beer for everyone and food from her childhood for herself, tasty treats that would definitely not fall under the category of 'clean eating' or 'paleo': fried meat empanadas (putting Cornish pasties to shame!), buñelos (their glorious sour yucca cheesiness! Their soft white bellies, hidden by the tough brown crust!). The lady gives her five different options for sauces and she requests them all. Mattías orders French fries draped in thick drippings of ketchup, Shauna orders a hamburger and Maryluz orders an enormous paper plate of greasy yellow potatoes. The new volunteer's order is the cheapest thing on the menu and the smallest serving, which makes her unbearably proud.

—Yeah, Mattías says as they all sit down, Shauna at the counter still waiting for her change. That Spanish food was good, but . . . I'm not really full.

She and Maryluz nod. The three of them in agreement. It's

a deeply satisfying feeling – to know she's on the same team as them. The Medellín natives.

—I kept wanting to add salt, Mattías says, waving down the man selling cigarettes and candy nearby, bumping fists as he asks him to bring them a bottle of rum from the shop next door.

As Mattías pours the rum into the four white plastic cups, the new volunteer ducks behind the corner of the bodega. She throws up quietly behind the building, splattering liquid all over a sad patch of grass. She uses her phone camera to check her mouth for any stains. When she returns to the table, wiping her mouth on the back of her hand, Maryluz is in the middle of telling a story. —At that point in my life, she says, I was still in that phase of making miniature houses – remember, Mattías? The ones out of hairpins and scrunchies?

But Mattías isn't listening. He's wiggling his fingers urgently at the new volunteer, trying to get her attention. —Put it away, he whispers, like he's trying not to interrupt Maryluz, even though that's exactly what's he doing. Don't carry your phone around in public!

—Oh, come on, the new volunteer says. It's not like someone's going to snatch it out of my hand.

Nonetheless she sticks it down the elastic band of her underpants, which is how she's seen Maryluz carry hers.

—Sorry, Mattías says. I just want to protect you.

Shauna bites into her hamburger, lettuce and tomato spilling everywhere. Maryluz pulls two cigarettes from her newly purchased pack, handing one to the new volunteer and keeping one for herself. —That professor, though, she continues. His comments were idiotic. He kept saying my houses looked like uteruses. What I want to know is, how does a miniature house made out of hairpins and scrunchies look like a uterus?

—Excellent question, the new volunteer says. I'd love to know myself.

Maryluz smiles, and there it is again, that slow feeling of warmth. If it had a word, maybe it would sound like 'belonging'.
I belong here.

Sitting with a drink before her. A plateful of fried food to scarf down. No PhD, no England, nothing in Europe could be as . . . as life-filled as this. As authentic. She can taste it, life between her teeth, the act of living her life to the fullest capacity, like a mother cat carrying around a kitten in her jaws.

Is this the feeling her own mother was looking for? Tramping up and down the unpaved streets all those years ago, with her evangelical church?

But Maryluz is still telling her story: —Anyway, so when I had a chance to visit my brother in prison, of course I wanted to go! I wanted to build a model of it, see, she explains, blowing smoke in the new volunteer's direction. And it was absolutely worth it. In the cell where they were keeping him, there were four cement bunk beds. Two on each side. One was for a former guerrilla. One for a former paraco, a paramilitary. One for my brother, the stupid mule who went and got himself caught. And the other one was for a – what's the word . . .

—Sicario? the new volunteer says. Delinquent? Narco? Mafioso?

—Street criminal, Maryluz and Mattías say at the same time. They look at each other, as if exchanging a mutual understanding.

—A common street criminal, Maryluz repeats. That room

was like a metaphor for this whole shitty country. She laughs happily, as if delighted.

—Was there a toilet in the room? the new volunteer asks. She's picturing buckets in corners. Or maybe a single toilet, exposed with no wall.

—Of course not, Maryluz and Mattías say at the same time again. She gestures at him as if to say *Your turn*.

—What's typical is a plastic bottle, Mattías says softly. They pass it around for everyone to use.

He raises his eyebrows knowingly at Maryluz, who smiles back.

And there it is again, that sour feeling in her stomach. Twisting.

Maryluz pours everyone another generous shot of rum. — My brother worked for Spirit Airlines. And if he hadn't been so hypoglycaemic, he'd have never got caught. What a fat fuck!

The new volunteer downs her rum as fast as possible, wiping her chin. —Maryluz? she says. What was it like for you?

Maryluz glances at her. Mattías is opening a beer with Maryluz's lighter, his plastic cup of rum still half full.

—Living here, I mean, the new volunteer says. In Medellín. Maryluz shrugs. —It was fine.

—Nothing ever happened? To you, your family?

—Something has happened to everyone who's lived here. Maryluz touches the piercings on her face, like she's making sure they're still there. We all have our scars, no? God knows that doesn't make them worth talking about, though.

She laughs hard, a disarmingly loud witch's cackle, as though she finds the whole thing deeply amusing.

The new volunteer looks down at her cup, disappointingly empty. —I'm just curious, she mumbles.

—Don't worry about it! Maryluz waves her hand through the air, an empress-like expression of generosity. I'll tell you my whole life story one day, I promise. All the gossip. And you can write it down for me. That's what I want, a Colombian woman to write out the soap opera of my life!

She raises the cup to her face, piercings glittering.

Moments like these, it's hard not to stare at her – to look at her as a physical thing. So young and hard and bright. So certain of her place in the world.

—Well, in any case, the new volunteer says, more stiffly this time, I'm not a writer. I study literature.

—Same thing. Maryluz is smiling without showing any teeth. He told us about you before you came here – didn't you, jefe? That you write and read for a living. That you're a very creative person.

They turn to look at him. He blinks quickly, as if his mind was elsewhere.

—What was that? he says. His voice sounds a bit hoarse, as if underused.

Maryluz taps her elegant nails on the table. —You've been very quiet all evening, jefe. It's your turn to talk now.

—Yeah! Shauna crows, lifting her head from her hands, where she's been temporarily resting her cheek. A story from the writer!

—He's not a writer either, Shauna. The new volunteer says this extra-loudly, like she wants to make sure she's heard. Neither of us are.

—Yes, he is, Maryluz says, interrupting. He writes all the

time. Come on, jefe, tell them! You have all those notebooks that you've filled. In the supply closet.

—What are you talking about? the new volunteer says. She laughs so hard her ribs hurt. That's silly.

—It's true! Maryluz says. He's always hiding in there, writing, when he thinks we're not paying attention. He pretends he's disappeared, that he's gone off to do other business, when what he's really done is locked himself away in there to scribble things down. Don't you, jefe?

The thought of Mattías locked in the closet, writing furiously, scrawling away, filling up pages and pages – it makes the new volunteer feel sick. Sicker than the hot vomit spewing from her mouth, the sickest she's felt all night. But Mattías is shaking his head and smiling. When he speaks, his voice still sounds croaky. —Oh no! he says brightly. It's okay – I'm happy listening to you guys.

—No, Maryluz says. No locked doors here – it's your turn to talk.

Shauna knocks the remains of her hamburger off the table in a dramatic sweep. —A story, she says in a formal-sounding voice, like she's reciting a quote. A story should be similar to love. Given freely without . . .

She hesitates, as though trying to remember. An insect flies by and hits the light bulb at a furious speed, kamikaze-pilot style.

—Without expecting anything in return, Mattías says quietly.

He crumples the plastic cup between his hands, then carefully uncrumples it, gently poking out the bumps with his fingers. They make loud cracking sounds.

—If it's easier, jefe, Maryluz says, pretend we're not here.

Or do what Esteban does – my cuentero friend. Pretend we're other people. Pretend you're someone else.

—Yeah, the new volunteer says, and maybe it's the rum, the twisted feeling still in her stomach, the sour aftertaste of vomit in her mouth that she can't quite get rid of, but her voice comes out sounding so mean it must be impossible for everyone to not notice. She says, Maybe someone like . . . Lalo?

—Lalo? Shauna says, furrowing her brow. Where is he? Is Lalo here?

—He didn't come, Maryluz tells her, touching Shauna on the wrist. Lalo stayed home.

—Oh, thank Christ, Shauna says, sighing loudly. The anxious, jittery look in her eyes is back as she puts her head down on her forearms. Jesus help me, she says, her voice muffled. I married a real asshole, didn't I?

—I think we should take Shauna home now, the new volunteer says. I think she's had too much to drink.

—Me? I'm fine! Shauna lifts her cup and drains the liquid inside in one gulp, throwing her head back.

—See? Maryluz says. She's fine. And regardless, jefe, it's your turn to talk. We want to hear from you! You've been very quiet all evening.

Mattías doesn't say anything. The new volunteer reaches across the table and takes the bottle from him, unscrewing it clumsily. —It's okay, she says, accidentally dropping the cap on the ground. I can tell one instead.

—No! Maryluz says. Her perfectly thin eyebrows shoot up her forehead. And it's only now that the new volunteer finally realises how drunk Maryluz must be, how out of control, how (to put it bluntly) completely fucked she is. Are they *all* that

173

fucked? How did they get this bad this fast?

—We've heard from you already, Maryluz is saying. It's his turn now. How did you two meet? You and Carolina?

The blood in the new volunteer's veins: ice-cold.

—Go on, Mattías! Maryluz continues. Man of mystery. Our secretive jefe! She tilts her head and smiles. He doesn't smile back.

—Am I secretive? he says flatly. I don't think so.

—You are! Isn't he, Shauna? It's always the same thing from him, and only ever to the volunteers: the orphanage, the nunnery, the reformatory. Working at the laundry place, climbing trees to steal fruit from the neighbour's yard. Blah blah blah. I have it memorised.

Shauna's playing with her bottom lip, pushing it into her teeth with her fingers, but as soon as Maryluz addresses her she immediately withdraws her hand. —Yeah, she says, slurring a bit. Mr Mysterious. International man of mystery.

Mattías closes his eyes briefly, then opens them. He arranges his face into a smile. The biggest grin he's had on his face all night.

—What do I have to say, he says, laughing, to get you bitches to shut up?

The new volunteer looks at him.

Shauna's eyes widen.

Maryluz says, —Excuse me?

—I'm joking! Can't you tell when I'm making a joke?

He turns towards her, a sharp, quick movement.

—Carolina, he says. You don't remember?

Maryluz picks up a napkin and touches it to her collarbone.

Shauna says, —Huh?

—You don't remember? he repeats. The dinner parties? The zoo?

Maryluz moves the napkin upwards, so that it's covering her lip.

—What about your mother? Her fun little living room game?

—Her *what*? says Shauna.

—Don't you remember, Carolina, Mattías says, his voice low and intense but never fading, never faltering. Remember my party tricks? he says. How I'd go around the room and finish the beer that was at the bottom of everyone's glass? Sometimes it'd be whisky and I'd get the hiccups and that would make everyone laugh. Remember how funny it was?

He's not laughing any more.

Maryluz brings the napkin to her forehead, momentarily covering her eyes.

Shauna says, —You two knew each other? In the orphanage?

And finally the new volunteer says, —There's nothing funny about it, Mattías.

He leans back. Away from the table, away from her.

—He didn't grow up in an orphanage, she says, turning to Maryluz and Shauna now. She speaks as clearly as she can. He didn't grow up in a nunnery. My mother – she took him from his home. From his family.

Maryluz and Shauna stare at her, like her words aren't registering. Like she's speaking a language they haven't heard before.

—She was visiting his neighbourhood, the new volunteer says. With her gross stupid evangelical church. And she took him home with her. Because she wanted to. Because she could. She thought he was cute, she felt sorry for him, so she brought him home with her.

175

Shauna says, —You two lived together? In the same house?

Shauna's cup has tilted over, rum trickling on to the pavement in a slim waterfall, but she doesn't seem to notice or care. Between her fingers, Maryluz has twisted the napkin into what would be the thinnest rollie ever.

—Oh, come on, Mattías says, rubbing his fingers into his temples. It wasn't like that! Your family was very good to me. It wasn't that bad.

—Yes, it was. It was exactly that bad. It's okay, she says, addressing Mattías now. Not the street lights, not the fireflies, not the sounds of the city and the night all around them. Him and him alone. I know you're grateful, she says. I know it was a good childhood and that you appreciate it. But at the same time, what she did to you – it was wrong. And it was bullshit.

She stops talking. Mattías is just gazing in front of him, at nothing in particular.

After a long moment, Shauna leans forward against the table. —But wasn't that . . . illegal? What your mother did?

She can feel how red her fingers are from scratching and picking – she doesn't have to look down to know.

—Of course it was. We didn't have his birth certificate, let alone adoption papers. He can't ever leave the country. She basically kidnapped him.

—Christ, Shauna says.

Maryluz still hasn't spoken. Her hands are fists, pressing into her forehead.

No one else says anything for a long while. Then Mattías says, —Your mother was very good to me.

—She was fucked in the head! She steals this kid, she says

176

to Shauna and Maryluz, who are both sitting very silent and still and straight. From his own mother, his family. Because she thinks it's going to make her life seem more fulfilling, or meaningful, or whatever. Because she's depressed about her dumb sad non-hippy life. Her stupid bourgeois guilt. I don't even care what the reason was. And then, when that doesn't happen, when her life doesn't become this instantly deep . . . thing, she gets herself killed crossing the street. By a motorcycle or what the fuck ever – I don't even remember; that's just what I was told. The most pointless traffic accident ever. What a dummy.

She lifts her plastic cup to her lips and empties it.

—She was good to me, Mattías repeats. She was good.

—Oh, she was something all right.

She reaches for the bottle and refills everyone's cups, even though Mattías and Maryluz have barely touched theirs.

After that, things get blurry. Maryluz makes a comment about Mattías drinking too quickly, which makes him immediately drain his cup, refill it, and drain it again. —Jefe, Maryluz says, touching his hand, and he slaps it away. And then Shauna needs someone to help her go to the bathroom, so the new volunteer goes with her. Except there's somebody in the stall already, so she bangs on the door with her knuckles as hard as she can.

—Is the room spinning? Shauna says, leaning against the wall. Is this room spinning or is it just me?

—It's just you, the new volunteer lies.

Somehow, the cashier guides her outside? (Or a security guard?) And then she's standing in a little shop? Holding cans of Poker beer? (Where did the money in her hand come from?

177

Did she go to a cash machine at some point?) And there is Mattías, pressing even more cans into her chest.

—I'll be right back, he says into her ear. He's standing so close she can see sweat glimmering on his upper lip. He whispers, I'm going to pee.

—In the street? The voice coming out of her mouth sounds awful, slurring. Somehow, deep within herself, she's able to feel the dull horror of having allowed herself to get this drunk – father-level drunk. Again. Struggling not to drop the cans, she manages to ask, Where's Maryluz?

—Shauna was having a family emergency. So Maryluz offered to take her home in a taxi, to make sure she got back safe. It's just you and me now. Just like it used to be. Isn't that good?

He squeezes her shoulder.

—Have you been avoiding me? she says, still in that awful thick voice, like her tongue has grown two sizes too big. Do you hate me?

He stares at her with those dark eyes that should be familiar but aren't. —Why would you say that?

—Because I never see you! You're never around! You never want to talk, and when you do it's just the Anthill this, the Anthill that . . .

Something is dribbling down her chin – spit? More vomit? Great, a new threshold in a life full of drunken low points. But he wipes the liquid away with his palm.

—I'm sorry! (A little girl's voice, thin and squeaky.) I just thought you thought – that you didn't want to be friends with me any more.

—I'll always want to be friends with you, Lina. If that's what makes you happy.

178

He moves his hands down from her shoulders, to her arms and waist.

—Lina and Matty. Lina and Matty's great adventures. Lina and Matty together again. Lina and Matty best friends forever.

It's like something has burst out of him. Uncaged, released. She doesn't like the way he's touching her, but she can't figure out a way to tell him to stop.

—The Lalo thing, she says. His hands freeze, but don't move away. Matty, why did you do that?

He narrows his eyes. —Lalo is the kind of man foreign girls like.

—So I'm a foreign girl?

He doesn't respond.

—And you're still writing? she says. In your little notebooks?

He still doesn't answer.

—I just wish you'd told me, she says. You can tell me, you know. Matty, why can't you just say what you're thinking?

He starts laughing. Mouth open, showing his teeth.

She tries to laugh too but her throat doesn't make a sound. —Matty, she says, is that you?

—Of course it's me. You made me. Remember?

She stares at him.

—You keep saying you want to remember, he says. But you don't. Not really.

She swallows.

—Well, I do, he says. I remember everything.

He yanks her towards him, hard.

—*I made you out of dirt*, he says. Speaking distinctly, as if quoting. *So that I wouldn't be lonely.*

—I don't—

179

His hand is clenching the flesh of her waist, fingers digging in.

—Matty, you're *hurting* me, she cries out.

His lips are by her ear. He opens his mouth, abruptly shuts it. As if he's literally swallowing his words. Turns and walks outside. Her waist feels strange when he takes his hand away.

As she steps up to the counter to pay, she points at a bottle of rum behind the cashier's shoulders. —One, please, she says, doing her best to pronounce the words clearly.

As she's handing over the cash, the door tinkles and a woman and a man walk in. The woman is wearing a pink unbuttoned shirt and nothing else. Even her feet are bare. As the woman walks past, following the man, the new volunteer can see the curve of her buttocks under her shirt. There's blood running down her legs, a thick trickle. And there's a hand-shaped bloodstain on her shirt.

The first thing the new volunteer does is turn and look at the cashier, who thins his lips. —Can you call the police? she whispers.

He shakes his head curtly, handing over the change and a plastic bag filled with alcohol.

The woman is following the man wordlessly around the store. Her hands are dirty, like she's been scratching at mud. The man (her boyfriend? Her pimp?) is wearing a brown leather jacket. The new volunteer takes her phone out from where it's been jammed in her underwear (what a Christmas miracle that it's managed to survive there this whole evening!). It makes a loud clicking sound as she takes the photo.

The man immediately spins towards her. —Did you just take my picture? he says. His voice sounds raspy, like he's speaking out of a hole in his throat.

—Have a beautiful night, she says. Is it the rum that's made her this bold?

—Bitch, are you photographing me? Fucking gringa bitch?

She turns towards the woman. —Are you okay?

The woman stares back with a hollow emptiness in her eyes. She isn't young: wrinkled skin under her eyes, saggy cheeks.

—Do you want to come with me? the new volunteer asks. Should I call the police?

The woman slides her eyes over to the man. She shakes her head, slowly.

—Come on, beautiful, the man says. His voice is suddenly soothing now, silky, which is far more alarming. Let me see that photo.

—So now I'm a beautiful fucking gringa bitch?

She stumbles over her own feet as she heads towards the door.

—Let me see it, the man says, laughing as though he's finding all this extremely funny, like he's gone from deeply enraged to profoundly amused at how charming and cute she is. He follows her out the door, the woman trailing behind. Come on, lovely, show it to me.

—I'm calling the police. I hope you have fun in jail.

—There's no need for that, beautiful, no need for that at all. Let me see your phone.

—You are a deeply fucked-up person. You need to see a psychiatrist.

That's when the man's arm darts out, horribly fast, like a snake lunging for the kill. She screams as loud as she can as his fingers press deep into her arm, as though her arm is

made out of putty from the Anthill art supplies. She's screaming and struggling, her sandals fly off and she's barefoot, she
steps on something wet on the ground that might be a gnawed
piece of corn or squashed tomato or soaked tissue or something worse, but the man is still holding on, grabbing her
with a terrible firmness, yanking her towards him. And that's
when Mattías appears from around the alley corner. Mattías
grabs the man and pushes him against a telephone pole. Mattías is raising his knee and bringing it into the man's face,
again and again, his fingers interlocked behind the man's
head as though he's pulling him in for a kiss, a loving embrace,
his knee darting up and down like he's doing the fastest high-
knee drills ever on the Anthill football field, and the man's
face is turning all mashed and pulpy and red like the tomato
she's just trodden on, it's awful to see it like that, like something that should be scraped off a plate into the kitchen trash,
a person's face isn't supposed to look like that. And now it's
the woman who's screaming as the new volunteer wraps her
hands around Mattías's arm and hangs off him, like a sailor
who's found the one piece of wood in the ocean to hang on to
without drowning. *Matty,* she begs, *let's go, let's get out of
here,* but what she really wants to say is *Who are you, what
are you doing, where did you learn to fight like this, who are
you and what did you do with my Matty? Come in, Arctic
Fox.* Scrabbling at his arm pleadingly. Looking at his face.
Over and out. Do you read me? But it's *him* she can't read, an
empty notebook, a blank page. And in one swift motion Mattías steps back, swivels around and starts walking away, dragging her along, and all she has time to glimpse as the man
falls to the ground is the woman still standing there, the

shop's dim lights shining on the blood on her shirt.

As they turn the corner, Mattías stops and bends over. He unties the laces of his running shoes and takes them off with one yank.

—Here, he says, passing them over.

—What about you?

—I'll be fine.

She shoves her feet into his shoes and ties the laces in big floppy bows.

—Where are we? she says. Do you have change for a cab? Where are we going? What should we do?

She keeps asking the same questions, over and over. Crying now, though it's hard to explain why; why are there tears rolling down her face, why is she so afraid? It's the same feeling she had backing out of the supply closet, stumbling down the stairs. It's been lying in wait for her this whole time, waiting to be released, and now it's finally come. What terrible darkness, what voice has been lurking there all this time, just out of sight, waiting for its turn to speak? —Matty, how are we going to get home?

But all he does is shake his head. His jaw is pushed out, like he's grinding his teeth.

—I've been lost, he says, for ages.

THAT NIGHT

She dreams he crawls into bed with her. He doesn't touch her, just lies stiff as a corpse, on the furthest-possible edge of the mattress. She keeps fumbling around, searching for his hand, but something else is in the bed between them, something is crawling around, burrowing under the sheets, touching her feet. It stinks of garbage, its skin damp and crumbly like wet newspaper. She keeps curling her toes inwards, but for some reason she's not afraid, not like in the supply closet when the voice said her name, not like by the bodega. Soon enough, whatever it is settles on her pelvis, a warm heavy weight. *Please don't let this be a sex dream*, she finds herself thinking as she feels hot breath on her ears, her neck, her breasts. *Please don't let this be a sex dream.* But when she finds Mattías's hand, she holds tight: it's floppy and limp. She keeps clutching and squeezing, like she's trying to crush him, like her hand is a torture device from medieval Spain, an iron vice trying to trap him, keep him close. But something is pulling him away. Violent, brutal tugs, like he's the rope in a tug-of-war game. Some force is vehemently dragging him across the mattress, which has now become impossibly wide, an impassable desert from the beginning of time, the infinite darkness of inter-galactic space. *I've got you*, she keeps trying to tell him, but whatever is sitting on top of her is weeping, sobbing and shak-ing, and then it's peed itself, a hot wet puddle spreading all over her stomach, the T-shirt she sleeps in sticking to her skin. *I've got you.* But then whatever force is tugging him in the opposite direction yanks so hard he's jerked out of reach, and all she can do now is flail around, patting the mattress frantically, her hands scurrying everywhere, like when she's running late and has to hunt for her phone in a terrible harried panic, except this time it's not her phone she's looking for, no, not Emma Green's phone either, it's something much more important and precious, something she didn't want to lose, she didn't get insurance on it, she didn't back up her data, she didn't save it to the Cloud, she tore it out of a photograph album in the middle of the night but she didn't save the rest of it and now it's gone for good, forever, and it's all her fault. All of her fault. All her fault. And that thing sitting on top of her, it spreads itself out on her torso, pushing her arms into the mattress, pinning her down with its dank wet weight. And whatever it is she was looking for (and she knows this with terrible certainty, the kind she only gets in nightmares): this thing that she's lost, it's gone for good. She'll never get it back.

When she wakes up, the sheets are on the floor in a crumpled pile. Her T-shirt is damp and smells terrible. Despite the pounding in her head, she immediately peels it off and lets it drop to the floor. Her tongue is so hot it feels like it's on fire, her head is full of baby seals getting clubbed to death, she is clearly still drunk as shit. Basically, she needs water. Immediately. She swings her legs over the side of the mattress, her phone still tucked down the band of her underpants – did she sleep with it there all night? She throws it into the suitcase. Somehow manages to pull on a clean shirt. Staggers towards the door, pushing it open.

What she sees:

Wallpaper torn

Bookshelf smashed

Couch cushions ripped

—Matty?

Chairs flipped upside down

Legs broken off

Splintered wood

—Matty, are you here?

She wanders into the kitchen, cat food kibble sticking to her feet. The kitchen where she's barely spent any time these past three weeks, as she's either in the Anthill, looking at her phone in the room or eating meals in the street. In the kitchen, cabinet doors are flung open. Plates and glasses and mugs shattered on the floor. The fridge and freezer doors have been opened too, lights flickering faintly. Even the fruit bowl has been overturned, limes resting on the floor like lost green golf balls.

—Mattías?

She picks her way carefully through the debris: shards of glass, overturned pots and pans. Did they . . . do this together? Were they really that fucked? How did they get home? Did they take a taxi? Was this them? Giggling and excited, bumping into the bookshelves, knocking over the chairs.

Or was it something else?

Something angry. Something explosive, released at long last.

This . . . is definitely a strong qualifier for the worst blackout yet.

She looks at her arms and bare legs, examining them for strange marks or cuts, but finds nothing apart from a few faint bruises on the underside of her arm, above her elbow. There's a streak of blood on the back of one hand (from the man's face, by the telephone pole? *No, don't think about it, don't remember*). She rubs it off with the awful-smelling sink sponge. The cats rub against her legs, mewing piteously, and she somehow finds the capacity to open the bag of kibble and pour more on the floor, the same way Mattías feeds the Anthill dogs, not really caring about the pieces bouncing everywhere; who cares about contributing even further to the mess, considering that everything's so fucked already.

—Matty, are you home?

She does what she's never done before: stand outside his room. The door, as always, is shut. It's in the very back of the house, a location that in other residences (their childhood home, for example) would have been used as the maid's room. There's a cement sink nearby, the same kind the maids from their childhood would have used to do laundry. She stares at the door. She touches the wood.

—Are you there?

She listens. There is a faint rustling sound. A sort of stirring.

Scratching at the wood?

Raspy breathing?

She keeps listening, but the sound stops, and doesn't begin again.

She touches the knob. She turns it slowly, so as not to make a noise, but she only needs a thin crack to see that the room is deserted, that there's no one inside. She pushes the door all the way open. The room is dim with shadows, by far the darkest room in the house. It smells like mould mixed with musky laundry, a deep salty scent like a man's sweaty hair, or the way the Anthill children smell after playing football. Like the rest of the apartment, it is sparse. A mattress on the floor covered with a single white sheet, which is dotted in muddy pawprints from the cats. The impossibly flat pillow is covered in tiny black hairs, which make her feel terribly embarrassed.

It feels like being in a museum. A museum where she's the only guest, one who's been specifically curated for. Except there's nothing on display.

She looks around. A pile of wrinkled clothes in the corner, identical exercise shirts and sweatpants. In a separate stack, there's the salesman outfit he wore when she first arrived: carefully folded, still immaculately white, as if untouched since that day (she finds this thrillingly, disturbingly moving). A thin blue-and-yellow toothbrush tilted on its side, the bristles frayed as a punk mohawk. And two books, stacked against the wall. She has to twist her head to read the spines:

Creativity Now! 365 Writing Prompts
Healing Your Life: The Power of the Present Moment

They're both in English. She crosses the room in two quick strides and picks them up, flipping through. There are no underlined passages or notes in the margins. Nor are there any pages with the corners folded over, marking the spot. But the spines are creased with thick white lines. They've clearly been read and held and used, often.

One of the cats rubs against her calf, startling her so badly she drops the books. —Good puss, she says, hastily kneeling and stroking its bony little spine. Good girl.

Pausing, she tilts her head again. Gets down on her stomach, pressing her cheek against the floor.

There's something shoved under the mattress.

She scoots forward. Listening hard for any footsteps in the corridor, the doorknob rattling, a sharp intake of breath. But there's nothing to hear. She shoves her hand under the mattress, fumbling around. She has to tug hard to get it to slide out completely, without getting it caught on the fabric. Holding it in her hands, it's surprisingly light.

It's a notebook. Child-size. Spiral-bound.

Her hands tremble, touching the cover. She hesitates.

She uses her thumb to lift the cover up. The words on the first page are surrounded by faint marks, as though someone was trying to get a pen to work.

> *Because the thing is, you made me. That's what you told me when we played in your parents' bedro*

She slams it shut. Jams it back under the mattress, careful not to let the spiral hoops snag. As she closes the door behind her, she pulls hard on the knob to make sure it's shut completely.

Because all the cups are in broken shards on the floor, she drinks water straight from the faucet, pushing her mouth against it. Water dribbling down her chin, she heads to the bathroom. As she pushes the door open, it hits Mattías on the back. Their eyes meet in the mirror. It takes her a beat to realise he's naked – at first, it looks like he's wearing a printed T-shirt, skintight.

But then she sees the tattoos. Curling up and down his back and buttocks and arms. Swirling, filling every inch of skin.

Foxes and oak trees. Jaguars and orchids. The New World and Old, smashed together. Big-eyed and enormous and colourful, like sprawling graffiti on a city street.

They almost hide the puckered burn marks, but not quite.

—Whoops, sorry! she says, in a squeaky voice that is somehow terrible to hear, a childish voice; it's awful to hear herself speak that way, even more terrible than the sight before her, that of Mattías's eyes staring at her, swollen and red (has he been crying?), eyes that are unblinking in the circle-shaped mirror, which is small enough to only reveal his face and the top of his chest. His back still turned to her, his torso of brightly coloured images.

He says quietly, —Could you please close the door?

She does so immediately, without speaking.

She sits on the edge of her bed. She puts her head in her hands, elbows pressing red marks into her knees. Then she turns her wrist over and pinches the skin over and over, until her veins stand out. When that's not enough, she puts her fingers in her mouth and bites down hard. Scrapes her teeth over her nails, or what's left of them.

This is it: the lowest she can possibly go.

And what's worst is how tired he sounded. As if saying without words: *Oh. Of course you want this, the one thing I asked to keep for myself. My privacy. Of course. Here you go. Have it. Take it. I can't stop you. It's yours.*

———

Monday's cable ride up to the Anthill is absolutely brutal. Twenty-four hours in bed (leaving only to stumble outside for sancocho and freshly squeezed juice) has barely helped. Hours of mindless YouTube videos on her phone, vague attempts at comfort that didn't succeed, occasionally poking her head out into the living room to see if Mattías was there – as usual, he never was. The mess in the apartment sat there, undealt with, untouched. She even tried calling her father in the evening, and as usual he didn't answer, her call going straight to the voicemail she knows he never checks.

In the cable car, she keeps closing her eyes as it rumbles beneath her. She arrived at the station late – they'll definitely be at the bakery by now, Shauna and the other new volunteers, whoever else is coming for the day. Eating snacks and waiting for the bus while Mattías finishes up last-minute shopping, errands, chatting with the men. So it's just her in the cable car and two middle-aged women, wearing brightly coloured baseball caps, clearly dressed to go hiking through the nature park at the Metrocable's very last stop. At one point (is her face that green?), the woman in an orange hat offers her a mint, which she gratefully accepts.

—I drank too much on Saturday, she explains, pointing at her head. I'm still recovering.

The two women cluck their tongues. The one in the orange hat says, —You shouldn't have said that, dearie. Now we don't feel sorry for you any more!

They laugh like happy witches. She smiles weakly, settling back. They offer to take a photo with her phone, so that she can have a memento of her time here. —Where are you from, dearie? They ask this as the cable car sways over houses crowded wherever they can fit, huddled to the very edges of cliff sides, squashed under telephone poles. A child carrying an armful of puppies, a man riding a bicycle, an ice cream vendor strolling with his big Styrofoam box. All those hundreds of thousands of little lives, the nameless and anonymous others carrying on. They ask, How long have you been visiting? Do you like Colombia? What do you think of Medellín? But for once it doesn't feel like a struggle to explain, or like she's excusing herself.

—I grew up here, she says. My mother was from here, but my father is English. I left twenty years ago – that's why my Spanish isn't so good any more, I'm afraid.

Which makes the two women frown deeply, shaking their heads, speaking in unison like a Greek chorus. —No, no, they exclaim, recrossing their legs, taking a sip of water from their plastic water bottles, slathering sunscreen over their cheeks and noses as if preparing for a hike is like preparing for a battle. They offer her a granola bar, a Tic Tac, a packet of graham crackers. Don't be silly, your Spanish is wonderful, we never would have guessed. How good of you to come back; it's wonderful to see Colombians returning and enjoying their homeland.

—I'm not Colombian, she whispers. But the women just look at her, confused. But of course you are, they say in unison, you grew up here!

As expected, there's no one at the bakery. —Which bus to the Anthill? she asks a man in a cowboy hat, and he tells her that he'll wait with her until the bus arrives, waving away her insistence that it's too much, it's not necessary, shaking his head at her offer to buy him a coffee. Just before boarding, when she thanks him one last time, he touches the brim of his hat respectfully, and stands on the pavement, waiting for the bus to pull away completely, as if wanting to make sure she's safe. She stupidly doesn't have enough change for the fare, but a woman in a plastic raincoat pays for her, tells her not to worry, it's not a problem.

—This bus goes to the Anthill, right? she asks her seatmate: a young woman in a sweatshirt and braids, playing the 'Despacito' video on her phone. The young woman wordlessly nods, switching to reggaetón. The reggaetón keeps playing during their entire journey, as the young woman says no, she's not from Medellín, no, she's not in school at the moment, no, she doesn't have a job, no, she's not in touch with her children's two fathers, no, she's not on good terms with either of them; her most recent ex was working in Miami but was recently deported and, no, she hasn't made an effort to get back in touch; no, she's never been to Miami herself; no, she has no thoughts on Colombia's growing tourist industry; yes, she's heard of the Anthill but doesn't have an opinion about it. But just when it starts to feel like the new volunteer has been on the bus too long, like she's missed the stop, the young woman taps her on the wrist, indicating with her head that here, this is it, and as she stands up the young woman says, —Thanks for chatting with me, miss; you be safe now and have a good day.

The sun feels ridiculously hot on her head, like it's trying to fry an invisible egg on her scalp. But what a pleasure it is: walking past the now-familiar buildings, the little grocery store. The house with the roosters on the balcony that other volunteers always want to photograph (and which, along with the dogs on the rooftops, seem to be the most Instagrammable features of the neighbourhood). What a joy it is to be a volunteer who 'knows' how things work, where things are, what things are like. What a pleasure to belong, to make small talk with strangers while travelling to your next destination, confident of where you're going and what you'll be doing. Who you are and what you'll be. A child waves shyly at her from a doorway and she waves back, smiling as best she can, even though the inside of her mouth still feels like the bottom of a dirty birdcage.

Could this be what it feels like – to live a good life? A life where moments seem meaningful, add up to something? A life that doesn't solely consist of looking at the time on her laptop or phone and closing all the browsers in horror? A life that fits, that connects, that matters?

Approaching the Anthill, she initially thinks that she's gone too far – she must have passed it already, oblivious, because the Anthill never has cars parked outside. But as she gets closer she sees the faded pink building, the hand-painted sign (*ALL WELCOME*), the mural of children holding hands.

But there are also two vans parked outside, big ones. New. Expensive. The kind you might get from an airport rental.

And inside the Anthill – sitting on chairs and at tables – are strangers. Young people, mostly teenagers, but some adults too. Clapping hands and chattering away, raising their phones high while the kids scream and make crazy faces. Their T-shirts are light blue and have a quote from the Bible, and a cross inside a giant heart.

—What do you think?

She turns around slowly. His head looks recently shaved, bumpier and sorer than ever. He's wearing a new exercise shirt, too: dark blue, long-sleeved. He's smiling, but his face looks tired, the skin under his eyes puffier than ever.

—Where's Maryluz? she says. And Shauna?

—I told them not to come.

She stares at him. He looks straight back. His face doesn't flicker. His skin could be made of stone.

—To be precise, he says, I told them never to return. Ever. I've made my decision, and it's final: for the benefit of the Anthill, it needs to rely on a less diverse group of volunteers. And a more financially committed one.

Slinging his arm around her shoulder. That old familiar feeling.

—It's better with just you and me, he says. And no one else. Don't you agree?

She can't speak. Him and her, together again. It feels like security. Like protection. It feels . . . right.

But deep inside the Anthill: the sound of singing hymns.

—I invited the evangelical church, he says. And they came.

THE ARCTIC FOX SPEAKS:

YAY
    WHEE
    HURRAH
    HOORAY
    FROM NOW ON IT'S
    LINA AND MATTY
    TOGETHER FOREVER
    NO ONE ELSE
    BESTEST FRIENDS
    LINA AND MATTY LINA AND MATTY LINA AND
MATTY LINA AND MATTY
    I'm coming for you, Lina!
    Can you finally hear me, at long last?
    Listen. Listen close:

PART III

LINA AND MATTY

HIGGLEDY-PIGGLEDY

It's the day of her wedding and Emma Green won't stop tell-
ing anybody who will listen about the time her parents' house
in Medellín got flooded. —The water came in under the door,
she says, gesturing with her hands. Streaming in. Think Titanic.
Think women and children first. It poured all over our feet –
God knows how we didn't get salmonella! It ruined the carpet.
It stained the furniture. We had to throw out all the couches
the next day.

—Goodness, says one of the older women at the table.
Mother of the groom, maybe: she shares his BBC accent.

—I was so scared, Emma says, touching the ring on her
finger. Medellín's thunderstorms were the absolute worst.
Worse than Guam. Worse than Wales, even.

The people within your immediate vicinity chortle. You
lift your hands on and off the dark wooden table a few times,
enjoying its stickiness. The inside of this pub is cool and dark
but fairly pleasant for this part of London. Wooden interiors,
seaside paintings, tasteful blue-and-white china from Corn-
wall. You're sitting in the weird middle section, with the other
awkward invitees, people you suspect were only included on
the list of guests to bump up the paltry number of attendees
to an even double-dozen. You seem to be the 'Colombian
childhood' representative, and Colombia itself seems to be
an amusing if brief chapter in Emma's globetrotting life (an

expected consequence with two NGO parents).

From what little you've gathered, Emma and her fiancé haven't known each other for very long, and Emma herself has barely been in England – less than a year (she's still paying rent for her apartment in Berlin). The wedding is only the second time you've made the effort to see each other in person. Otherwise your communication has been restricted to cordial WhatsApp messages.

—I've never forgotten it, Emma is now saying. And I never will.

You shuffle in your seat. It's almost time for the third course; everyone's forks and knives are resting on their plates. On the peach-coloured checklist you received in the mail a few months ago, listing meal options, you put a black 'X' next to Beef Wellington, but now you're wishing you'd gone for Salmon Salad instead, like the other women you hear whispering to each other ('Oh good, I got that one too!').

—Caroline, Emma says, do you ever have nightmares?

You tug at one of your fake nails. It's loose enough to flick back and forth, but it's still in the stage where it'd be painful to yank it off completely.

—I have them all the time, Emma says. I can't hear a helicopter without feeling like I'm going to have a panic attack. And forget about someone zooming past on a motorcycle. I jump every time. That's how they assassinated people, babe.

She touches her newly declared husband on the arm, but he remains absorbed in conversation with someone else.

—Motorcycles, Emma continues. That's what the assassins used. They'd drive right up to you and bam, shot in the head. Remember Doctor Bonillo, killed in the mall? Remember Lala

Pereira's uncle? One shot, and then the motorcycle would just zoom away. Wasn't it awful, how we weren't allowed to go anywhere as children? Primitive. Savage. I spent days locked up in the house. I couldn't walk the dogs without the body-guard following me up and down the block. I didn't freaking ride on a bus till I moved to New York.

—Yeah, yeah, you say, it was all very Anne Frank. Emma's plate is still half full of pasta, the little ravioli pieces smashed to bits by her fork, that classic mushing-it-up strategy to make it seem like she's eaten more than she really has.

—And then every time I had permission to leave, Emma says in that light-hearted voice of hers, I had to take one of those vintage nineties cell phones with me. (Her words seem meant for the entire table, but her eyes are fixed on you.) They were as big as my head. If I see them in old films now I just laugh. God, and my dad's interrogation routine! 'Where are you going, who will you be with, when will you be back.' Even though I was only going to be wandering around the shopping mall like a cow in a pen. All those kidnapping threats on the phone really fucked with his head. Did your family got those too? The threatening phone calls? Do you remember?

—Uh-huh, you lie. Of course.

She leans back in her seat, allowing a waiter to swoop in and take away her pasta-smeared plate. You look around the table in an effort to make eye contact with someone else, a vague attempt at escape. This conversation, this crowd: it's making you tired. These English women and their perfectly shaven pale legs: such a creamy colour you can never believe they're not wearing see-through stockings. How do these

English women do it? Does being genetically half-English make you an English woman?

—Caroline, Emma says again, and you look up. Her insistence is verging on pleading. But how could you blame her? Who wouldn't want to remember, to get the verbal nod and assent from someone else that yes, your experiences are valid; yes, that's what it was like for me too. What was that game, Emma continues. The one we used to play after church in your living room. The one with your mother?

The waiter reaches for your plate, brushing against your arm. You pull your hands rapidly into your lap.

—Higgledy-Piggledy! Emma says, answering her own question. That was it! Babe, please listen to this, it's really cute.

She touches her husband's arm again – at some point, you'll have to start thinking of him and Emma by their newly-wed names, 'Mr and Mrs Bundren'. The ease with which some people become someone else! Slipping into new names, new identities. New lives. This time, he turns towards her gamely.

—For Higgledy-Piggledy, Emma says, we'd lie on the living room floor, all fancy and dressed up in our church clothes, with tons of blankets and couch cushions piled on top. God, it was sweaty! Quite frankly, I'm surprised your mother let us do it. So there we'd be, trying not to suffocate, and Mattías – he was the maid's nephew, or cousin, or something – he would come and sit on top, and shout, Higgledy-Piggledy!

You whisper, —Oink, oink.

The uncle sitting across from you, with white hair growing out of his ears, grins a little harder – though out of amusement or alarm, it's hard to say.

—That's right, Emma says, fingering her fork. Her husband has commenced an attack on the Beef Wellington that the duke himself would be proud of, busily sawing away. We would answer, Oink, oink. And then Mattías would have to guess whose voice it was. Who was speaking.

You look down at your fingers again, the white crescent moons. Fake nails are a reality of your life in London. You can never, ever expose what they're really like underneath.

—You know that he emailed me? Emma says. She has to talk over the clatter of white gravy jugs being placed by waiters across the table. Mattías, I mean.

Your nail scrapes involuntarily at your index finger. Digging deep. The sour liquid taste of carsickness rises in your throat. —That's nice, you manage to say.

—Actually, no, it wasn't. Emma makes a noise that is maybe supposed to be a laugh. Her hair is tied to the top of her head in a tight bun, earrings swinging like Christmas-tree ornaments. She always did know how to dress for every occasion, Emma did. It wasn't nice at all, she whispers, still in that highly amused tone. He was asking for money.

—Money for what?

To your left, the Italian cousin is telling a story to one of the groomsmen. He's speaking in a hushed tone about having sex with a pregnant woman in Tokyo. —When I slipped it in her, he murmurs, fork and knife clinking against the plate, I was really worried about, you know, poking the baby's head. So I had her lie on her side, to change the angle. That probably would have been safe, right?

As the Italian cousin laughs, you keep your eyes fixed on Emma. You say it again, louder this time:

—Money for what?

She raises and lowers her shoulders, earrings swinging. — He called it a 'donation', to be fair. He's working for an after-school club or something. It was such a creepy message. So random.

She leans back in her chair, allowing the waiter to place the salad before her.

—Who's creepy? her husband interrupts, chewing noisily. The maid's son?

—No, you say, even though they're not listening to you. That's not who he was.

—But wait, the groomsman says, still speaking low, what if there's a baby walking around in Tokyo right now with this, like, dent in its head?

—No way, the Italian cousin says to your left. I'm always careful about things like that. I always follow up. Leave no trace, you know? That's my motto. I always make sure, the Italian cousin says, his arm brushing yours as he reaches for his pint, to follow up on my mistakes.

The gravy has finally been passed down to your section of the table. Emma has picked up her phone to take a photo of her meal and is typing out her password. You watch her fingers move over the screen: tap, tap, tap. And then the father of the groom pushes back his chair and clears his throat, raising his glass of see-through liquid. —I'm not one for storytelling, he announces grandiosely, waving his glass around, but I'm going to give this my very best shot.

But all around you, everyone is still chattering away. Not willing to fall silent and let another voice speak. Not yet.

In an hour or so, you're going to do it. I know it for a fact, *the same way I know everything about you, and have all along. You'll see the opportunity, and you won't hesitate. Emma and her husband, they'll be posing for photos outside in the courtyard: smiling and laughing by the picturesque brick wall, arms around each other's waists. Most guests will be clustered around the bar at this point, gravy-smeared plates abandoned at the table. Emma's phone will be left at her seat, turned face down by her napkin, so trustingly, so innocently. What a safe country England is. So secure. So stable.*

As quick as anything, your hand will dart out. Your hand, that clawed sneaky creature, will snatch Emma's phone into your lap. You will then immediately take your leave, an unhesitant Irish exit. And then, in the Uber ride home, hands trembling, you'll type out her password: tap, tap, tap.

But all of that will come later. Because I'm watching you, Lina: then and now, inside and out, I can see and hear you anytime I want. I know it all, better than you know yourself. So for the time being, it's Emma smiling at her friends and family. It's Emma surrounded by loved ones, raising their drinks to the past, blessing the present, toasting the future. And it's you, scratching away with your fake plastic claws, drawing first blood.

Soon enough, though, you'll seek me out. You'll hunt me down. And I'll be waiting, Lina. I've been waiting for you to find me for a very long time.

Because the thing is, you made me. That's what you told me when we played in your parents' bedroom. We played *The Secret Garden*. We played *A Little Princess*. We played dolls. We played hide and seek, especially when the electricity went out thanks to the FARC setting off bombs at the electrical plant, and the entire apartment was cast into darkness, and Florencia had to light candles like we were Oliver Twist and Fagin living in a stinky rat-infested building. We played *Little Women*. You were Jo, I was Beth and the stuffed animals filled in for everyone else. I died of scarlet fever, again and again, and no one could save me. We played *The Count of Monte Cristo*: posing as corpses, hunting down those who'd done us wrong. We played *Free Willy*, which we watched over and over on VHS tape. Why was Jesse living with a family that wasn't his own? Why was he so angry at his missing mother? What happened to her; why did she give him away; where had she gone?

We played *The Amazon Trail* – with each other, not on the computer. I hung on to the raft for dear life as we went over the waterfall, clutching the cinchona we'd worked so hard to collect. *Hold on*, you said, *don't let go!* We played FIFA World Cup, running through the house in an attempt to flee the assassins hired to gun us down, due to us scoring a goal against our own team. *What a terrible way to go*, you said. *What do you think it feels like to get shot?* We played FARC. We hid in the jungle from communist guerrilla soldiers who wanted to kidnap us and hold us hostage for decades, just like they did to Lala Pereira's uncle. I got shot by the FARC in the stomach as we tried to escape. I lay on my back on the balcony for ages, staring up at the sky, flies buzzing around my wound, waiting for you to come and find me. *What took you so long?* I said, when you finally scrambled up on your belly, sweaty from crouching behind the potted plant. We had no garden in the apartment, just a small balcony – those were the days when we were still permitted to play on it, before your mother started telling us to keep away from windows, to stay in the middle of the room. We examined my mortal wound: the blood had turned black and crusty and smelled like coins. You pried the wound apart with your scalpel, poking around for the bullet, but it was nowhere to be found. *I can't find it,* you finally said tearfully, throwing your medical kit to the ground in weepy frustration. *There's no clean exit wound. That's okay*, I said. *I'll just live with it inside of me.*

Could someone do that in real life? We wondered. We crept into your parents' bedroom to look at your mother's medical dictionary, the only book she'd kept from the degree she'd never finished. Sneaking into your parents' bedroom, we crawled over the snowy-white carpet, shirts pulled over our noses, speaking into our radio-controller fists. *Come in, Arctic Fox,* you said, squatting by the bookshelf. *Arctic Fox, do you read me? Loud and clear*, I said. *Over and out.* Why did we choose it, that code name in particular? What was it about foxes, and arctic ones at that? Maybe because the end of the world was icy, and we survived it together by burrowing in the snow, seeking out underground caves. And even when we transitioned into a world on fire, with belching volcanoes and dusty clouds of ash streaking across the sky, the code name still stuck. It meant nothing and everything; it had always been with us; we never questioned it; what mattered was that it was us and us alone and there was nobody else in the world included and nobody else in the universe that mattered. You and me.

But instead of your mother's medical dictionary, what we ended up pulling from the shelf was the photograph album. The dark-green one with enormous hoop binding, as big as the earrings your mother wore. You liked how the photos were in order, how they told a chronological story, a straightforward one that was easy to understand. The thirty or so photos that summed up her life. Your mother at the Universidad de Antioquia, orange-brick buildings and palm trees, clutching her medical books tightly to her chest. The faded pencil scrawl of her handwriting in the margins, informing us of her movements, the years she spent abroad after dropping out of her programme: Thailand, feeding monkeys in the temple. The Aleppo marketplace, head bound in a glittery scarf we recognised from her closet. Jakarta was motorbikes and mangoes and a gritty haze. And then, in England, your father made his first appearance. England was all cloudy skies and unfamiliar trees, crescent-moon bridges over rivers, and your father's arms wrapped around your mother's waist, her head thrown back in laughter. In the photographs, your father had square glasses and shoulder-length hair and a slightly stunned expression, like he couldn't believe his good fortune, his luck in meeting this woman. Your mother, wearing long dresses covered in sparkly sequins and hair down to her waist. *A hippy.* That's what you liked to say, touching the photograph reverently, quoting your father's term of affection for her. *My mother's a damn hippy.*

And then, back in Medellín, you came along. Red-faced and wrinkly in your mother's arms at the hospital, surrounded by her relatives. Your father hovering nervously in the background, so pale he looked ill. Your mother looked at the camera, smiling uncertainly. *Me,* you said, sounding unconvinced as we stared down at the puckered-up creature in your mother's arms. *That's me.*

There were only two more photographs in the album after that. As though your mother's interest in documenting her life from that point onwards had completely faded, evaporated to nothing.

Or, to be accurate, only one photograph left: the second had long since been peeled away, leaving behind a faint ghost on the page of sticky tape resin.

I wonder what happened to this one, I said, touching the empty space. *Do you remember what it was?*

You said nothing.

The last photograph in the album, then: your mother, sitting at a chair in a dark house with clay walls. She held a child in her lap: maybe a baby, maybe a toddler. Your mother's hands were under the child's armpits. She looked directly at the camera, lips peeling away from her teeth in a broad smile. The child's head was turned away, looking off to the side, as if there was something beyond the camera's sight he wanted to see.

Look, Matty, you said, touching the page. *That's you.*

I looked at the photo but didn't touch it.

That was taken after I made you, you said, in that careless, amused tone you liked to use when you were inventing a story.

I made you out of dirt. You used your fingers to thoughtfully pull your lower lip away from your teeth. *With a magic spell. I made you,* you said, *so I wouldn't be lonely.* And then you laughed to let me know that what you had said was ridiculous and sad and really rather stupid. But you said it every single time, anyway.

I kept looking at the photo.

Your mother's story was slightly different: *She didn't want you, sweetie.* That's what she told me on the balcony, striking a match repeatedly against the rough side of the box, frowning as it failed to light. *She couldn't take care of you. She begged me to take you. Begged! But if she ever wants you back* (she said, the match finally sputtering into life between her fingers), *she knows where you live. If she really wanted you, love, she could come down to the city and get you. At any time.*

I reached out again and touched the shadow of the missing photo, the tape stain on the album pages. *I wonder what this was,* I repeated.

You still didn't answer. You pushed the photograph album back on the shelf. You pushed the medical dictionary back on the shelf. You pushed away whatever book it was we were reading, the two of us together in a hundred different moments, a thousand different memories, a million different lives.

Come on, you said, rising to your feet. *Let's go.*

And I followed close behind, eager and excited to do as you said. Happy to make you happy.

But I never told you that I walked around with that bullet in me for years. It rattled inside me, like a ball in a pinball machine, or a football across a field. At school, I never played football. If anybody ever asked me to, my eyes would fill with tears. *Jesus,*

Paco would say as tears streamed down my face. *What's wrong with you? You're such a girl!* The other boys rarely approached me – they'd learned long ago to not recruit me, not even for the despicable, unwanted role of goalie. Whenever one of the Recess Monitors forced me to 'participate', I'd stand in the furthest corner of the field, as close to the dusty chalk line as possible. Sometimes you were forced to 'participate' with the girls, standing in line at the swing set or turning the jump rope. But then you'd sneak away, wait patiently by the hedge. Waiting for the moment when a goal was scored, or the ball got kicked out of bounds, and in the ensuing distraction I could slip away and join you. We loved playing with the leafcutter ants, the long line they made marching by the fence. We'd pinch the leaves they were carrying between our fingers, bring the ones at the back of the line to the front. One time, we got stung so hard welts appeared on our fingers, which your mother mistook for the beginning of chickenpox. *Matty,* she said, covering my thumb with lumpy white cream so cold it gave me goosebumps, *you need to be careful with Lina. Don't make me worry.*

Your mother. The irony is that *we* worried about *her*. She came bursting into the house at any and all times: carrying an armful of shopping from the new French department store; a hundred bags of popcorn she'd bought from a street vendor, every single bag he was selling. She'd come home sweaty from running dance classes at the Down's syndrome school; she'd return with icy water trickling from her hair after a morning swim in the river, with the club that only swam in moving bodies of water. She was getting certified as a yoga teacher and a personal fitness instructor; she was taking a course in nutrition; she was applying to get a master's in business administration; she was going to a weekend get-away for entrepreneurs with small business ideas. She usual-ly materialised a few days later in a tearful explosion, pulling stiff bags of frozen guanábana juice from the freezer, ranting about sugar, sugar was now officially banned from the house-hold, sugar was a sin, it caused rising glucose levels and warmed the blood; she'd learned all about it during her med-ical degree; she was going to be a doctor at one point, didn't we know? She'd studied medicine for two semesters at the University of Antioquia; she'd attended at the same time as the current governor, Álvaro Uribe. She could have really been someone at one point. Did we know that? She could have really done something with her life, something mean-ingful, something that mattered. The shakiness of her voice, the rising tone. Wide-eyed, we pressed ourselves into the corner, eyeing her warily as she slid down the fridge to the floor, burying her face in her arms. *Why is everything so hard*, she snuffled, speaking into her own skin, as Clara silently brought her tissues. *Why is everything so goddamn impossible? Don't tell the Doctor*, she'd say suddenly, grab-bing Clara by the wrist. Even though no one was paying attention to us, we'd nod solemnly as well, clutching each other in an imitation of her melodramatic gestures. Weeping, your mother cried out, *Don't tell him a goddamn thing!*

The Doctor: your father. You called him *Papa*. Your mother called him *darling* and *love of my life*, but only when directly addressing him. Florencia and Clara and Yolanda and everyone else who rotated through the household over the years called him *The Doctor* as a term of respect, even though he was tech-nically a lawyer. We wondered and worried about him. He was different from everyone else's father. He spoke Spanish with an accent and never went to church, not even to the evangelical services with us (until your mother quit going, started attending Buddhist meditation instead). He never watched football or danced salsa. He didn't drink coffee and smoked the same kind of cigarettes as the doorman, and he was stooped and grey-haired like a grandfather even though he couldn't be *that* old already? Surely not? Most other fathers cycled by the river on Sundays, when the highways were closed and transformed into bike lanes, but your father went jogging instead, while your mother lay in bed with her eye mask and ice pack until late afternoon.

When can we get a pet dog? you asked him once, and he said, *When we don't have to hide in this apartment like a couple of rats.* Laughing as he patted you on the head, as he was never the hugging type. He mainly seemed either alarmed by us or stunned by Colombia in general, the situation he'd somehow found himself in: watching us warily from the far side of the room, holding his whisky glass and surrounded by papers. Most of the time, he was at work.

Papa and Mummy. You called her *Mummy* with an English accent, like the Railway Children. Sometimes you called her *Ma*, like *Little House on the Prairie*, but if she was listening, that term would usually elicit a frown. This still basically counted as attention from her, though, and was thus desirable.

Ma, you asked her at the dinner table, purposefully chewing with your mouth open, *is Matty an Indian?*

I was picking at the edge of the table mat, trying to see if I could get the edge to peel upwards, but immediately withdrew my hands into my lap.

No, lovely, your mother said. *He's just dark. Matty, keep your hands to yourself.*

Yes, ma'am, I said. You chewed even louder, smacking your lips.

Love, your mother said, *for God's sake. For the last time. You can call me 'Mummy', sweetheart. Or 'Mami'. Whatever you prefer.* She smiled and tucked a strand of hair behind my ear.

I said, *Yes, ma'am.*

Your mother's hand withdrew. She swirled the food around on her plate, making it look like she'd eaten more than she really had, and rang the bell to alert Yolanda that it was time to come and clear it.

Mummy and Mami. *Mami* was less frequent, but not unheard of – usually you only called her that in front of her mass herd of relatives, who descended upon the household during their biannual Easter and Christmas visits. Your mother's dinner parties: they rarely lasted long, and gradually stopped altogether. The screaming matches! The shouting! Not even my party tricks could soothe people, my frantic glugging of the leftover beer at the bottom of everyone's glasses. We'd sit there quietly, watching the juice from the beans soak into the rice, as one of your uncles nasally insisted to your mother that the last thing Colombia needed was to become Venezuela. Or, God forbid, Cuba. God, what an embarrassment it had been, the way your mother had briefly joined the Communist Party in university. What a joke she was. So pathetic. Thank God she finally got her shit together, started focusing on being a good mother and wife like a proper Colombian woman, at long last. *Watch out,* they said to your father, *she might still move on to socialism, or even anarchy!* And your aunts and uncles chortled and slapped their thighs while your father smiled in alarm and your mother hid the food she hadn't eaten under her napkin.

But it was obvious (your relatives told your father): the Colombian people had spoken up in the recent election – the country needed change. They'd spoken loud and they'd spoken clear, their voices rising in perfect unison, through their unanimous election of Governor Uribe. It was obvious (one of your uncles said, pointing a meat-stained knife at your mother, who drained the contents of her wine glass in one quick gulp) what this childlike, underdeveloped country needed was a firm hand, a father figure, someone to whip it into shape and guide it into the future. Someone who was going to clean things up, transform this childish country into an adult. How wonderful it was, your aunts and uncles said, the transformation this country was going through, the newfound safety and urban renewal.

Your father opened his mouth to say something in his accented Spanish. But your mother interrupted, her voice rising high above the squabble, louder than anyone else in the room. Your mother said what was obvious to *her* was that too many Colombians had already died unjustly. Silently. Right in the middle of city public plazas, while everyone else stood around without saying a word. And she'd be God-damned if she stayed silent too; she couldn't live with herself otherwise, couldn't *not* do her volunteer work in the mountain neighbourhoods. That's what she had learned about Colombia by leaving it; that was the value of travel; she could see things more clearly now that she was back. Just because the papers didn't bother printing it, just because the massacres had become so common that *Semana* magazine only covered them in a small box at the bottom of the page. The mothers whose children were suffocated in plastic bags by the paramilitaries. The caretaker for the priest who'd had his skin peeled off, nose removed. The maid dragged through the street until her face was reduced to a purple mess, left to die in the pigsty, tied to the wooden fence. The owner of the coffee shop, the woman who worked at the Centro Cultural, the young man who worked at the hospital: they opened the door and were whisked away by armed men, never to be seen again. And all the others who were never recognised, never acknowledged. They were Colombians too, your mother said, calmly adding ají sauce to her steak. Even if they were never given a voice or a chance to speak; even if nobody ever talked about them or noticed or cared. Even if they were invisible and never known. The others, they were part of this country just like us, and we all had rights, *human* rights. If she didn't believe that, how could she get up every day? It wasn't about doing what made her happy, your mother said, wiping her mouth with a napkin. It was about doing what was right. And if that meant risking her life for justice, fine.

Justice! Your aunts and uncles screamed, as you and I patted our piles of rice into sticky white faces, providing eyes and eyebrows and mouths with the beans. But how could she say that? Was your mother not aware that members of the FARC were hiding in Medellín *at this very moment*, disguised as civilians? Explain it to her, they'd say to your father, who silently emptied what remained of the wine bottle into his glass. You poor man. Can't you make it clear to your wife – that there's nothing wrong with the government trying to strengthen national security? That's all the paramilitaries were doing – cleaning the city up, washing it clean. For something to be clean, you needed someone to remove the garbage. The guerrillas, the gays, the communist street children gathering cardboard. Medellín needed to be treated the same way you'd treat an anthill: pour water over it until all the filth is washed away, sweeping the undesirables of this country where they belong, out of sight and mind. And besides, your aunts hissed, touching your father urgently on the sleeve in an effort to get his attention, as a foreigner, you need to be careful. Things for foreigners were getting tense these days, especially for those in his line of work, consulting for land reform lawsuits. Think of your safety, your wife and daughter. Is her so-called leftist volunteer work worth that?

Your father never said a word. Your mother just uncorked a new wine bottle, laughing as she said, *What do I have to say to get you bitches to shut up?* So on and on they went, while you and I shoved potatoes into our cheeks, trying to see how many we could fit at one time, like squirrels in *Redwall* storing nuts.

After dinner, your mother slammed the door behind her relatives' retreating backs. *Never again,* she said to your father as he took out his cigarettes. *They're banned from the household, officially.*

Your father's hands shook so hard he dropped several matches on to the floor, which we silently retrieved for him. *Lover,* he said simply. *We need to leave. We need to go to England.*

Your mother shook her head. *I'm never leaving Colombia again. Not now. If this country knew the truth of what's going on – about what happened to its neighbourhoods, what's still happening – the truth would make it fall apart.*

She turned to us abruptly as Yolanda brought out the whisky. *Lina and Matty. Listen: if anyone talks to you anywhere outside the apartment, or outside of school – don't speak. Pretend you're mute.*

You and I looked at each other. We looked at her.

Even in the elevator, she said. Even though she was slurring, we could still understand. *Even in the hallway. This is very important. For your own personal security. I don't want to go into details, because I don't want to frighten you, but do you both understand? Do you promise?*

We nodded.

Good boy, your mother said, addressing me as she unscrewed the bottle cap. *You'll protect Lina. Won't you, Matty?*

I nodded as hard as I could.

She sloshed a bit of whisky into my glass. *That's a good man. Go on, this'll put hair on your chest, have a glug.*

I drank it down obediently, even though it burned my throat.

I want some too, you said, but your mother shook her head: *Whisky's not for young ladies.* She let you have a puff of her Cuban cigar instead, which she didn't smoke in front of her relatives due to their scandalised reactions. She laughed nervously when you coughed. Her laughter always went on for far too long; it made us look excitedly around the room, as if there was something funny hidden somewhere, something we hadn't yet noticed.

As Yolanda cleared the table, you asked your father if it was safe in the apartment. If armed men were going to come and knock on the door, like they did at the farm with Lala Pereira's uncle. Knock on the door and snatch us away.

Your father lit another cigarette, spilling matches all over the floor again as he did so. *Don't worry about security*, he said, flicking the ash into the hair of a My Little Pony we'd left on the table. *There's no point. If somebody wants to kill us in this country, they will.*

He laughed so hard his forehead almost touched the table. And then, right before leaving the apartment to return to the office, he gave us permission to go outside and play on the balcony. In those days, we were still allowed. Pacing back and forth as the crickets sang and the fireflies came out, swarming around that tiny enclosed space. At the end of the world, after everything exploded, we lived together in a cave. Nobody ever found us. When enough time passed, our original memories of both Spanish and English faded away and we were left with a strange blend that only birds and animals could understand. In my cart of supplies, we kept only the essentials: tinned food. Geiger counter. Plastic ziplock bags. As the Arctic Fox, I was your bodyguard, patrolling the nuclear wastelands, protecting you for life. And so we stayed like that, alone together, safe, for the rest of our lives. You and me, Lina and Matty, the only two people left in the world.

THE GRASSHOPPER
AND THE ANTS

—I'd let him in, Tomás says. But I wouldn't let him eat.

Craning their necks, they study the ground. Six pieces of paper lie in a row before them, held down by dusty rocks. Tomás twists his shirt as though wringing out a wet towel; Rebecca and Dafne link fingers and swing their arms; Gabriela stands stiff and tall.

And Lina stands there too. Arms crossed over her chest, as if for protection.

—Gabriela? she says. What do you think?

—I disagree with Tomás, Gabriela says, with the polite formality of a political candidate. I wouldn't let him in the house.

She kneels and flicks a speck of dirt off the first page. In this one, the grasshopper lazes about in the sunshine, cheerily playing his fiddle. Around him, the ants sweat and pant, carrying enormous crumbs of whatever it is that ants carry around with them.

Gabriela repeats, —I wouldn't. I'd leave him outside and let him die.

She grins toothily, as if the thought deeply pleases her.

Lina says, —Even if you had enough food to share? Enough so that you and the other ants wouldn't go hungry?

Gabriela shakes her head, lips curling. —He doesn't deserve it.

A chorus of whoops drifts over from the open Anthill door

– someone must have won at Bible Trivia. Rebecca shoots the building an anxious glance; Dafne whispers something in her ear. Lina uncrosses and recrosses her arms.

After two weeks of American volunteers, the new routine is firmly established. No more assembly. No more art. No more activities that the children get to choose to attend for themselves. No more daily reminders of *make good choices*, or *ALL WELCOME*. Instead, the American volunteers show up daily (five days a week, punctual as anything). The teens arrive with assigned buddies and Nalgenes full of water. High-protein granola bars are carried at all times, in case blood sugar runs low. The boys have biceps swollen from rowing, the girls have curved calves from track and cross-country, and all of them are tall from years of non-powdered milk and richly flavoured cheeses. Back in the US, they take extracurricular activities like musical theatre and debate. They have investments in stock shares, acceptances at Georgetown and Harvard and Yale are pending, they're future politicians and tech giants and they never, ever bite their nails. Freckles are sprinkled on noses, skin is the colour of office printer paper, and the Anthill children can't tell any of them apart (Gabriela has invented sly nicknames for a random few: *Kilo. Yucca. Sancocho*).

Every time the American volunteers arrive at the Anthill, they busily get to work: they move around tables and chairs, bring out papers and crayons. The daily activities vary. Bible stories. Bible colouring. Bible singing. And Free Time. Lots and lots and lots of Free Time. Every Friday, for Community Meal, they bring massive amounts of Carrefour-purchased food – baguettes and iceberg lettuce, stacks of packaged meat. Initially, the single mothers would hover uncertainly by the wall, banished from the kitchen by the bustling volunteers. They'd file their nails, look at their phones. By now, the single mothers have stopped attending Community Meal altogether. So instead Community Meal is fully staffed by the teens: dashing back and forth between the tables, handing out sandwiches with the thrilled delirium of bestowing lottery tickets, a winning one each and every time. *Here you go, here you are, enjoy! God bless you, and you, and you.*

Gabriela's knees crack as she stands up. —He's a bad person, she says airily. He needs to be punished.

—Rebecca? Lina says. Dafne? What do you think?

The two girls glance down at the papers, as if expecting to see the answer there. The grasshopper dances and fiddles and sings through the seasons, summer to spring to autumn. A chronological sequence, nicely ordered. Throughout it all, the ants keep working: dragging the crumbs, burrowing underground. In the winter picture, though, the grasshopper shivers in the waist-deep snow. He's waiting outside the ants' home, knocking on the door. Waiting to see if they'll forgive him. If they'll let him in.

The last piece of paper is blank, waiting to be filled in by the children's interpretation. Whatever they choose as an ending.

—I wouldn't let him in either, Rebecca whispers. He's bad. He's lazy. He didn't work. She wipes her hand on her dress, repeating Gabriela's phrase: He doesn't deserve it.

—Dafne?

Dafne runs her fingers through her hair, stopping when she gets to a knot. She nods in agreement, looking bored.

—Well, Lina says, raising her voice to be heard over yet another burst of yells and whoops emerging from the Anthill entrance. *Good job, Brian, go Team Corinthians!* Since we don't all agree, we're going to need a vote.

Tomás's face wrinkles up in misery, as though being the sole dissenting voice in a democracy was the last thing on earth he wanted. —Wait, he says, can I change my mind? But Lina has already nudged him, indicating with her head that he should carry out the extra-special task of running inside and fetching the plastic cup full of crayons.

—Miss Carolina? Gabriela says as Tomás scurries off. She wraps her hands around Lina's arm and hangs off like Tarzan on a vine. She's wearing the same dull-coloured shirt and shorts she always wears, her ever-present scent of smoke. The strap of one of her sandals has broken off and been fixed with a twisted-off bit from a plastic bag. Miss Carolina, what would you do?

Lina looks down at the drawings, at the grasshopper's withered face. The children watch, waiting patiently for her answer.

It's perfectly acceptable to rearrange the images in a story – to make it say what you want it to. Like the order of photographs in an album: you can take one out, keep it hidden for years, and no one would ever be any the wiser.

—I'd take him home with me, she says slowly. I'd take care of him. And I'd let him stay.

—Well, I wouldn't, Gabriela repeats, shaking her head vigorously.

—You don't think he deserves to be forgiven? For making a mistake?

This time, the children's voices are unanimous.

—No, Rebecca says.

—No way, Dafne says.

223

—Absolutely not, Gabriela says.

Tomás reappears with the cup full of crayons, rattling them like coins in a medieval beggar's cup. —Can we draw it now? he says. The grasshopper turning into a butterfly?

—What the hell are you talking about? Rebecca says, and Dafne starts laughing hysterically.

Lina steps off the dirt road, allowing a trio of young men with baggy jeans and shaved heads to walk by. —Sorry, Tomáso-man, she says, Gabriela still clutching her leg. We need to vote so that we can decide.

—Ugh, Gabriela says, flopping her head back dramatically. The ends of her hair trail on the ground. Can't you just tell us what to do?

—Nope. That's not how it works in a democracy, unfortunately. And that's what we have in this country.

—Democracy's dumb, Dafne says, jutting her hip out in that unsettlingly sassy way she's been doing more and more of lately.

—Yeah! Dumb! Rebecca repeats excitedly. Both girls start giggling and clutching each other, imitating the female teen volunteers.

—In democracies you have debates, Gabriela says, her head still tilted back. Like on TV.

—That's right. Like on TV right now, about the peace negotiations.

Gabriela frowns. —What's that?

She almost laughs at Gabriela's blank expression, but doesn't. —You haven't heard about the peace negotiations?

Gabriela shakes her head. So do Rebecca and Dafne. They shrug, scrunch up their faces, look up at her indifferently.

They've never heard of it before in their lives.

—What's a debate? Tomás asks, tentatively approaching Lina's other leg to grab it. But Gabriela's fist flings out in an attempt to punch him, and he jumps back.

—Gabriela, Lina says warningly, but Gabriela keeps talking, in that breezily airy tone of hers, the same one she uses when she tells Lina her random anecdotes (*That man down the hill? He walked me home last night and told me I was beautiful. My grandmother has a new boyfriend. The people in that house, the one over there? They fought with the people in this house over here, so these men came at night and set fire as revenge. The kittens went blind and lost their voices from the smoke.*). Gabriela and her stories: it's so hard to tell if they're calculated, deliberately narrated and carefully constructed by her, or if they're just spilling out, uncontrolled. Deeply personal testimony as opposed to irrelevant, flippant remarks.

—A debate is like a fight, Gabriela is saying. Like my mother in New York with her boyfriend. My mother was twenty-one and he's, well, he's not her boyfriend any more, but he was thirty-six. They were arguing in the park where we were having a picnic. A picnic with a picnic basket. We had bread and salami and he punched her in the face.

One of the young men has turned to look back at them. He has light eyes and a U-shaped scar on his forehead. He's carrying a megaphone in one hand, the kind advertisers use to sell lottery tickets. When he and Lina make eye contact, he puckers his lips to send her a kiss.

—Gabriela, where was this? Lina says. Were you in Central Park?

—She called the police, Gabriela says. And the police made

225

us go back to Colombia. They put us in a cage and we had to wait for hours and hours and hours and it was freezing cold. I was VERY young then. She holds her fingers up, a tiny distance from each other. I was just a baby! A stupid little baby!

—The police sent you back? From New York?

But Gabriela is now poking her finger into Lina's leg, as though trying to press a button that doesn't work. —Miss Carolina, can I ask a question?

Lina sighs. —Of course.

—Why don't Miss Maryluz and Miss Shauna come any more?

—They became very busy, she says quickly. Gabriela stares up at her with those fuzzy eyebrows, the ones that make her look automatically angry regardless of the conversation. Maryluz is very, very busy teaching her art classes. And Shauna is very, very busy with her son.

Gabriela exhales loudly. —When are they coming back?

—Oh, that doesn't matter. It's much nicer having so many new American friends here, isn't it? So many new people to practise English with!

Gabriela doesn't say anything. Her fingers keep tapping on Lina's leg, trying to punch in a secret code.

—And me and Mister Mattías are still here, aren't we? That's pretty fun, huh? Having me and him in charge?

Gabriela still doesn't speak. Neither do any of the other children.

Lina takes a deep breath. The men have clambered up the wooden steps of a house a few doors down, the one with a wire fence built out of scavenged mattress coils. They're taking cigarette packs out of their pockets, bringing out chairs to form a circle. Shaved heads. Tattooed arms. Surveying the scene, keeping watch.

Always the men in this city. Waiting and watching on every corner.

If she didn't know any better, Mattías could be one of them. He'd fit right in.

He could be anyone, really.

—*He* doesn't come around any more either, Gabriela says.

Lina blinks, startled. —Who?

Gabriela lets her head flop back once more. —The dirty boy. I haven't seen him in *ages*. Nobody comes to the stupid Anthill any more and it's SO. BORING! BORING. BORING.

—I'm glad he doesn't come, Tomás whispers. He smelled awful.

—Yeah, Rebecca says, while Dafne exaggeratedly pinches her nose. He stank. Almost as bad as you, Gabriela! And your crackhead mum!

Gabriela's eyes immediately fill with tears. She presses her lips together.

—Dafne, Lina says, in a tone so icily reminiscent of Mary-luz that Dafne immediately bows her head. If you say something like that again, I'm afraid you'll have to leave Leadership Club and not be invited back.

Dafne's head still bowed, she mumbles. —Good. Leadership Club sucks.

Lina opens her mouth to retort but is able to stop herself just in time. —Come on, she manages to say instead. Let's pick up the papers. We can vote on the ending and draw it inside.

Gabriela's mouth is still trembling, but she obediently unclenches her hands from Lina's leg and leaps to her feet.

Not for the first time, watching Gabriela's nimble, quick movements, Lina can't help but wonder: if provided with the proper resources, would Gabriela want to study gymnastics? Or would she go for track and field, cross-country races? Ice hockey, lacrosse? Would she make the debate team, or would she go for musical theatre instead? What would she be like; what would she be doing, if things were a tiny bit different?

In an attempt at redemption, Dafne has crouched down and scooped up the papers, careful not to wrinkle them as she hands them over.

—Thank you very much, Lina says, patting each child on the head as they pass by. Gabriela, however, nimbly ducks her head away, swift as a bird.

—It *was* Central Park, she says.

She skips away so fast one of her sandals flies off. Trailing after her, Tomás picks it up. He carries it raised high, like a runner with the Olympic torch.

Inside the Anthill, the American volunteers are preparing for today's raffle (which is now done daily, as opposed to once a week). They're folding T-shirts, rolling up baby socks, stacking the brand-new footballs and dolls in their see-through plastic boxes. A few slender-legged teens have snuck doughnuts out of the boxes and stand with their backs to the wall, munching away. The youth pastor nods at Lina when they make eye contact; Lina nods back.

—How'd it go? the youth pastor says in badly accented Spanish.

She shrugs. —It went okay, she says in English.

He replies, still insistently speaking Spanish: —That badly, huh? He blows air out from his nostrils like a bull. He has a bug-eyed, intense way of talking that makes Lina feel slightly on edge, similar to the first-year postgraduate students back in London, interrogating her about her 'academic career path' and 'planned path to publication' (where are these fantastical, mystical paths that seemed to obsess them so much? In the middle of a lost and lonely wood? On top of a faraway icy mountain?). Like her, he left Colombia as a child: his father worked as a political cartoonist for a newspaper. After receiving threatening phone calls for months, his father was kidnapped and held hostage for over a year. However, he'd been careful to emphasise that, in contrast to the majority of immigrants nowadays, he and his family had fled for 'legitimate', 'respectable' reasons; for safety, not to find work. He talks very earnestly and straightforwardly about his childhood in Colombia: he uses terms like 'trauma' and 'PTSD', and talks about how much safer everything is, now that the war is over. He makes it sound so straightforward, a clear-cut story of cause and effect: enemies and victims, with a decisive ending. The country has moved on; the past is a completed chapter, a closed book. Via his job at the Christian high school, he's gone abroad every summer for the past eight years, running the service trips: Peru, Ecuador, India. And now Colombia. A new addition to the list of acceptably safe countries.

Lina says, reluctantly switching to Spanish. —They put the scenes in the right order. We're going to take a vote on the ending now, before drawing it.

—A vote? he says, frowning and nodding at the same time, like he can't stop himself from simultaneously agreeing with her while deeply disapproving. That's a strange thing to do.

—We couldn't agree what it would be.

—Just tell them! Listen, you need to be careful. Children don't like to have too many responsibilities. They get drunk on power.

He tears open a giant bag of Festival cookies and starts stacking the individual packets in wobbly little towers.

—I'll bring more activity sheets tomorrow. Have you guys done the Good Samaritan one yet?

—We have, Lina says. Last week. Thank you. Have you seen Mattías?

—Who? The youth pastor's frown deepens. Oh, him? The guy who helps you? He took the blankets to get washed. They were kind of funky – grit or something from the suitcases – so I asked him to get them cleaned. I just feel, what's the word, embarazado giving something that dirty to the families here.

He shakes his head, as if feeling embarazado, pregnant, rather than embarrassed is too much emotion for him to handle (she knows better than to correct him). She's already started to turn away when he asks if she can do him a favour.

—Two favours, actually, he says briskly. If it's not too much trouble. The bathroom sign, you see: it keeps falling down. The tape here doesn't work very well, does it? Are you sure you don't have any Scotch tape tidied away somewhere? Don't worry, we'll bring some tomorrow; we were going to make a supply stop at Carrefour anyway. Gosh, it's a mess in those art cupboards, isn't it? I can't believe how you guys can ever find anything! He laughs before immediately becoming serious, like a mask with two expressions that can flip back and forth at the speed of light. But whatever you need to get done, he says, with the firm commitment of a Green Beret in Iraq, we'll do it.

We're here to help. I want to make the most of our time here. I can't believe we only have one day left!

—Time flies, Lina says, resisting the urge to twist around and check on the Leadership Club kids, whose murmurs are steadily rising in volume behind her: *No, not like that, you're doing it all wrong, ugh Gabriela, you're RUINING IT!*

—Second favour . . . (he drops his voice, low and confidential) . . . About the gang members: they're making the girls nervous. Do you think you could ask them to leave the vicinity?

—Excuse me?

—The gang members. The men who just walked by earlier. They kept looking over when the girls were turning the jump rope. He pauses for dramatic effect. It wasn't good, believe me.

—How do you know they're gang members?

—Because that's what they look like! He jabs at his arms, tracing the skin, drawing the tattoos. Isn't it obvious?

Mattías – he'd fit right in.

She says, —Is it, though?

He holds up his hands, don't-shoot style. —Hey. I'm not here to tread on your toes. You're the jefe here. You're in charge; you know how everything works.

Lina looks across the street, but the men are no longer on the porch. All she can see are the houses, rows and rows of them, and the mountains beyond, looming over the city like its most trusted, thuggish bodyguards.

She says, —I believe they're locals from the neighbourhood and aren't necessarily gang members. But! (Because the youth pastor's eyes are getting particularly buggy now.) I'll talk to them. I promise.

—Thank you, he says, frowning again.

One of the wobbly cookie towers he's built tumbles down, spilling over the rows of Sparkies packets.

She has to dig through the endless mess of art supplies in order to find the Scotch tape. The American volunteers like to put out as many art supplies as possible for children to use, paintbrushes and markers and stickers, as opposed to rationing them out one day a time, Maryluz style. *It's important for them to have routine* – that's what Maryluz liked to say. *For some Anthill children, here is the only place they get it.*

She re-tapes the sign on the bathroom door, flattening her fist over the English words: DON'T DRINK THE WATER! That's what the youth pastor announced, way back on their very first day. Two weeks ago now, when Lina led them on an introductory tour of the Anthill. Mattías faded away into the background at some point (an issue with where the vans were parked? A need to reschedule the sewing class with the single mothers?). Who knows where he went, what he got up to – in the end, it didn't matter, because Lina stepped up.

This is the kitchen, she said, waving her arms at the sink, the refrigerator. *And there's the supply closet. No one else has keys for the supply closet but me. And there's one thing I would like you to please keep in mind*, she said, showing them the computers, the ESL tables. *It's something I ask of all volunteers, so no need to take it personally. Please don't accept any contact information from the students. No Facebook, no email, no phone numbers, no nothing. You especially*, she said, turning to the male teens, their eyes widening in alarm. *Please don't flirt with the students, female and male. Don't invite them on dates outside of the Anthill.*

The American volunteers often look to Lina for advice. They frequently ask Lina about the Anthill, how it works and what to do. And it's hard to deny it: the feeling inside her, rotating like a rotisserie chicken on a stick. The juices of it dripping into the deepest, darkest, most secret part of her gut.

The rich pleasure of pure triumph.

Of being the one who *knows*. Where everything is and how it works. Someone who belongs. *I've made so many mistakes with the Anthill*, she told the youth pastor, tentatively, hesitantly at first, like her tongue was just experimenting with the words (his words? The words of him?). But as the youth pastor nodded and looked at her, eyes wide with patient interest, the words started coming faster, flowing more easily. *So many mistakes! I can't even begin to get into all the mistakes I've made!* Ask her a question, she can tell you the answer. If an American volunteer has a problem that needs solving, Lina can point them in the right direction. Tell them where to go; what to do.

Is this how it feels to be an adult? The pleasure of being decisive, of knowing one's place in the world? As opposed to nauseous with uncertainty?

And oh, how glad it makes her! The feeling of goodness, washing over her! Glad! Glad! Glad!

Is this what her mother felt, all those years ago? Tramping around in the hillside neighbourhoods with such a clear sense of purpose?

And how could feeling happy be anything other than a good thing?

—Miss Carolina?

Gabriela is tugging on her fingers. —We need tape, she's

saying. But good tape, the see-through kind. To put the story together.

—We finished the last scene! Tomás shouts, throwing his arms up like a victorious World Cup player.

She doesn't bother sliding into a chair, just leans over the table to get a look. Dafne and Rebecca have long since moved on to their current main interest, hissing and whispering gossip to each other ('gossip' seems to have become their new favourite game recently, since the teens' arrival). Tomás is smiling in a way that shows all his gums. His fingers are stained red from the marker, which he still grips in his clenched fist.

On the page, the grasshopper lies dead. Headless, liquid spurting from the stump. Red like the blood Lina left on Rebecca's page all those weeks ago. She touches the scribbles, like she wants to wipe them away. The ants carry machine guns. They march in straight lines, surrounding the corpse.

———

In more ways than one, the Anthill's first floor has become a refuge for Lina – a general's barracks, a site of rest when she needs a quick break. That's where she heads now, Churchill retreating to his headquarters, taking a deep breath and scratching her fingers. She bumps into Mattías at the top of the stairs.

—Oh! she says, sounding more startled than she means to. He takes a nimble step sideways.

—Apologies, he says. I'll get out of your way.

—No, please don't.

How thin he is these days! A sunken cheek sort of thin. Like something's been sucked out of him. He isn't around much at the Anthill these days – not that it's a problem. After all, he's an adult, a grown man, isn't he? He's free to go off and do . . . whatever it is he does all day.

And to be honest . . . sometimes it's easier having him gone: out of sight, out of mind. When he *is* here, she sometimes catches the youth pastor and other adult supervisors smiling too wide and shuffling away from him, the same way they respond to certain men who sometimes come to Community Meal. The men who arrive black with grease, and with wild empty expressions. Walking on crutches, bags of collected rubbish dangling from the grips.

Because Mattías is just like those men in a way, isn't he? A bit intense? Too much to handle? Somewhat off-putting? He is! He really can be! He can be (she says to herself, watching him shuffle into the furthest corner of the room, as far away from her as possible as she rummages through the ESL materials) a bit overwhelming. And who can blame the volunteers for wanting to protect themselves? For wanting to feel comfortable?

—I'm just looking for the Scotch tape, she says, and he nods, pointing wordlessly at a scuffed plastic container by the fridge.

It's no wonder he's got thin, though, overworking himself like he has. It's no surprise, really. And here she is, getting larger and larger! Colombia has been good to her; there's no denying it. Putting shorts on now involves huffing and puffing and determined yanks; the soft flab of her belly is hard to ignore when she steps into the shower. But ignore it she does, with the same mean thrill she gets when hitting the button to delete her PhD supervisor's emails, which have transitioned over the past few weeks from polite enquiry to aggressive curiosity to genuine concern. It doesn't matter! None of it matters! England and everything there feels tiny and far away, and not very interesting or important. Because what could be more important than here, now, the present moment? It feels good to not care: about England, her studies, the life she tried to build there. Because how could it possibly compare to what she's made for herself here?

—What are you up to? she says, tucking the Scotch tape into her armpit.

He gestures towards a swollen black garbage bag at his feet. —Oh, I was just heading out. The pastor asked me to do some laundry.

—Perfect! she says, scooping the bag up. Don't worry, I can do it.

He smiles but doesn't respond.

On their way back downstairs, she tells him the latest update, how the American volunteers have brought bags of apples and pears for Community Meal tomorrow. It's a bit sad, isn't it, how the Anthill children rarely have access to Vitamin C or vegetables, doesn't he agree? They shouldn't be eating so much sugar. So many cakes and desserts during Community Meal! It isn't healthy, in her opinion. It does things to the blood. How long ago was the no-sugar rule abolished? Has he ever reconsidered the possibility of reinstating it?

—Whatever you want, Lina, he says. If that makes you happy. He's walking slightly behind her, in a way that's almost . . . servile.

—Hey! she says. It's not about making me happy; it's about doing what's good for the Anthill.

—Of course, he says. He comes to a stop against the wall,

watching the children at the tables. They both fall silent. Or rather: she does.

As it was mainly her who was doing the talking. Her stories and opinions and thoughts. Not his.

The American volunteers have taken the board games out of the cupboard, spreading them over the floor. As with the art supplies, instead of rationing them out daily, Maryluz style, the games are now available at all times for any child to play with. Connect Four and Memory, Sorry! and Candy Land, dominoes and playing cards – all day, every day, all the time.

—I'm sorry, he says. You're right. No sugar at the Anthill is definitely an idea worth considering.

She leans against the wall beside him. The two of them together, in charge. —Okay.

Sometimes . . .

. . . it's moments like these . . .

. . . lurking on the edge of her mind . . .

. . . that she can maybe?

Kind of?

Hear a tiny voice talking to her?

A voice that sort of sounds like a scream?

A scream that's saying,

Lina. What . . . are you DOING?

But oh, it's so easy to talk to him. It's so wonderful, the two of them together. He's always been a good listener, Mattías has. And who would know him better than her?

In the end, it's much easier to not look at the screaming feeling. To not examine it. Better to just keep on rushing on: Lina, getting things done. Why . . . in the end . . . she's become her mother after all! Abandoning her studies, just like her mother fleeing her medical degree decades before, leaving it all behind, for *this*. For him. It's like the past has flipped forward, superimposing itself on to the present, like one of those colouring books with transparent paper. Her mother in the clay house, wandering through the dirt-road neighbourhoods. Deciding what was best for the little boy before her. How best to help him.

What has she been so afraid of, all this time?

Shouldn't she just accept it – her inheritance, who she's meant to be?

—Matty? she says, but he doesn't look over; he's intensely watching the room as if there's something urgent that requires his attention. At a nearby table, Gabriela and Tomás are playing Memory. Tomás is debating over which card to choose, while Gabriela lets out an enormous yawn.

—Ugh, she says, loud enough that her voice carries over. Memory is so BORING.

She speaks as fast as she can: —Matty . . . are you okay? With how things are at the Anthill?

He answers promptly, his eyes still elsewhere: —Of course.

The youth pastor has started clapping his hands. He's calling out in English to the Anthill children: —Come on, boys and girls, come line up! Come get ready, come get in line! And don't forget to say your special phrase in English, or you won't get a raffle ticket!

—Are you sure? You're not . . . tired?

—Don't worry about me, he says. I'm fine.

The youth pastor is still clapping his hands. The Anthill children have begun organising themselves into two lines: girls in one, boys in the other. Only Gabriela and Tomás remain seated. Gabriela is drumming her fingers, Tomás has just picked up three cards instead of two, but she doesn't protest, no squeaky cry of *Hey, only two at a time, no cheating, you cheater!*

—Good, she says. That's . . . good.

In order to get their raffle tickets, the Anthill children now have to recite a phrase in English. They repeat it incorrectly, mangled from the original version, but none of the teens ever bothers to correct them. One by one the children say it, and one by one an American volunteer presses a raffle ticket into their sticky palms.

God bless please my name is thank you very much.
God bless please my name is thank you very much.
God bless please my name is thank you very much.

—You know what? she says suddenly. I'd like to make a donation to the Anthill.

He finally looks at her. Directly, in the face.

—I mean it. She laughs shakily. I can make the transfer whenever you want.

He stands there. Listening.

Her voice is rising: —Because it'd make a big difference, wouldn't it? For the Anthill? I want to help, she says. I want to help you.

—If that's what you want, he says. If that would make you happy.

He steps away from her. The children keep moving, shuffling forward in line.

God bless please my name is thank you very much.
God bless please my name is thank you very much.
God bless please my name is thank you very much.

—Come on, you two! the youth pastor shouts, waving his arms at Gabriela and Tomás. Everybody come participate!

Tomás just looks bemused. Gabriela's lips are starting to curl upwards in that familiar contemptuous expression of hers, the one she gets right before a tantrum. It's the same one she had during Bible Trivia the other day, when she shouted at the top of her voice that it was two murderers on the cross with Jesus at the end, not thieves, and then she yanked Veronica's hair so hard, Veronica fell to the ground.

—There she goes, Mattías says. He's watching Gabriela too.

—Argh, Lina says, already picturing the scene: Gabriela knocking a chair over, Gabriela cursing, Gabriela throwing Connect Four coins into a volunteer's eye.

She follows him over to Tomás and Gabriela's table. They look up at him with their usual expressions of wide-eyed respect. Even Gabriela tends to be stunned into submissive silence by the grace of Mattías's presence, like she's meeting the Pope, or a member of the Atlético Nacional football team. She can't help but be touched by it – their utter, undying respect for him. He fists-bumps Tomás with one hand while scooping up the Memory cards with the other.

—Come on, soldiers, he says. Time to clean up.

Gabriela nods solemnly. Tomás holds up his hand again, eager for another fist-bump, which Mattías willingly provides.

—How's your grandmother?

Tomás opens his mouth but Gabriela interrupts before he can speak: —Fine, she says. She has a cold.

He pats her on the head. —I'll see the two of you later. You be good with Miss Lina here, and do exactly what she says. Okay?

Gabriela and Tomás nod again, simultaneously this time.

But as he's walking away, Gabriela calls after him. —Hey! she shouts. When are Miss Shauna and Miss Maryluz coming back?

But he doesn't look back. He turns his body sideways to slide through the half-open, half-closed Anthill door. And just like that, he's gone.

—Come on, Lina says, pointing at the closest teen with a candy bag. Go and line up.

But Gabriela doesn't move. She just stands there, pressing her chin into Tomás's shoulder. Lina sighs. She picks up the drawings of the grasshopper and the ants, flicking through to make sure the scenes are in order.

There were different versions of the fable online. A variety of endings.

But what did the Leadership Club kids know? Who were they to say that the version with forgiveness wasn't the best? After all, how did that phrase go again?

Forgive and forget. Not forgive and remember.

When she gets to the last piece of paper, though, her hands stop. She stares. She bites her lip.

There it is again: the entire page filled in, scribbled black lines. The marker has been pressed down so hard in places it's torn right through the paper. A harried, raw mess, like the ugliest lump of scar tissue ever.

As if she hadn't been able to stop herself. As if she hadn't been able to hold it back.

—Gabriela? she says.

But Gabriela is already moving away, as if sensing the trouble that's brewing, pulling Tomás towards the last remaining children in line. Lina's hands shake as she approaches them.

—Gabriela! she repeats, and there must be something different in her voice this time, because when Gabriela turns in her direction, it's with an expression of mild alarm. You ruined the assignment, Lina says, in that same low voice that doesn't sound like her, a voice that she can't seem to stop. This drawing – it has nothing to do with the story we were discussing. It has nothing to do with anything. You did it wrong on purpose and you've ruined it. That's very, very disrespectful of you.

Gabriela scowls. She tugs Tomás so hard their hips bang into each other. Tomás keeps his gaze fixed forward, intensely staring at the bag of sweets in the teen's hand.

—Come on, little girl! the youth pastor calls out cheerily. Girls in the girl line, boys in the boy line! Line up correctly if you want to get your candy!

—Gabriela, Lina says, keeping her voice to a whisper, though it sounds hot and hard in her ears. If you can't be respectful . . . and if you can't do activities correctly . . . then you shouldn't come to the Anthill. And if you can't follow instructions, then you shouldn't bother coming at all.

Gabriela folds her lips inward. She doesn't let go of Tomás – they've reached the front of the line now. The American teen is looking back and forth between them, smiling invitingly. —Come on, little dude! he says chirpily. Boys stand in the boys' line and girls with the girls!

—I mean it, Lina says. The Anthill is not a place for people who are rude and mean and ungrateful and . . . and who ruin very nice, carefully planned activities on purpose. It's not a place for anyone like that.

She steps forward and peels Gabriela's fingers off Tomás's

arm, one at a time. Tomás dashes forward, holding both his palms upturned. —Thank you very much, he says in hurried English.

The teen shakes the bag of candy up and down encouragingly. —Say the full phrase, little amigo! You can do it!

—Thank you very much, Tomás repeats.

That's when Gabriela starts to scream.

The turning of heads. The widening of eyes. Her voice is filling up the Anthill, every inch of it, every corner: it's there, it's loud, and nobody can deny it. But before anybody can do anything Gabriela is already on the move; Gabriela is already half-gone. She's turning her body sideways, she's slipping through the half-closed door, her sandals flapping and darting. The youth pastor frowns, muttering something about inappropriate behaviour, what a shame; the teens nudge each other and hoot, man, did you hear that one, what a pair of lungs.

But Lina stands there alone, papers in her hand. Page after page of gaping darkness. Of scribbled rage. Of a monstrously dark presence that no amount of good cheer and optimistic determination can hide. You can't pretend it didn't happen. You can't pretend that it hasn't been there all along. Urban transformation and twenty-first-century innovation can't hide it, can't keep it from seeping in, it's here, it's big, and it's not going away anytime soon. Has it been lurking in the background of this country the entire time? How could she not have seen it; how could she not have known? And still, the Anthill children keep heading to the front of the line, mouths moving automatically, repeating the phrase they're seemingly compelled to finish, like they've joined something that they

243

now have to follow through to the very end, whatever that may be.

God bless please my name is thank you very much.
God bless please my name is thank you very much.
God bless please my name is thank you very much.

Thank you very much. That's what I said when you shared your enormous bag of birthday candy with me. Your mother always bought one cake for you and a smaller one for me, and I would say, *Thank you, ma'am.* Your father gave me a plastic cowboy gun, which he must have bought in the French department store. *Thank you, sir,* I said, not daring to confess that I'd have been happy with a doll like yours; that wasn't the sort of thing boys were supposed to admit. I held the gun in my lap throughout dinner as you opened the rest of your presents. *Thank you, Lina,* I said when you allowed me to blow out some of your candles. I was a good little boy. I was, I was. I was very appreciative and grateful. I came when called. I sat; I stood. I kept still as your mother, in one of her frenzied displays of attention, combed my hair down so flat and wet from the shower it looked like a wig, while you squirmed around and said *Ouch, you're hurting me* as Toña tied your hair back into tight pigtails. *Mummy, do me!* But your mother didn't answer, tilting my chin up to make sure there weren't any smears of egg yolk by my mouth. She pushed us by the bottoms out the front door, watching us clamber into the chauffeured car with tinted windows your father had begged the law firm to provide. *Off you go now,* she called out as the car rumbled away. *Be a good little boy, Matty!* We were good little students. Ms Cadence liked to have boys sit with boys and girls with girls, so instead of you I had to sit with

Eduardo, a worried-looking boy whose hands were always wet when he came back from the bathroom. But at least that wasn't as bad as sitting next to one of the Gómez twins, excellent at football, or someone like Paco, who told stories about his father taking his older brothers to see prostitutes. Paco regarded me with the same kind of disdain typically reserved for the dead black beetles that fell down from the straw roof of the cafeteria kiosk, like he knew a terrible secret about me, something that meant I needed to be picked last for football, and bumped into accidentally-on-purpose in the bathrooms. I kept my head down; I didn't complain. I kept quiet; I stayed out of the way. I did, I did.

I will not act out. I will not act out.

That's what I had to write, the first week of school when we did our name tags. We wrote our names down in giant capital letters, coloured in pictures that best represented us and our lives, the good young citizens of Colombia. We used our very best markers, our brand-new crayons. We drew things that we liked and things that we wanted to be. The boys drew footballs and tanks, grenades exploding and killing those evil FARC rebels. The girls drew dolls and flowers, colouring in the pointiest, blackest high-heel shoes possible. You drew a figure in a dress, sitting at a desk with a pencil in your hand. You were surrounded by stacks of books, which you drew as fat squares. Above your head, you wrote down the job of the people we admired most, Roald Dahl and Jack London and Anna Sewell, the thing we both wanted to be: *WRITER*.

I drew the same. It wasn't copying, because we never copied. It's just that we were the same, you and me, just different versions of each other.

When Ms Cadence strolled by, though, she frowned at my drawing. Lala Pereira covered her mouth with her hand and said, *You drew yourself wearing a dress?!* The Gómez twins started to laugh, nudging each other. *You need to draw something different, Mattías,* Ms Cadence said. *Don't just copy Maria Carolina.* As she walked away, Paco leaned forward and poked me. *Did you draw your vagina too?* he whispered. *I can smell his vagina,* Eduardo said, twisting around excitedly in his seat, frantic to get Paco's attention. *He doesn't wash it properly.* As we waited in line for Ms Cadence to staple our drawings up on the bulletin board, I hurried back to my desk and fumbled through my pencil bag. I chose a black marker, since ink wasn't erasable. Scribbling hard, it was easy enough to change. The desk became a tank, the books squat grenades, the pencil a rifle. Once a writer, I was now a soldier. *Good job, Mattías,* Ms Cadence said when I passed it to her. I kept the marker hidden behind the elastic band of my underwear, where there was no chance of it being seen. The stapler went *click* against the bulletin board.

During recess you waited for me for ages by the fence, and when I finally appeared you said, *What took you so long? What were you doing? Never mind, the leaf-cutter ants are waiting.* And so we continued like we always did, carrying them forward to the front of the line, one at a time, leaves pinched between our fingers. But when we came back into the classroom, Emma Green and Lala Pereira put their hands on their cheeks and started to scream. *Ms Cadence, Ms Cadence, come look, somebody's ruined the bulletin board!* Ms Cadence had to come running from the back of the line, and along with everyone else she stood and stared at the name tags.

Jagged black lines.

Wrinkled torn paper.

On each and every one: the marker scribbled furiously, uncontrollably, darkness spreading to the edge of the page. For all of us – the young, good citizens of Colombia – our identities had been transformed into a wild clump of stitches, barely holding back the wound. Uncontainable, irreversible. There it was, right in front of us. Everyone whispered and gasped and nudged each other, pointing at the ink stains on my fingers, and even you clutched my arm and whispered, *Oh, Arctic Fox, how could you!* But I stood there; I didn't move. I looked right at it, and I didn't look away.

That's how your mother and I ended up sitting across the table from Ms Cadence, while you waited tearfully in the hallway, ordered there by your mother: *Don't be such a baby, María, go and wait outside.* Ms Cadence showed your mother the name tags I'd ruined, while I tapped a pen against my mouth. Without glancing at me, your mother snatched the pen from my hand, hissing, *Don't be cheeky.* Without missing a beat, she then explained the situation very patiently to Ms Cadence, how she could never do that to her daughter, have me move to a different grade, a different school. As she was sure Ms Cadence could recall, even having me in a different classroom at the beginning of the school year had made you a hysterical mess. It was important you and I stayed together; it's what we were accustomed to, we'd never known anything different. I kept quiet as your mother explained to Ms Cadence what she may or may not have already known, the fact that I didn't have a mother of my own, but that I lived with you. Your mother had rescued me, saved me from the awful poverty of Medellín's very worst neighbourhoods, the streets filled with criminals and drug addicts and Pablo Escobar's henchmen and Lord knows what else. She had brought me here instead, to benefit from the excellent education system, to bless me with a wonderful childhood and a future of opportunity.

My husband's work keeps him away from home quite a bit, your mother said, touching her hair, which she'd recently chopped off into a bob. *And I've been busy myself too; I have a very important showing of my photographs next month, in the Intercontinental Hotel.* She laughed in that nervous way of hers. I pressed my wrist to my mouth and chewed gently on the skin. With your mother watching, I apologised to Ms Cadence, saying, *I will not act out. I will not act out.* And with that, your mother pulled her cigarettes from her bag and thanked Ms Cadence for her time. I shot out of my seat and thanked Ms Cadence as well, in the nice polite way your mother wanted me to.

I will not cause trouble. I will not cause trouble.

We never played with the leafcutter ants again after that. Even though your mother liked telling the story at her parties, laughing as she puffed on her cigar, waving her hand through the air as she described the intensity of the scribblings, the darkness of my destruction. *He ruined the whole fucking room, the little shit!* After that, I was more careful. I protected you. I made sure to not get attention, to not stand out. You and Emma and all the rest of them: they could be the centre of attention, not me. I was a good little boy. I was, I was.

I will not be rude. I will not be rude.

I'd sit in my seat as quietly as possible. I was good at staying silent, at not being noticed. But then we had the school-wide event to collect food for the landslide victims. The flyer for the event had photos of children on it, and Paco had started laughing when he saw them, jabbing his finger at the page again and again, talking loudly enough to make sure everyone could hear him: *Look, Mattías, dirty Indians like you! Look, everybody, he's famous, his picture's in the newspaper!*

Across the room, your eyes filled with tears as Paco laughed. Watching your lip tremble, your hands shake, I knew in that moment what I had to do.

I will not cause a fuss. I will not cause a fuss.

I didn't complain. I wrote down the right answers for pop quizzes. I wrote book reports, I studied for exams. And then, one day, Paco came to school wearing shorts. When he came back from the bathroom and sat down, I pushed my chair back. I got down on my hands and knees, as if looking for a dropped eraser. I crawled towards him, keeping low. And I leaned forward and sank my teeth into his calf, as deep as possible. I didn't let go. Not when he screamed. Not when he cried. Not when I got pulled on and yanked on and slapped, dozens of hands all over me, trying to pull me away. But I kept my jaw clenched tight.

Oh, Matty, you said, hours later, when your mother came with the driver to take us home early. We sat in the back seat of the car together, my head resting in your lap. The inside of the car stank of exhaust fumes and French bread. We were driving past a group of men at a traffic light, their arms and collarbones dark with ink.

Criminals, your mother hissed, twisting around in the front seat, while the chauffeur stared straight ahead. *Sicarios. Look, María – tattoos are how you identify them: the gang members, the assassins, the men for hire.*

But instead of looking at where your mother was pointing, you carefully touched the bruises on my face, one by one. *Oh, Arctic Fox*, you said, sighing. *What are we going to do.* You said it like a statement, as opposed to a question.

I'll protect you, I said. *Forever and always.*

You smiled. You put your hand on my hair. A quick, light pat of approval. *Over and out*, you whispered. And later that evening, after your mother had slapped me on the face with the back of her slipper, I wrote down what she told me to: *I will not be cheeky. I will not be cheeky.*

Oh, it's so hard to know how to put any and all of this in order, isn't it? Such a mess, such a disaster! Which is better to start with, which one should I choose, who should I follow? It's like when the Anthill children are waiting to be picked for a team, swarming around, crying and begging: *Choose me next, choose me, please.* No matter how much I try to reassure them, *Don't worry, wait your turn, I'll get to you in time* – they shake their heads. They moan. They tremble with terror at the thought of being left all alone, forgotten. *When is it my turn. When do I get to speak. When, when.* So many to choose from. What order to put it in? *Stop fighting*, I want to tell them. *Stop rushing in. One at a time; I'll get to you. Stop bickering.*

That was an English word your mother liked to use with us. *Stop bickering!* That's what she shouted at us at the zoo in accented English, standing in the Ice World. Your mother loved British words. We loved the zoo. We loved getting our faces painted, although when I asked to have a butterfly drawn on my cheek like yours, the woman laughed: *Butterflies aren't for boys.* She offered to draw me a lion instead, or a tiger, but I shook my head. Your mother stood under a tree and smoked her Cuban cigars while we ran into the Night House, our absolute favourite section, since it had bats like *The Deptford Mice*, a badger like *The Animals of Farthing Wood* and a barn owl just like Plop. We loved the deer in the Petting Area, feeding it stale bread your mother bought from a vendor. Their damp black noses! Their sticky pink tongues! You said their eyelashes looked like mine, which caused me to throw my bread on the ground in anger, for reasons I couldn't quite understand. How could I tell you that I didn't want to be told that I had eyes like a baby deer's, since Paco and Eduardo and all the other boys would want to be like lions and tigers? Hardened animals from the Predator section. Fighters. Warriors. That's what boys were supposed to be, wasn't it?

After the Night House, our second-favourite section was the Ice World. It had no arctic foxes or penguins, but it did have bears – even though they looked dirty green rather than white, like they had moss growing in their fur. They paced back and forth in their metal cage, claws clanking on the barred floor, eyes crusty with black gunk. We kept a respectful distance as we watched, but the bears took no notice of us, kept pacing over and over, the same repetitive gesture. They wouldn't stop.

What's wrong with them, you tentatively asked. Your mother stubbed her cigarette out on the gawking eyeball of the clown-shaped bin.

They're fucked in the head, she said, shaking her cigarette packet to make the next one easier to pull out. *That's what being in a cage will do to you.*

She gave me some coins to buy her a Club Colombia, and when I returned a man was waiting for us up ahead by the flamingos. As we walked past, he immediately began walking in the same direction, following behind at a distance. I could hear his footsteps on the tiles. Your mother took you by the hand and quickened her pace, and I kept up as best I could without tripping.

You pulled on your mother's sleeve. *Mummy,* you said, looking up at her piteously. This sometimes got her attention, like Laura Ingalls when brave Jack the bulldog dies and she wants to know if he will go to Dog Heaven, like all good dogs do. *Mummy, is there anything we can do for the bears? Can we adopt them?*

Don't be stupid, María, your mother said, looking over her shoulder. I looked too. The man was still there. Another one had joined him. They were still following us, hands in their pockets.

Can we talk to the zookeeper? Can we give them money to build them a better cage? Please, Mummy, you kept saying, your fingers creeping up her arm, touching her wrist as though there were buttons there that you were trying to push, like she was a robot and you were trying to punch in the code that would make her do what you were asking. But whatever code you must have punched in that day didn't work, because your mother just grabbed you by the hand, yanking you close.

I'm done with helping, she said. *Your father's much better at helping than me.* She was still looking over her shoulder, at the men. To distract you, I pushed my face into the cotton candy. *Matty!* you screamed. *Stop being so beastly* – like Peter yelling at Edmund in Narnia. The men behind us started to walk faster, getting closer; your mother started to breathe more rapidly. I pushed my face into your neck, and you screamed even louder. In English your mother shouted: *Stop fucking bickering!*

She dragged you through the zoo exit, panting and rushing towards the parked car. Scurrying along, I looked behind me one last time. But the men who'd been following us were gone.

We never went back to the zoo after that.

I will not upset Maria Carolina. I will not upset Maria Carolina.

I will not be ungrateful and rude. I will not be ungrateful and rude.

That's what I was writing when the phone rang. Your mother was in bed with the empty wine bottle and ice pack, your father still at work, and Nataly out at the grocery store, so I was able to answer it. The man's voice on the other end was a deep one, talking calmly and steadily. The voice explained how it was in your father's interest to keep his wife safe. It seemed your father still hadn't got the message, despite the notes delivered to his office. What with being a foreigner and all, and with the kind of legal work he was involved in, your father needed to be careful, especially with a patriot like Álvaro Uribe currently in power, a potential presidential candidate. And yet your father still hadn't left the country, hadn't been able to restrain his wife from indulging in such leftist insurrectionary activity, running around in those neighbourhoods as brazen as anything. She should learn her lesson before it was too late, stay in her home instead of acting so scandalously, be happy and safe, a good Colombian wife. Don't you agree, little boy, that it'd be awful to have something happen to your mother?

At first I didn't answer. I kept my jaw clenched tight. But then my mouth opened, and the words came out. *She's not my mother*, I said. And then I said it. I said it out loud.

HE SAYS HE'LL GET REVENGE
WHEN HE'S OLDER

—Don't you, *mijo*?

Lina wiggles on the wooden stool, turning to look at him. Sitting on the edge of the mattress, Tomás doesn't answer. He starts fiddling with the blanket tassels.

—Yes, he does, Tomás's grandmother says, answering her own question. He says it every day, don't you, kiddo?

She presses her lips together and shakes her head – approvingly or disapprovingly, it's hard to tell.

It took them less than five minutes to walk here. Tomás led the way, his Crocs squeaking as she followed him wordlessly down the street. They walked past half-open windows, an unattended sputtering motorcycle, a wooden crate with two bewildered-looking hens inside. At one point, they passed a group of kids she didn't recognise from the Anthill, who appeared to be . . . sledding? Lying flat on a plank of wood, using their bare feet to push themselves down the dirt slope. Unlit cigarettes jutting from their mouths, laughing and whooping. They seemed around Tomás's age, eight or nine.

—Tomáso-man, she said to him when he finally came to a stop by a bright-green house. The Anthill was still within sight, just up the street. So you've lived this close to the Anthill? This whole time?

He shrugged and pushed the door open without knocking.

As she stepped through, she couldn't help but remember

with a low thud in her gut: one of Mattías's rules during his orientation talk, all those weeks ago. *Do not – I repeat, do not – go into their homes.* But it shocked her when she followed Tomás inside. How . . . *nice* it was. Sure, there was a stack of bricks by the wall, and an eye-watering smell (incense mixed with burnt rubber mixed with cement). But there was an enormous bed, plump with cushions and a fuzzy fleece blanket. There was an elegant wooden wardrobe that wouldn't have been out of place in *Beauty and the Beast*, and a television with a DVD player. Laminated cards of saints were taped to the cinderblock walls, and the floor was cement, not wood (albeit scratchy). Styrofoam heads adorned with floppy wigs lined a wooden shelf, along with other hairdressing supplies: hairspray, slim scissors, a single black plastic comb.

It didn't seem . . . poor.

The shock came first. Then the embarrassment.

—He goes on and on about it, the grandmother is saying. How he's going to shoot them in the head when he grows up and get revenge.

As she talks, Tomás's grandmother takes the scuffed pot off the stove and pours the boiling water into two mugs. Unscrewing a lid of instant coffee, she scoops up one heaped spoonful after another. Lina swallows her *That's enough for me, thank you.*

—That's the problem with this neighbourhood, the grandmother says, spoon clinking on the side of the mug. Trash! Garbage, everywhere! Little boys with guns! That's all we got from this disarmament, these negotiations. We're still living under the command of small children!

She shakes her head again as she pours in the sugar: this time, it's definitely in disapproval.

—And the way they killed his father. An orphan! Not right. It's not right.

Lina accepts the mug of coffee. It's hard to know what to say. Is the grandmother telling her this because . . . this is just her style of talking, to anyone and everyone? Is this her typical conversation-starter? To open the door with Tomás's life story? *Come in*, the grandmother said after Lina introduced herself, *thank you for coming*, before immediately plunging into a rapid-fire monologue, a rushing stream of sentences: welcome, come in, you're a new volunteer at the Anthill? What a good place, what a good man, that Mattías, what a blessing he's been for the neighbourhood. What a help he's been, bringing them groceries, helping out with the rent, lending money so that she can take the bus to the hospital. She has a problem with her leg, see, the grandmother explains, and it's only then that Lina notices she walks with a limp. But what a help the Anthill has been for her poor grandson, a poor boy who's an orphan with his family all dead, all killed, all gone, an orphan, the poor thing, his father killed by the government as a suspected member of the FARC, when they brought the American helicopters here in 2013, Black Hawks you know, there are still bullet marks in the walls, but he says he'll get revenge when he's older, don't you, *mijo*?

Tomás nods his head, his toad-like eyes wide in the dim room. He whispers, —Yes.

And then there's the awkwardness of being told to take the most comfortable-looking armchair, the grandmother nudging her towards it.

And yet – the familiarity of it.

The comfort of getting to sink down and wait patiently

257

while the grandmother bustles around, knocking over cans of hairspray as she prepares the coffee.

The recognition of servitude. And her automatic acceptance of it.

What else has she been accepting unquestioningly, all this time?

—Thank you so much, she says, taking a sip. The oil-dark liquid burns her tongue. It's been a long day.

—Hasn't it just? Tomás's grandmother straightens a chunky plastic Barney toy on a nearby wooden shelf. Uff, what a horrible thing, so sorry you have to look at it. He never plays with it any more. And the baby's too young for it.

—Baby? It's hard to keep the startled note out of her voice. But Tomás's grandmother presses an index finger to her lips, the universal sign for *Be quiet.*

—In the next room, she says. Sleeping. But Willem, my goodness, why don't you take all these ugly toys you don't play with any more to the Anthill? Let some poor child benefit from it, somebody in need!

Tomás doesn't answer. He's still focused on twisting the blanket tassels around his finger, the blanket bunching up in his lap.

The grandmother raps her knuckles loudly on the wooden shelf —Willem Edison, I'm talking to you!

Tomás looks up and nods vigorously, as if a screw in his neck has come loose.

—Willem Edison? Lina says.

—That's who he is, girlie. What, did you think you were bringing some other kid here? Tomás's grandmother looks amused, letting out a throaty chuckle.

—Gabriela calls me Tomás, he whispers. Like the inventor.

He looks down at the floor. It's her special name for me.

He's wrapped the tassels around his fingers so tight his skin is turning purple.

Lina says, somewhat faintly, —I didn't know Gabriela had a special name for you.

She looks down at her coffee.

What else has she not known, all this time?

What questions, exactly, has she been failing to ask?

—That's right. The grandmother lightly touches the back of her neck, as if checking to make sure her kerchief is still tied. Willem Edison, just like his father. That's who you're going to get revenge for, aren't you?

Tomás rotates his ankles, like a runner warming up for a race. —Yes, he says again, louder this time.

—That's right, the grandmother repeats. That's exactly right. She fiddles with the see-through curtain that separates the kitchen from the bedroom. It's white and lacy, like something the ghost of a dead virgin bride would wear.

—Well, Lina says, as calmly as she can, I don't want to take up too much of your time. I was hoping you could help me with something.

—Of course, girlie, the grandmother says. She crosses her arms and leans against the doorframe. The curtain stirs behind her.

—Tomás's . . . um, Willem Edison's friend, Gabriela. Do you know her?

The grandmother's expression doesn't change.

—She went running out of the Anthill just now. She was, uh, upset. I was . . .

Lina swallows.

—I'd like to talk to her. Is there any chance you know where she lives?

It comes out high-pitched and wavery. The same voice she used earlier, when she grabbed Tomás by the arm and pulled him urgently away from the American volunteers, the last of the children standing in line for candy. *Tomás,* she said shakily, as he calmly unwrapped his sweets and shoved the entire palmful into his mouth at once. *Gabriela – do you know where she went? Where she lives? Where would she have gone?*

Shrugging, the candy banging against his teeth as he spoke: *My grandma might know.*

And now, Lina is saying to her, —I want to go and check on her. To see if she's okay.

The grandmother looks at Tomás, frowning. Tomás immediately freezes, his legs still sticking straight out in front of him, ankles in mid-rotation.

Lina keeps going: —It's my fault, you see. I wasn't . . . I said something I shouldn't have.

—To who? the grandmother says, finally speaking. To that dirty, lying little girl?

She crosses the room towards Tomás in two quick steps. She slaps Tomás hard across the face. Two, three, four times.

In another world, Lina stands up and says, *Ma'am. With all due respect. That is not necessary.*

In another world, Lina takes Tomás aside afterwards and whispers to him, *You know what, Tomás? That really wasn't okay. I know it's not my place or business to say so or to judge, but I just want you to know that in the UK grown-ups generally don't hit children.*

In another world, Lina never put her hands on Gabriela at

all. Never lifted her fingers up from Tomás's arm, one by one. Pulling them apart.

In this world, though, Lina sits as still as possible. And she keeps her mouth shut.

Tomás's mouth turns downwards into a U-shape. He closes his eyes. Water begins brimming out from under the lids. But his grandmother grabs him by the arm and starts shaking him, so hard he's lifted off the bed. Lina automatically jerks her legs away, because of course it's herself she's concerned about in this moment, herself and no one else. And again, who is she to judge? She hadn't even asked for the grandmother's name. And now Tomás's grandmother is shaking Tomás hard, and she shouts, —You stay away from her. That filthy, lying little girl – she was made out of dirt. Dirt is where she came from. And dirt is all she'll ever be. You hear me? I'm not going to tell you again. We've already had this conversation.

Tomás stares down at the mattress, tears streaming down his face.

—He never listens, God damn him, the grandmother says, exhaling hard. Crying like a girl.

She lets go of his arm and wipes her hands on her dress, which is ankle-length and shimmery with sequins, like something a fortune-teller would wear.

—That child, she says, and it takes a second for Lina to realise she means Gabriela. That mother of hers. That crackhead! That witch! They need to stay out of this neighbourhood, both of them!

Lina's lips feel hot and puffy as she speaks. —But – isn't Gabriela's mother in New York?

For a second, Tomás's grandmother looks confused. But then she shakes her head briskly. —New York? No, no, no. What are you talking about, girlie? You haven't seen them? She and that poor little girl – they beg on the pavement down in Centro, by the traffic light. They sleep on a pile of cardboard; they don't even have a bed. That poor child, running around! Begging on buses, to get the fare to come here!

She frowns so hard the skin between her eyes bunches up.

—I bought those from her, she says, pointing at the laminated saints' portraits on the wall. From that poor girl. That dirty little thing. I felt sorry for her! So sorry! But it did no good. You can't help anybody in this life, the grandmother says. You can't. There's no wickedness that crackhead mother of hers wouldn't do, with whatever money she gets her hands on. Bad people, the two of them.

—But you're wrong, Lina says, unable to restrain herself. Gabriela's mother is in the States. In New York. Gabriela told me—

The grandmother claps her hands together, as though there's something in-between her palms she needs to trap. —No, *mija*. The people in this city, they're – how should I put it? Trust! You can't trust them. You can't trust anybody, dearie, the grandmother explains, carefully touching her kerchief yet again as if to make sure her hair is still contained, not spilling out. You'll never get the same story twice from anyone here. People are tricky in this country, my dear. If you stay here long enough, you'll see. People will do and say things to get whatever. Nothing is ever straight; nothing is clear. That's just the way things are. And especially with you, honey. You need to be careful in this place. It's a different world.

The bluntness of it.

—Actually, Lina says, sighing, I grew up here.

—Yes, Tomás's grandmother says. But you're not from here.

———

On the walk back, she stops at the grocery store to get Tomás a popsicle. He slurps on it cautiously, running it over his lips like he's applying lipstick.

—Tomáso-man?

He looks up at her with his serious dark eyes, that perpetual mournful expression. He's holding the popsicle between his index finger and thumb, the same way the sledding children smoked their cigarettes. His tears have formed clean streaks down his face.

—Tell me the truth. Does Gabriela beg on the street?

He shrugs. He sticks his tongue out and moves his popsicle up and down against it. His tongue slowly begins to darken.

A dog barks; a radio blares. A few plastic bags scurry across the dirt, as if alive.

And then there was the night you had a nightmare. Your mother didn't hear you and your father wasn't there so I crawled into bed with you instead.

I don't want to die alone, you said, pulling the blanket up to your nose. *I'm afraid.*

You never said what exactly you were afraid of. Maybe it was the way your mother jerked you away from the window, snapping, *Stay away from the glass!*

Or the way your mother fired Nataly, the last maid we ever had, chasing her out of the house while shouting that she was a spy, she was an informant for the sicarios, God damn it, she'd seen the tattoo on her calf, and as Nataly cried and pleaded, your mother slammed the door in her face and locked it, ranting that she couldn't trust anyone in this city any more. Nataly, with her smell of onion and fresh coriander. We went into our room and cried wordlessly, stunned by the force of our own sadness, by how quickly someone we had taken for granted could disappear, and it was too late, we didn't realise it in time; just like that, she was gone for good.

Or maybe it was the night your father didn't come home from the consulate appointment in Bogotá, didn't even call. Your mother took all the glasses out of the cupboard and threw them on the floor, screaming that this was it this time, it had finally happened, he'd been shot in the street. You and I pressed ourselves into the corner by the stove, as far away from her as possible, pieces of glass bouncing near our feet. *Gunned down,* your mother said, *killed like a dog.* No job was worth this, human rights her ass. She'd seen the light now, understood how serious things were, her former idealism was gone. Why was it taking so long for their passports to arrive, when were they going to get out of here, when were they going to be able to leave?

She didn't mention me.

I don't want to die alone, you said to me in the bed. *I don't want to go to England.*

You pushed your face into my armpit, the same way I'd pushed my face into the cotton candy at the zoo.

Please don't let him send me away.

I put my arms around you. And I made a promise. *If you go away,* I said, *I'll wait for you. I won't leave.*

You sat up. We played the game we liked, the one where we sat back to back, trying to line up the bones of our spines.

(How would our bones line up if we tried it now?)

But what if I'm gone for years? you said, your pelvis banging against mine.

I'll wait for you, I said. *I'll wait a hundred thousand years.*

That's when the strangest feeling came over me. Like I was inventing a story for us to play together, a make-believe game. I'm not sure if I'll be able to put it into words, but I'll try. It was like the mattress underneath us had become a raft, *Amazon Trail* style, and the crumpled white sheet was the water streaming past, carrying us away. We might have been getting pulled towards a waterfall, or a whirlpool, or out into the great expanses of the ocean, but that didn't really matter. What

265

mattered was that, for a moment, we had to press against each other, as hard as possible, because that was the only way to prevent each other from getting swept away into the blackness that surrounded us. But just as quickly as the feeling came over me, it was gone.

You pulled your knees into your chest. *Good,* you murmured. Our vertebrae clicked together; my skull bumped against yours. *That's why I made you, Matty.* You whispered it in the dark. *I made you out of dirt.* Reciting the words as if talking to yourself, a magic spell uttered for comfort, for protection. As if whatever had happened to me beforehand didn't matter, as though, if it weren't for you, I wouldn't even exist. *I made you,* you said, *so I wouldn't be lonely.*

It's funny – you'd think that memory is a safe place, something desirable. That the past is a comforting location you can always return to – childhood as the only homeland, the one true nation we can all migrate to. But what exactly is so good about bringing out what's hidden? Doesn't looking into the light cause your eyes to burn?

Personally, I prefer the dark. Personally, I prefer to stay here, hidden away.

Because otherwise, what ends up happening is always this.

I get out of bed.

I leave you behind, without me.

And I'll wander the hallways of your mother and father's apartment, opening one door and then another. I'll open one door, and in this one it's you and me and Emma Green and your mother. It's after church (several years ago, when we were still allowed to leave the building), and we're all playing a game. I'm lying on the living room floor, couch cushions piled on me. The three of you clamber on top, still dressed in your church clothes, crushing me underneath. *Higgledy-Piggledy!* That's what you and Emma shout, screeching it over and over. And rising above it all is your mother's voice: her laughter, her pure delight. *Higgledy-Piggledy!* She shouts it in English, over and over. And underneath her I reply, *Oink, oink,* barely more than a whisper.

The three of you laugh even harder.

Oh, how funny it was, to have all of you on top and me underneath!

It was wonderful that you all enjoyed and benefited from my company so much. That I provided so much support.

I can keep going. Keep exploring. One door after another. But sooner or later, it happens.

Sooner or later, I always end up at the same place.

In this one, we crawled into your mother's bed. We sat on top of crushed cigarette packs, happily kicking the wine bottle off the mattress with our feet. Your mother pushed away the sheet and stood up, her legs shaking like Bambi's. Her night-dress was all droopy down the front. *Don't look at me, you pervert,* she said playfully, thwacking me on the head. I turned away and stared helplessly out the window, at the grey clouds and rain, the violent summer storm crashing overhead. *Look, Mummy,* you shouted, picking up one of her bras and pressing it against your chest, *I'm like you!* But your mother didn't pay you any attention. She went into the bathroom instead and sat in the shower without turning on the water. We brought her a Diet Coke from the fridge, with a few pills that she called her 'medicine' dissolved in it, and she thanked us both. *You're a good boy, Matty,* she said, weeping as usual. *Such a good boy. I don't deserve you.* Pressing her wet face into my arm and

267

crying. I stared at the mirror, watching you. You played unhappily with your mother's bathrobe, pulling it over your head like a hood.

But then the water started coming in. Streaming in under the bathroom door. Outside the apartment, the thunder cracked. The two of you screamed when the water poured in, soaking the bathmat. Your mother leapt up. She shouted for us to go and put our bathing suits on, hurry, hurry, grab a broom, close the balcony door, we had to get to work sweeping the water out, sweep it off the balcony, sweep it out of the apartment. We all had to help, we had to save the furniture before the Doctor got home! It was the most excited we'd seen her since her photography classes; it was the most motivated she'd been since dropping out of her medical degree. *Wait here*, your mother told us, heading to the door still in her nightdress, without a jacket or even an umbrella. She's heading to the store to buy extra brooms, extra buckets; we need to save the apartment, save the family, hurry, hurry, your father will be home soon!

Be a good boy, Matty. That's what your mother called out over her shoulder, dashing into the hallway. *Take care of María Carolina!*

The water spewed over our feet. It rushed past our ankles. It moved as if alive.

And this is where the memories fail me. Right at the moment where I need them most. Turning their dirty snuffling faces away, as I open door after door. I could talk about the moments that came before, and the moments that came after, but what would be the point? Does telling mean overcoming?

Because after your mother ran downstairs, out into the

street, we went to change into our bathing suits. *Don't look at me, you pervert,* you said, experimenting with the phrase as you headed into the bathroom, locking the door behind you so that I couldn't get in (something you'd never done with me before, not even with Emma Green).

I waited for you on the balcony. I made sure to keep the sliding glass door shut, so that the water wouldn't pour into the apartment. I stood there, letting the rain fall on me, soaking me through as I stared out at the city – my city. The mountains where I had come from – not just me, but my mother. My real mother.

I made you out of dirt, you'd whispered.

Down in the street below, there was some sort of commotion going on. I leaned over the metal bar. Pressed my stomach against it. The line of traffic had come to a stop, despite the lights turning green. A crowd of people had gathered by the traffic lights. They were forming a circle around something – something or someone, lying on the ground.

A figure in a nightdress. The surging water in the road carried away the redness, but I could still see it. Crumpled up and bloody, half the head missing. The raw sticky mess, mother-shaped no longer. Not any more.

Somewhere in the distance, the men on the motorcycle must have been racing away.

———

She's not my mother. That's what I told the voice on the other end of the phone. I said: *And if you want her – fine with me.*

———

She didn't want you, your mother tells me. Lighting her cigarette on the balcony, striking the match. *If she really wanted to, sweetie, she'd come back and get you. At any time.*

———————

I left the balcony. I left the scene outside, the people gathering around your mother's body. I put a chair against the bathroom doorknob, just like I'd seen in the movies, so that you wouldn't be able to get out, no matter how hard you tried. In the living room, I pushed over the armchair. I swept the vases off the shelves. I tore down the curtains. I ripped the paintings from the walls. I smashed every dish in the kitchen cupboard (your mother had already taken care of the glasses). I went back into your parents' bedroom, ignoring your voice on the other side of the door, calling and crying. Weeping in confusion, over and over. *Matty, what are you doing? Matty, open the door!* Fumbling at the lock. Scratching at the door until your fingers bled, your nails torn to shreds. *Arctic Fox, do you read me? Over and out.* But I didn't answer you; I didn't respond. Instead I tore the sheets off the bed. I threw the pillows on the floor. I pulled out every drawer and flipped them over, spilling the contents. I yanked every book out of the bookcase. I tore out the pages and crumpled them into balls. I went through the albums, shredded every photo to bits. I went back into the hallway. I punched a hole in the wall. And then I opened the balcony door. I let the water come in, pouring into the house. I let it all in. It stained the walls. It soaked the furniture. It filled the house till it came up to my ankles. Because it was better to tear it all down. It was better to ruin it, destroy it completely, everything we had. I'd leave myself, rather than have you leave me. Leave me here, all alone.

So I turned and ran. I ran out of your mother and father's apartment. I ran down the stairs and into the street. I ran through the stagnant puddles and the road that was now a river. I ran away and I kept running. I'm running still, Lina.

But I kept my promise to you. I did.

THE DIRTY BOY

When she wakes up from the dream, she immediately rolls over and pulls her knees into her chest. She looks at the wall. She looks at her suitcase, the one she's barely unpacked since her first night here, apart from pulling out necessary clothes and toiletries. She looks at her fingers, the pieces of skin she's peeled away, the raw bits of flesh left behind. She looks at her phone, charging on the other side of the room. She looks at herself, and she thinks.

————

Her father calls when she's on the Metrocable, suitcase jammed between her legs. She can tell it's him from the long string of numbers, the +44 code. He calls just as she's unscrewing the cap off her water bottle. In her frenzied attempt to answer in time, she ends up spilling water over the arm of the lady sitting next to her, but by the time she's able to try and answer, the ringtone has stopped.

—I'm so sorry, she tells the woman, who holds up a well-manicured hand as if to say *No worries*. But as she settles back to stare out the window, at the red-bricked buildings of the city under her feet, the ringing starts up again.

—Hello?

—Well, her father says. If it isn't Mary. The one and only. My beloved child who never calls.

—I called the other day and you didn't pick up.

It's going to cost her a fortune (does she get charged for incoming international calls, or just outgoing?), but she stays on the line.

—Mary Caroline. María Carolina. My only daughter.

—I've called several times, actually. At least three.

She keeps her eyes fixed on a grey smear of clouds, the afternoon storm. It's going to rain later. She can hear traffic sounds on the other end, cars on a road. British cars. It seems like a miracle, Harry Potter magic, that she can hear England blaring through the tiny speaker of her phone.

She says, —Are you outside?

—How is he, he says. How's the boy.

—Where are you?

She presses the phone hard against her ear. Honking? Is he walking by a motorway?

—That poor boy.

He's slurring his words. The cable car grinds through a stop.

—He told me you came over. That you're with him now.

She scoots over so that a group of high-school students can squeeze in.

—Tell him I sent it, he says. Tell him I sent as much as I could. To the usual account. I sent—

A gust of wind, British wind. It's hard to hear what he's saying. He sounds almost as bad as he does on the anniversary of her mother's death. Worse, even.

—Papa. Can you find somewhere to go inside? A building or something?

—Could have sent more. Tell him sorry.

—Is there anyone around you? Her voice is rising: the

273

other passengers are starting to sneak looks at her, but she doesn't care. Is there someone you can ask for help?

—Help?

He lets out a groan, a sound like an injured animal, the worst noise she's ever heard in her life. It takes her a moment to realise that it's supposed to be a laugh.

—Help, he repeats, laughing and laughing. Nobody can help anyone.

—Papa?

He hangs up. She has to double-check the screen to make sure the call is really gone, that she hasn't accidentally muted it. She goes into incoming calls and taps on the number, calling him back again and again, but she already knows that he won't pick up.

———

Her suitcase rattles so loudly on the stony road, it's a wonder people don't peek out of their windows to see what the noise is. When she gets to the Anthill, he's not out the back at the former assembly site. Nor is he upstairs in the kitchen, by the ESL tables and supply closet. He's not downstairs by the art cupboard or Education Corner (that's where she leaves her suitcase, tucked under a table). And he's definitely not in the street outside, saying goodbye to the American teens. As the teens hug and take last-minute selfies with the squealing, wiggling children, Dafne and Rebecca solemnly present the youth pastor with a giant poster they've drawn (when? Where?). *THANK YOU BEST FRIENDS LOVE*, the poster says. The youth pastor accepts it with tears in his eyes. As Dafne and Rebecca stand on their tiptoes to kiss his cheek, it's hard to deny it: how happy the children seem – how much they've enjoyed having the teens here. *We'll miss you!* the Anthill children cry out. *Come back soon!* And when the youth pastor makes the teens form a circle and go around one at a time, sharing their favourite Anthill memory, memories that make the Anthill children screech with joy and clap their hands, she can't deny it either: *He just wants to help*, she thinks, watching him lead the group in a Goodbye Prayer. *He's just trying to be good in the way that he can.*

And so she stands in the doorway with her arms crossed, watching the teens clamber into the van (driven here with epic determination by one of the adult supervisors, to make sure they return it to the rental agency on time). The Anthill children wave goodbye, gradually trickling away, wandering off to go and do Lord knows what. Lina is pretty much the only one left as the youth pastor rushes up to her, Dafne and Rebecca's poster rolled under his arm.

—Lina! How do I even begin? Thank you so much for everything. He takes her hand and pumps it up and down. Really, I mean it. I can't imagine having had a better time.

—Thank *you*. She squeezes his hand hard, sneaking a glance up the street. But there's still no sign of it: Mattías's dark, solitary head.

—We're off to Hacienda Nápoles tomorrow. You know, the Escobar ranch? And then our flight leaves Sunday. The youth pastor cheerfully wipes sweat from his forehead with his REI bandana. Any recommendations about the best sights?

She can't help herself. —You're taking them *there*?

He looks at her like it's obvious. —Of course! He starts laughing. They all love the TV show, you know. We'd promised them we'd go before we even left Miami! They've been look-ing forward to it all week.

She presses her hands into her hips. Leans forward slightly.

The youth pastor is still talking: —We're taking a chartered bus, of course – since we're returning the van today, it's what makes the most sense. And the discount helps too, ha. We'll defi-nitely do the tour – entry gate – abandoned swimming pool – water slides. He ticks the sights off on his fingers, one by one. Oh, and hopefully we'll get to see some of the animals. The kids are especially excited about that. Do you know how many hip-pos Escobar kept originally? Do they still live at the theme park?

She opens her mouth. The vomit dribbles down her chin, hot and thick like juice in a blender that hasn't been liquefied properly. His eyes widen; he takes a step back. Coughing and hacking, she spews it all over the ground. It splashes on the bare skin of his sandalled feet.

—Oh my! He rubs his foot on the telephone pole, but instead of cleaning it off, grit and dirt get stuck to the vomit. She starts shaking her head, trying to apologise. But what comes out instead is a laugh. Sputtering and heaving, but laughing.

—Theme park! she keeps saying in-between breaths. *Theme park!*

Speechless, the youth pastor backs away. He clambers hur-riedly into the back of the van. And that's how the American volunteers depart, wide-eyed behind windows as Lina hunches on the ground, hacking and gagging until the sour liquid com-ing out of her mouth is nothing more than a trickle.

When she's done, it's Rebecca and Dafne who touch her arm. They've brought her a wad of toilet paper.

—Are you okay, Miss Carolina? Rebecca whispers.

Lina smears the toilet paper over her mouth. She accidentally drops it, picking it back up immediately with pinched fingers.

—Don't forget, she rasps, as Dafne and Rebecca stare (God, the post-vomit voice really is the worst, isn't it?). Remember, girls, what Maryluz always said. Don't litter. We want to be good to the planet and not create extra trash. We need to take care of Planet Earth, the only thing we all share.

Dafne and Rebecca nod. They hold up their palms. She hesitates – it'd be easier and quicker to just do it herself – but she places the wad of dirty tissue into their hands. They scurry inside, straight to the garbage.

—Thank you, she says, following them. Thank you so much, girls. Do you think you could help? Could you help me clean up?

They nod and grab her hands. They're smudged and smeared with the expelled liquid from her stomach, but they don't seem to mind, don't seem to care.

And the two girls say, —Yes. We can help.

————

The Anthill has been closed for an hour by the time he finally shows up. She's never stayed this late, past five o'clock. It'll be getting dark soon, six thirty on the dot, the ever-reliable equatorial sunset. She sits at the table, staring at her suitcase, its smooth grey skin. When she hears the door scraping open, she quickly pushes it under the table with her knees.

—Hey! he says as he enters. He's carrying a stack of papers in one hand, seems genuinely surprised. And possibly . . . not

277

pleased. I was wondering why the door was unlocked – you're here late.

She wipes her chin with the back of her hand, even though she's checked and rechecked her face via the phone camera a dozen times. —I was waiting for you, she says. Where have you been?

He sits down next to her – if he notices her suitcase, he doesn't comment on it. Instead he says, —I had some business to attend to.

—Ah, of course. Man of mystery. The secretive jefe.

She only realises when they leave her mouth: Maryluz's words. But he just shrugs, hands over the papers he's carrying. —You never asked.

The papers are flyers. Simple black-and-white photocopies. *COME TO THE ANTHILL*, they say. *FREE OF CHARGE*. Stick figures holding hands, the Colombian flag. And right in the middle, a giant peace sign.

—Advertising, he says. I go door to door.

She flips the paper over:

ALL WELCOME!
BE SAFE
BE RESPECTFUL
BE KIND

She can picture it easily: him, walking door to door. Ramshackle wooden houses, tarpaper huts. Entering one house after another, passing scraggly roosters, petting mangy dogs.

And once inside the house, his eyes: scanning, searching.

Looking for something.

A familiar flicker of a memory. Recognisable.

Because houses don't change that much over the years, do they? And even if they did, there's always the possibility of neighbours. People like Josefina in the ruffled pink shirt, or Tomás's grandmother. People who've lived here for decades and decades, not leaving. She understands it in a flash.

Do you remember? That's what he'd be asking them, painstakingly but persistently. *Twenty-five years ago. There was an evangelical church group that came here. They went door to door.* Waving his hands through the air, describing the scene, recreating the photograph in the album from so long ago. *A woman was with them. Long hair, hooped earrings.*

Her mother, sitting in a dark house with clay walls. Holding another child in her lap. Half-baby, half-toddler.

—Do you think I should laminate them? he says. I dunno. On one hand it'd be a lot of extra work. But on the other hand it might make people less likely to throw them away. I'd hate to think I'm just creating a bunch of extra garbage.

—Matty, she says. Do you think your mother lived near this neighbourhood?

He fiddles with the papers, trying to line the edges up with each other.

—Your real mother?

—I know who you mean. He says it very calmly, like it's nothing. Why would you ask that?

—Fuck, she says, turning her hands into fists and pressing them into her forehead. This is so hard to talk about.

He settles back into his chair and tilts his head, like a policeman listening to a prisoner break down during a climactic interrogation sequence. —Why?

—*Why?* She wants to laugh, but it's clear he's serious. Because I feel really bad about it!

—Why? he repeats. He seems genuinely curious.

—I just do! Tears are filling her eyes. She presses her knuckles against her face.

—Well, don't, he says. It's a waste of time.

—But we could try to find her. If that's what you wanted. I could ask my father. He might remember something – my mother might have—

—I don't see any point in that whatsoever.

She forces her hands down on to the table. His eyes flicker down to her fingers, to the red bits she's bitten away. His forehead furrows slightly.

—Lina, he says, and his voice is so patient, so understanding and so kind. He was always so good at comforting her, Mattías was. I have no interest in contacting my real mother. *Your* mother was like a mother to me. Why is that so hard for you to accept?

—Okay, she manages to say. Well.

If only her voice wasn't so wavery, her eyes so drippy! More like a child's, rather than a grown woman's. She says, still shakily, —So I stayed late today, because there was something I wanted to give you. And I wanted to do it in person before I leave.

Now she has his attention. Absolutely nothing in his body language has changed, but the air around them feels different. As if even the molecules have tensed up.

—Leave? He smiles, as if what she's just said is very amusing and entertaining indeed. What are you talking about?

—Away. I'm going away. I haven't decided yet. Back to

England? She starts laughing, even though what she really wants to do is weep. I shouldn't be here, Matty. I need to leave.

—What are you talking about? His voice is rising.

She starts shaking her head. —It's not good for you, she whispers. Having me here. I'm making you unhappy.

He starts laughing too, incredulously.

—I am, she says. You're not ready. I'll come back one day when you are. I swear it. I swear it on my fucking life. But having me here is causing you harm.

How can she explain it? What would be the right concept, the correct term? Maybe something like 'sacred'. And 'duty'. Choosing his well-being over her own comfort. She and him.

Even if nobody else in the world ever knows it besides her.

—I need to leave, she repeats. But that's not the point. That's not what matters. Look – I have something for you. I brought it from England and I've had it with me this whole time. Look.

She drags the suitcase out from under the table. Heavy as Santa Claus's sack hauling ass through the snow, distributing presents to millions of sleeping children. How worried she and he were as children, that their apartment didn't have a chimney! *Will Santa still be able to get in?* That's what she asked her mother, watching the hired men prop up the Christmas tree in the living room. *Where will he leave the reindeer?* Her mother chugged her whisky and said, *He'll leave them at the petrol station.* And then she laughed, stubbing her cigarette out in the tree pot. The tree got some kind of weird fungus and died within days. Oh, her mother! What a child! What if she just forgave her? God. She realises it as she zips open her suitcase: she could forgive her mother, and that could be that.

It doesn't have to be a collective or symbolic forgiveness. It doesn't have to be approved by an institution or defined by a clinical term. She doesn't need to write a book about it, or announce it on social media, or experience any sort of catharsis or change. It could be a useless and quiet sort of forgiveness: pointless, but necessary. *I forgive you, Mother,* she thinks, silently sending the thought deep into the earth, jabbing it down into the dirt that made them, her and her mother and Mattías alike. This dirt they're all made of, this country that has created and taken away so much, filled with graves and mines and rifle cases and indestructible plastic, all of which will never biodegrade, will never fully fade away or disappear, not in a hundred thousand years. The bones of the massacred anonymous dead, the nameless and voiceless others who will never be recognised, never be acknowledged, never be given a chance to speak. But just because something doesn't speak doesn't mean it's not there.

Forgiveness can't change the past. In the same way that tearing a photograph from an album can't change it. But maybe, just maybe, it can change the future.

—Here, she says, flipping the suitcase open. Remember what I told you, the very first night? About the security, and my suitcase? And how they thought I'd brought boxes with me?

She takes them out one by one. It's not about giving them back. It's about acknowledging they were there in the first place – that they existed all along. Even if nobody else ever knew about them, or noticed, or cared.

Instead of spreading them out over the floor like a deck of cards, she stacks them like a tower. He sits there, watching.

—I didn't read them, she says. I promise. I swear. I swear on my mother's grave. Pinkie swear. I swear on the Bible. I swear on a blade of grass.

A playground litany, recited. He still doesn't say anything. She stacks the very last notebook on top. They're child-size, spiral-bound. The covers are a series of different cute little animals. Rabbits with fat ears, chubby dogs riding bicycles, cats with googly eyes. And inside the pages, his voice. The voice of him.

—I've kept them in a box all this time, she says. I took them with us. When we left.

She wipes her nose on the back of her hand. It's dripping.

When he finally speaks, it's barely more than a whisper. — You went into my room, he says. You looked under my bed.

He sounds stunned.

—I did, she says. But only because you were gone. My father, he said you just . . . ran out of the house! That he couldn't find you! You disappeared!

—You looked under my bed, he repeats. You looked at my journals.

—I never read them. I swear to God. She swallows. I did look at the first page of one, the first sentence. In your room here.

His expression doesn't change.

—I'm sorry, she whispers. I know that doesn't make a difference. The second I found them, I knew that was the last thing you wanted – that they were yours and no one else's. Matty (she scoots forward, chair screeching against the floor, but she doesn't touch him, doesn't lean in; she lets him have it, his privacy, his space), I was a kid. I was just a kid and so were you. We didn't understand. I don't even remember.

(God, if only she could remember! The smears of baking soda in her shoes eventually faded, but this never has – carrying his journals, dragging his secret most private thing from place to place. A physical embodiment of her childhood to lug around, the most tedious literalised metaphor ever. Boarding school to friends' houses to university accommodation; from freegan apartment to her current London flat. Sitting in closets, under beds, on shelves. Most of the time she kept them stored away, hidden – out of sight, out of mind. But sometimes – every once in a while – she'd open the suitcase and reach in. Touch the covers, trace the images. But she never turned the pages. Never glanced inside. Only that one time, that one moment in his bedroom here. Even if he never believes her, *can't* believe her. Even if she's the only one who ever knows it's true.)

She says, —All he told me was just . . . he didn't know where you went. I didn't know what happened to you. I didn't know if you were ever coming back.

—Your father, he whispers. The furniture.

—Yeah, he probably was upset about that or whatever. But I don't know how he reacted or what he did. I don't! I really don't! I think about that time and it's just like . . . a black hole in my mind! It's a blank space, nothing! She raps her knuckles against the side of her skull for emphasis. It's so fucked what you do and don't remember.

—Yes, he says evenly. It is.

—We were just children, she repeats. We didn't understand. He put me on a plane. I didn't know what was going on. I thought I was coming back. I thought *you* were coming back. Her nose is dripping for real now, along with her eyes. I missed you. I missed you my whole life.

—Of course I came back. His voice is still a whisper. I came back and everything was gone. The apartment . . .

Poor Matty. She can see it now, as clear in her head as a memory, or a story she's invented. Like one of those colouring books with transparent paper, where you could lay one image on top of another to change what's underneath. Matty, wandering through the vacated apartment, stunned by its desertion, the sudden emptiness. The place she can't remember, the one she has to invent: the desk there, the window here, the bookshelf way over yonder. Over there, that's where the brooms were propped up on the couch; that's where the water streamed in under the balcony. And there was the door where her mother must have run out, down the stairs, into the street. Matty, alone: no radiation suit to protect him from a world gone up in flames.

Maybe the doorman had let him in. Maybe he'd found out somehow, had found someone to ask, to tell him: that she and her father had gone to England. Left.

But what about Mattías? Where did he go after that? Will she ever know; will he ever tell? Would him telling her directly make things better? Should he lie, like Gabriela? (About her mother, her grandmother, about who knows what else.) Is telling the same thing as healing, or is lying just as good?

—I didn't know you came back, she says, as steadily as she can. If I'd known, I would have waited. I would have waited for you forever. But look.

She taps on the notebook. Tap, tap, tap.

—I didn't read them, she says, because I know that's not what you wanted. They're not mine; they're yours. And I'm sorry. I'm so sorry.

Finally, he looks her straight in the eye. Finally, he's facing her directly, confronting her head-on. But it's not what she was expecting. What it is is a look of pure ice. There's no movement in his face, no water-like rippling. Just nothing. Worse than nothing.

He says, —You should be.

But before she can say anything, that's when it begins. The banging.

The banging makes the Anthill door shake. It quivers. It rattles. She automatically reaches for the keys hanging from her neck, but Mattías is already standing, he's heading for the door. Someone is pounding and banging on the door, as hard and fast as a drum, like it's a musical instrument, like it needs to be kicked down.

—Don't, she says. Don't open it.

But it's too late; he's grabbing the metal handle and yanking it. He pulls the door open.

The two figures by the door jump back. She immediately sees that one is Gabriela. Same knee-length shirt, same battered flip-flops. She has some ashy grey smudges on her face, but otherwise she looks the same.

—Gabriela!

Gabriela lets herself be hugged. She solemnly wraps her hands around Lina's neck, kissing her stickily on the cheek. That familiar smoky smell. And then Gabriela tilts her face upwards. In a breathy whisper, she says, —I brought him, Lina!

They turn to look at the other figure. Mattías has already turned to look too. And then there's a smell of wet garbage, so strong Lina can't help but press her nose into her arm. Up the street, the dogs have started barking, Eight-Bras and all her daughters, a louder, more aggressive barking than she's ever heard before.

It's a small boy. He's impossibly thin, scarily so. She had no idea a person could be that thin and still be alive. He can't be older than five, though perhaps he's so emaciated he looks younger. He's wearing no shirt, and his shorts are little more than rags. His skin is grey and veiny, like something that's been kept underwater for too long. There are dents up and down his skin, as though it's lost all its elasticity, like a deflated ball.

And on his arms and torso there is writing. Angry scribbles running up and down, filling every inch of his skin. Furiously, uncontrollably, like someone trying to fill in every possible inch of white space in a notebook. Like a voice struggling to speak.

—See, Gabriela says, stepping towards the little boy and grabbing his hand. She raises his arm upwards, an Olympic-victory-style gesture. You didn't believe me, so I made him come!

The little boy opens his mouth. His teeth have been filed. Each and every tooth is pointy, razor-sharp. There are dark clumps on the corner of his mouth that could be dirt, could be dried-up blood. His fingernails are raw red patches, as if torn clean off. He moves his mouth up and down, as if trying to figure out how to talk.

—You didn't believe me, Gabriela repeats, as if deeply satisfied. You thought I was lying. But now he can tell you himself.

Lina looks at him. She looks some more. She says, —Matty?

She holds out her hand, which is shaking. Neither the boy nor Gabriela moves towards it. Mattías still hasn't spoken.

—Go on, Matty, Gabriela says. Tell them.

—Oh, Matty, Lina whispers. She falls to her knees. Swallowing, she opens her arms as wide as she can. She says, It's okay.

Beside her, she can hear Mattías swallow. Some foamy liquid spills out of the little boy's mouth. There's a gurgling sound. The little boy coughs.

—It's okay, Lina repeats. You can talk.

The Anthill sign behind her: *ALL WELCOME.*

And just like that, Mattías steps forward. He moves towards the boy and smacks him hard across the head.

Gabriela screams but doesn't let go of his hand.

Lina cries out, —What are you *doing*, you're *hurting* him!

But Mattías doesn't stop. He uses his fingers to jab the boy in the eye. He uses a clenched fist to smash his jaw. The boy crumples in half. Mattías kicks him hard in the knees to make him fall on the ground. He raises his feet to stomp down on the boy's body, again and again. Lina rushes forward and grabs Gabriela, pulling her away, and as Gabriela's hand is dragged away from the little boy's some awful spongy material comes off with it, long and streaming like seaweed, or wet plastic bags that have been rotting in a river for centuries. Lina touches it, recognises it: that soft squishy wetness, from deep inside the supply closet.

—Stop, Gabriela is screaming. Stop it!

Lina is shouting out too, shouting at Mattías, words she can't even hear herself say. A chunk of skin falls off the boy's torso, plopping on the ground, and she can see the sharp white curve of his ribs, and there are words written there too, small cramped handwriting, angry and deep and dark, as though a pen has been pressed down all the way into the depths of his skeleton, like words written in the most secret and hidden of journals. The voice is there; it wants to be heard, but the words are blurred and she can't read them. She can't read a thing; she'll never understand. The dirty boy sobs and howls, the wounded cry of an animal. And throughout it all the dogs up the street never stop snarling.

But then Mattías is stopping. Mattías is stepping away. He's backing away so fast he almost trips; Lina grabs his arm to steady him. The sounds die away, her sounds and Gabriela's and the barks of Eight-Bras and her children and the dirty boy's most of all, abruptly cutting off, until the only voice left is Mattías's. Slow and steady and perfectly clear.

—Go away, Mattías is saying. I told you before. And don't come back. Ever.

—No! Lina screams. She steps towards him: the dirty boy, cowering.

On all fours, he scurries away. His rump raised high in the air, he darts into a gap between two houses up the road. A few doors have started to open, people have come out to stand outside. Have there been others, standing and watching all this time? Who else has witnessed, who else knows? Lina wraps her arms around Gabriela in an attempt to give her a hug but Gabriela is already slipping out of her grasp. The spongy black material from the boy's skin is still stuck to her hands. —Wait, Lina cries out, but Gabriela has already turned to run in the same direction, running, running, her sandals flapping against the dirt. And when she turns around, Mattías is nowhere to be seen, vanished back into the Anthill's depths. His fortress.

She follows the boy down the alleyway. Struggling to fit in the gap between two houses, scraping her shoulder. She stumbles over planks of wood, stubs her toe on a cement block. A sticky spiderweb smears across her knee. Gasping and panting, reaching her arm out, fumbling around in the near-dark.

—Matty?

She knows it when she touches it. That dank sour smell. It's trembling. There's a shift beneath her palm, a movement. And then she sees its eyes.

—Come with me, she whispers. Come back.

It's so much worse than anything she could have possibly imagined. It pants and whimpers, trembles and shakes. But she looks right at it, and doesn't look away.

She lets her hand stay for a second. And then she withdraws it. Pulls it back towards her torso.

She hasn't said anything, but hopefully it'll understand. If not now, then someday. Someday soon. Breathing its hot sour breath over her legs, it sighs. Long and slow.

Backing away, her sandal is stabbed by a nail. A beetle crawls over her foot. A stack of wet cardboard smears something foul and crumbly over her shorts. But she keeps moving.

Giving it privacy. A space for no one else, until it's ready.

———

When she re-enters the Anthill, she has to stop and slump against the doorway.

Standing. Staring.

She whispers, —Oh no.

Board games snapped in half. The art cupboard overturned,

contents spilled every which way. Paint, glitter, glue. Tables flipped over, legs snapped off.

The Anthill has been destroyed. Smashed to bits. Only one table hasn't been damaged – and there it is, the stack of his childhood journals. Untouched.

She turns and looks up the street. One more time, just to be sure. But Gabriela is nowhere to be seen. The evening lights of people's houses have come on. There are even some people standing in the street, smoking and chatting. Children turn jump ropes and dogs run uphill. Life is moving on; life hasn't stopped. How wonderful, how terrible, that life can still go on despite everything.

She strokes the frame of the door where she's standing. As if to say *There, there*. As if to say *It's okay to be angry*.

He's gone. Run away. Again.

This time, though, she knows where to look.

———————

He's hiding in the back of the supply closet. Sitting like a child in time out. She crouches down but doesn't touch him. He doesn't look at her. But he doesn't move away either.

—Fuck, he says. His hands are covered in blood and scratches. She waits.

—I think . . . He pauses. I believe I'm a little bit tired.

She says, —You've been working really hard.

He looks up. Half his face is hidden by his arms, so that all she can see is his eyes. The very same ones in the alleyway, the ones from her childhood. Bloodshot and puffy, but still him. It's been him this whole time.

If only she could have recognised him earlier!

He says, —I know I'm annoying.

—No.

—Yes. I know I'm irritating to be around.

—Sometimes. But who isn't?

He swallows. —I know . . . you want me to talk more.

—You don't have to do anything you don't want to.

—Lina, he whispers. Your mother.

She waits.

—I said . . . on the phone . . .

His mouth moves, but nothing comes out.

If she asked him to, he would tell her. She knows it more clearly than she's ever known anything in her entire life.

If she wanted him to, he would tell her everything.

But what she says instead is this: —You don't have to tell me.

He lowers his face again. His shirtsleeve has been pulled up. She reaches out and touches the tattoos, the scars.

—I should tell you how I got these, he says, his voice muffled. It's a good story.

—I can't wait to hear it. She squeezes his arm. Tell me when I come back – when you ask me to come back. Okay?

He closes his eyes.

She squeezes his arm one last time as she stands back up. Heads downstairs, her fingers trembling as she pulls out her phone.

———

It's terrifying how much random crap was being kept in the art cupboard. Crêpe paper. Wrapping paper. Tracing paper. Walking through it is more like wading. Scissors with the handle missing. Dried-up markers. A wrinkled deck of UNO cards. All of it thrown everywhere, scattered over the floor.

—What the hell is this?

Maryluz picks up the cards, flipping through them. Sighing heavily, she lets them fall, fluttering from her hands like she's done a magic trick.

—What the hell, she repeats. Why were the cards here and not in the games cupboard? Is the art shit and games shit not separated any more? Are the footballs now being kept with the ESL textbooks? Is that, like, an official thing now?

Shauna doesn't answer. Her forehead is lined with concentration. She's screwing the tops back on to the paint bottles, one by messy one. Paint has been spilled all over the Anthill floor, forming horrible lakes of every colour imaginable, the last water sources available after a nuclear explosion. The glitter has been poured out too, all over the cement floor where it will never, ever come out, sparkling for as long as the Anthill stands.

—Everything everywhere, Maryluz says. My God. Those fucking gringos sure know how to make a mess. She reaches down and picks up a magazine that's been collaged to death, shaking her head. Shit. He really let this place go, didn't he?

Lina doesn't answer either. She's still in the phase of standing numbly in the middle of the room, cradling her elbows. She can't stop staring at the jagged glass of the smashed Anthill computers, thrown down the stairs. They look like broken astronaut helmets, letting in the dark air and blackness of space.

—You know what? Maryluz says. Fuck it. Do either of you have cash? I only have large bills; the bus driver let me ride for free. Let's go to the shop and get some garbage bags. Let's throw all this away and start again. *All* of it.

Lina picks up a ball of yarn in an attempt to hide her hands, burrowing her fingers deep inside.

Shauna opens an egg carton and makes a face at all the painted eggs inside. —Oh my God, the Easter eggs! Maryluz, look! I thought the kids hid them somewhere we would never find them. Will they smell if we break them?

—Shauna, Maryluz says, touching the tip of her braid, we can never . . . ever . . . let the children break them. It'll be like when the rat drowned in the toilet but worse. Remember how we couldn't figure out what that stink was, for weeks? And then Mattías pulled it out with a clothes hanger and Dafne threw up on her shoes?

Shauna closes her eyes. —Don't remind me.

She's smiling, though. Like the memory is a good one.

It can be a good place, memory.

Yet there he sits, shut in the closet, and he's not coming down anytime soon.

Does forgetting pain allow you to move on? Or is talking about it the only way forward? Is it one or the other, or could you have both at the same time?

Maybe this is adulthood after all – the not knowing.

Lina says (more like a whisper, really), —Thank you for coming.

They both turn towards her.

Maryluz says, —Of course. I'm sorry I couldn't come sooner. I came as soon as you called.

Shauna says, —It wasn't a problem at all. I left Arturo with the neighbour. He likes it better there anyway – she lets him eat refined sugar. Haha, he probably prefers her to me.

Lina says again (a little louder this time, but barely), —
Thank you.

They both nod. Lina lets the ball of yarn fall to the floor,
exposing her hands.

—My God, Maryluz says. What's wrong with your nails?
Jesus, Shauna. Look at her fingers.

Shauna sucks in her breath. —Oh my God, Carolina! What
did you do?

Lina wipes the blood off on her bare leg. It feels too exhaust-
ing to hide it.

Maryluz puts her hands on her hips. —Come on, she says.
We need help.

————————

—You shouldn't bite them.

That's what Leidy tells her, reaching across the wooden
table and picking up her hand, inspecting it. Lina's fingers curl
automatically inward, like a crab flipped over on its back, but
it's too late.

—Oh, girlie, Leidy says, whistling. Juana! Juana, come over
here and get a look at these nails!

Juana has a wispy fringe, thin as insect antennae. She keeps
brushing it away with her fingers as she leans over to look. In
the background, the single mothers hustle and bustle, whispering to each other as they open the garbage bags, preparing
the military campaign: cleaning the Anthill.

—They're so short, Juana says, in a voice that truly could
only be described as awestruck.

—I bite them, Lina whispers. I have anxiety. I'm a very
anxious person.

Leidy wags a finger, scolding-teacher style. —You shouldn't, girlie. It's bad for your teeth.

Juana nods vigorously in agreement. —I've never seen nails so short.

The skin under Leidy's eyes wrinkles as she frowns. —Wow, she says. Oh, no. No need for that! No, no, no. Ay, girlie, don't cry. Oh dear. Juana, get the tissues.

Because her nails are so short, the polish mainly ends up on her skin. As Leidy holds her hand, poking at what remains, Lina says (trying so hard to keep her voice from shaking it ends up shaking anyway), —I know they're disgusting.

Leidy waves her hand briskly through the air, batting the words away like an annoying fly.

The single mothers talk in loud voices. They call out to each other as they sweep up the glass and make coffee on the stove. As they clear off the tables, Juana and Piedrahita argue about local football teams they remember from the eighties, with names so intricately complicated they sound like specialised armies. —What was his name, Piedrahita says, throwing the rotten food from the fridge on to the ground for Eight-Bras to chomp up. The player who died in the plane crash. What a tragedy that was! His funeral was held in my hometown. Everyone brought guaro and was drunk for days. Sandra (wiping sweat from her brow as she untangles a giant clump of string), she says she remembers that party; her cousin attended. He was part of the search party that wandered the jungle for days but they never found any remains, not a trace of the plane, it was like it never even existed at all. —Hey! Melida shouts from her station at the chopping board, did they hear about that player from the Cali team who's now playing for

Equatorial Guinea, on a team called the Vegetarian Lions, can you imagine! They laugh so hard that Rebecca and Dafne anxiously poke their heads in. They dash in and sit at Lina's feet, fiddling with the straps on her sandals, picking at the buckle.

—What are you doing, Ms Carolina? Rebecca says. Lina waggles her fingers at them so that they can see.

—That's very beautiful, Dafne murmurs, leaning her head against Lina's calf.

—No biting! Leidy says, screwing the top back on the polish. Not any more. You're better than that. You're a grown woman, not a little girl. What was your name again, honey?

Lina doesn't say anything for a minute. When she finally answers, she says, —I don't know.

Leidy looks briefly confused. Understandably. But then Rebecca and Dafne are clambering over her: *Paint ours now, paint ours!* A thankful, well-timed distraction. And Pastora and Leticia are carrying on their own conversation as they cook a big pot of chicken soup for dinner; ruined Anthill or not, it's getting late and people need to eat; cleaning the Anthill is a big task and they need to keep their strength up. Hey, Leidy, did you know this person or that person, she went to Spain and married a Scotsman, he became a miner and his middle sister died along with the baby. They have to raise their voices to be heard above the crowd, who in turn have to raise theirs, and so on and so forth, until it's like everyone is yelling at each other. Except it's a good kind of yelling, like their yelling will form a sort of wall, something that will keep them all safe, protect them. It's a wall made of hot mouths and raised voices and quivering tonsils. It's many voices instead of one, and they're made out of sampling the broth and peeling the garlic and letting the annoyingly fiddly wisps of onion skin drift to the floor where no matter, don't worry, someone will sweep it up later. Do you remember, what's his name, Gabriel Jaime Santamaria. The human-rights worker shot and paralysed, what a shame that was. That was the first election I ever voted in. No way, me too, I also worked in the sugar-cane fields in the south. If you tap on the wall with a high heel, that's how you make the scorpions come out; trust me, it never fails. My mother walked in to find him wearing my clothes, bra AND panties, what a scandal that was, she'll never recover, I'm sure that's what gave her dementia. They found the little girl with her head cut off. My God, completely decapitated. And you know what the strangest thing was? Her eyebrows had been shaved off. My God, my God, was it the witches, was it the cartels, have the cartels become witches? It's as bad as Mexico. It's as bad as ISIS. And there was a cut in her stomach with dried-up semen on her skin. So they'd fucked her through the hole they'd cut in her. My God, those animals. Those beasts. You have to feel the fear, but you can't let it become a part of your life. You have to keep moving forward, because what else can you do? My God, Pastora, what have you done to that poor chicken, it's absolutely destroyed. I don't care how blunt your knife is, I wouldn't feed that mess to a dog. —Well, Pastora says, defiantly raising the chopping board and scraping the mangled bits there straight into the soup pot, you don't have to!

And with that the women laugh, and laugh, and laugh.

There's one last task Lina needs to carry out. Three.

—Maryluz? she says, touching her arm.

298

Maryluz looks up. She's mopping up the massive puddle of paint, which is slowly reducing in the style of a sped-up map of Arctic ice receding.

—Here, Lina says, handing over the Anthill keys, for both the building and the volunteer headquarters. Can you return these to him?

That's task number one. Now for number two: she shows Maryluz the journals, which have remained stacked on the table all this time, a steady tower among the mess. Maryluz examines them but doesn't touch. —I'll put them with the others, she says decisively. When he comes back out. He always does, you know.

Number three can be done quickly, quietly. She has time, she's not in a rush. Her suitcase is all packed and she'll take a taxi from the Metro station, which she assumes is the custom of all new volunteers on their very last day. *The new volunteer*: who is she now? Sooner or later, she'll figure it out. The same goes for what she should tell the taxi driver, airport or bus station. Which one? So many doors to choose from. One could be London. One could even be for staying right here. It can be an unfashionable, untrendy sort of travel; a search for self rather than experiences. Sooner or later, she'll have to decide.

But for now, standing by Matty's journals, the Anthill children whooping around her, she unzips her suitcase one last time, reaches inside. She looks at the photo in her hands.

That long-ago moment in her childhood. The moment she'd dreamed about the night before. Pulling the photograph out of the album. The back of the photo was so sticky it stuck to her hand. Keeping it secret from him, all these years. Carrying it in the suitcase with his notebooks from place to place. Hidden away.

But just because it was hidden didn't mean that it didn't exist.

In this photo, Mattías and his mother look at the camera. Mattías's expression is grave and serious, and so is hers. She's young. She has bony cheekbones. She holds him in her lap. But her eyes are bright. And her chin is lifted.

She flips the photo over and looks at the back. The name of Mattías's mother is still written there, in her own mother's cursive handwriting. In pencil, admittedly, but it's still somewhat legible. If someone really wanted to, they could make it out. Time hasn't faded it. Time hasn't made it go away.

Wherever you are, I will find you. No matter how far ahead into the future. No matter how far back into the past.

PART IV

THE ANTHILL

THE OTHERS

After you leave me

(alone in the dark)

(again)

I search for you.

Shivering, crying.

I curl up into a foetal position. Centuries pass. The lights of the city flicker away; buildings crumble and turn into sand. My body grows layers of dust; my feet turn into stone and fossilise; I become encrusted.

Why did you let me go? Why didn't you want me around any more?

I start crying, kicking. Punching everything within reach. Destroying everything I touch, tearing it apart. Just like I always have. Just like I always will. Oh, Mother! Why did you leave me; how could you do it? I scratch at the door and wail.

But then – something happens.

Something I didn't expect.

In the silence that follows, there's a voice.

Several voices.

Speaking.

They say, *Hello?*

Tentative. Searching.

I frown. I wait.

And just like that, the lights of the city come back on. Like a switch that's been flipped. I don't know how I didn't see it before – how that's all a city is, tiny flashes of light in the dark.

The individual lights are swirling together now – becoming indistinct, blurred – many and one at the same time. And in that moment I can see it. I see it all perfectly, like a story or a dream.

It wasn't just me who'd been lost, had lost.

There's dozens of them with me. Hundreds, thousands. They come out of the earth and rivers. They swell over the mountains. They fill up the streets.

This whole time, I wasn't alone.

They nod in agreement. They open their arms and gather me in.

And into my ear they whisper, *We're here.*

Acknowledgements

Muchísimas gracias a Elyssa, Edgar, Mambo, y Samba por prestarme el apartamento en Agosto 2017, para escribir el borrador de este libro.

Thank you so much to my parents and siblings for their love and support. Love you guys.

Thank you to Emily and Laura. LOVE YOU GUYS!

Gracias a las chicas de Cali – LOTS OF LOVE!

Thank you to Clare Alexander, best agent ever.

Thank you to my editors – Emmie, Margot, Melanie. Thank you for your profoundly insightful advice, edits, and support of this project. It means so much to be read so attentively. Thank you to Silvia Crompton, heroic copy-editor who improved the book immensely. Thank you to everyone involved in the process and labour of making this book a physical object and supporting it.

Thank you Rachel Mendel – LOVE YOU GIRL!!

Thank you Eliza R for reading my cards, Sara S for meeting up with me in pubs, Kiare L for your feedback on a super-early draft.

Lauren and Hamish – love you guys SO MUCH!

Thank you Anna M, Jon Cook, and the UEA PhD Creative-Critical workshop for your feedback on an embarrassingly early chapter of this.

Thank you to my former tutors and current mentors at

UEA, especially Andrew Cowan, James Scudamore, Jean McNeil, Philip Langeskov, and Trezza Azzopardi.

Gracias a Ceci – ¡¡¡ESTOY MUY AGRADECIDA!!!

Gracias al taller de traducción en Buenos Aires 2018, una experiencia que cambió mi manera de escribir y editar totalmente.

Thank you to the Salesian priesthood and volunteer network in Tijuana, the Boys & Girls Club in Vancouver WA, Los Angelitos de Medellín, y la organización Mi Sangre (specifically Ariel Safdie). Thank you for your work. Anything bad, negative, or shitty in this project comes from me (for the purposes of creating a fictional experience), and does not accurately reflect, mirror, or comment upon any of the good and important work that you do.

As an additional FYI, anyone expecting an accurate geographic representation of Medellín from this book may be disappointed and irritated. I have taken particular liberties with the zoo.

Thank you to the authors and translators of the books below, all of which fed into the process of writing this:

Affection (Rodrigo Hasbún)

Before (Carmen Boullosa)

The novels of Santiago Gamboa

There Are No Dead Here: A Story of Murder and Denial in Colombia (Maria McFarland Sánchez-Moreno)

Born to Die in Medellín (Alonso Salazar)

An early excerpt of this novel was originally published in the Sheffield Hallam *Matters* anthology. Thank you to my Sheffield Hallam MA students, and to my former colleagues Conor, Harriet, Chris, Shelley, and Maurice for all their support and encouragement during the time that I worked there.

Thank you to the Society of Authors, whose financial support meant I could buy a plane ticket to Medellín.

Thank you to all my publishers and translators, especially Camilo J. and Felipe. Gracias al equipo de Bogotá Contada (especialmente Camilo, Noé, y Alejandro) y el equipo de Planeta (especialmente Christopher).

Gracias a Padre P, inspiración original para este proyecto.

Nick Bradley – thank you so much for your constant love, reassurance, encouragement, and edits.

Thank you, Pansy, best friend and constant companion.

I would like to dedicate this book to Doris Salcedo and Clemencia Echeverri. Thank you for your work.